2ND EDITION

Fairy

SILVER

FRANCES-MARY BROWN

Frances-Mary Brown

Printed and bound in Canada by Art Bookbindery
ArtBookbindery.com

ISBN 0-9781056-0-5

Truth is stranger than fiction, but that is because fiction is obliged to stick to the possibilities. Truth isn't.

—*Mark Twain*

Contents

CHAPTER ONE
Once Upon A Time

Once upon a time I met a fairy at the bottom of our garden. Connal wasn't airy, adorable, and sparkly. He was swift, scruffy, and dangerous. Fate stranded him in our strawberry patch one summer and my life changed forever.

On a fiercely hot June day I discovered Connal half hidden by a leaf. It was almost the turn of the year and the sun blazed down, blasting everything that could not escape. A sensible person would be indoors having a siesta, but my mother wanted strawberries for a pie and I could not persuade her to postpone this chore until it was a little cooler. I'm only twelve years old and this happens a lot.

I turned my ball cap backwards so the visor could protect my already sunburned neck as I stooped over the berry patch. Kneeling on the ground allowed the earth's radiant heat to pour into my bones. I began to fancy it might be possible for me to melt into the earth. The lawn clippings my dad uses to mulch between the rows tickled my toes where they poked through my sandals and gave off the same peculiar odor as our compost heap. It was a scorcher.

When I glanced toward the neighbor's yard, I could see heat shimmers in the air. That's why I didn't really pay attention when the small action figure, partially hidden under a pumpkin leaf, seemed to move. I thought is must be some kind of miniature mirage.

Our garden grows wonderfully well, but everything tends to get mixed together and pumpkin vines wander everywhere. In the fall visitors have been surprised to find large pumpkins hanging from branches in our pine tree.

As I worked my way closer to the small figure, which was tangled in a stray tendril of a pumpkin vine, I was impressed with its lifelike detail. I stooped even closer and shook my head. I thought it must be a mirage or heat stroke because I was sure I'd seen its eyes blink. Then the little arms began flailing and I distinctly heard a small but very clear voice say, "Oh, no!" I think he can see me!"

Most people can neither see nor hear tiny fairies. Until I met Connal, I never knew I could do both. It was fortunate for him I was out in the garden that day. Small fairies find it very useful to have a 'friend' in the big world. I am somewhat less enthusiastic. Talking to small beings other people cannot see or hear can cause problems. It can be a recipe for disaster and there have been more than enough disasters in my life. If you like, I can show you the scars.

I was not scared, but surprised and very curious. I decided to believe my eyes, not logic, and act accordingly.

"Keep still and I'll untangle you. How did get caught by the pumpkin vine?" If I could get him talking, he might stop being so upset.

"I was very tired and thought I would lay down for a moment to rest on this beautiful sunny day. I needed shade and made the mistake of lying under this large pumpkin leaf. When I woke up, I was entangled in this blasted vine."

I finished releasing him and set him beside the leaf. "By the way, my name's James. What's yours?"

"Connal O'Connal at your service," the fairy replied with a deep bow and a fine flourish of his tattered cap. "The name

Connal means 'high and mighty' but at the moment I'm feeling very 'low and weak'."

His name didn't really match his appearance either, but it wouldn't be polite to say so.

Then a worried look crossed his face. "You won't try to capture me will you?"

"Why would I want to do that?"

"Some people confuse us with leprechauns and won't let us go until we give them a pot of gold, which is a crock, if you'll excuse the bad pun. Unfortunately, fairies are allergic to most metals except silver."

"Well your secret's safe with me," I assured him. "Gold isn't used as money here, so I couldn't spend it. If I suddenly acquired a piece of real gold, some well meaning adult would probably take it away from me for safekeeping and I'd never see it again."

Connal looked relieved.

"You said you were allergic to metals? So's my mom."

"Oh, fairies are allergic all right. We get what looks like a bad burn if we touch most metals without some kind of protection. It causes us no end of trouble and is partly responsible for my present sorry state." He shook his head sadly. "I lost all of my tools and other supplies crossing the creek, so I had no silver knife to cut myself loose from that pesky vine."

He began brushing himself off and it was plain to see he was definitely the worse for wear. His face and body were covered with tiny cuts and bruises and his sleeveless green tunic was badly torn. He had tried to repair it by tying the fabric together with wisps of string. I guessed he didn't have any silver needles either.

"How can you get another knife?"

"Well, I could make another one, if I could find a small bit of silver. That used to be fairly easy to do when you big folk used silver coins, but I'm told money today is made from other metals and we shouldn't go near it."

I remembered a few years ago when my Dad gave me several old coins made from real silver.

"I can get a little silver for you, but it will take a while to find it. It's at the bottom of a drawer somewhere."

"You can! That's wonderful!" He was so excited he leaped high into the air, and then he quickly ducked under the pumpkin leaf.

"Look." He pointed skyward. "The sun is so strong today I could become ill if I don't return to my shelter. Can we meet here again tonight? Fairies are much happier out in the moonlight."

"Sure, I don't have school tomorrow so I should be able to slip away. What time will you be here?"

"See that pine tree across the yard? When the moon is directly over the top, I'll come here again."

Suddenly, he was gone and I could only shake my head and wonder if I had imagined everything. Then something caught my eye. There on the earth beside the pumpkin vine was a very tiny, but very real, fairy's cap.

That evening I went into the back yard early and found a comfortable spot beside the old willow tree where I had a clear view of both the pine tree and the moon. A small silver coin nestled snugly in my pocket. The golden light from our family room spilled across the deck and onto the grass. The warm June air was heavy with the sweet, sweet fragrance from the white nicotina in the nearby planter.

Perhaps the strong perfume caused me to doze off because the next thing I knew something hit me on chin. My eyes flew open and there was the moon shining directly over the pine tree. I turned my head and saw Connal sitting on the rim of the planter throwing very small pebbles at me.

"Ouch! Stop that!" I cried. "There must be a better way to get my attention."

"I didn't want to get too close. If you started to thrash about when you woke up, I might not have been able to duck fast enough."

I reached into my pocket for the silver coin. That afternoon I'd taken a soft cloth and rubbed it until it gleamed. If Connal really was allergic, I thought a clean coin would be safer for him. The polished disc seemed to glow in the moonlight.

There was a soft answering glow in Connal's eyes. "Real silver and almost pure," he murmured. "This is a great gift and you are a true friend."

He had fashioned a little bag to carry it, and I helped him stow it away. I expected he would leave, but he stood there, his head tilted to one side, as if he were trying to make up his mind.

Finally he said, "I have another favor to ask. Would you mind if we stayed in your garden until winter?"

"Before I say 'yes', who is 'we'?"

"The old friend I'm traveling with was hurt when we tried to cross the creek. He should rest and recover for a time before we journey onward."

"Well, if there are only two of you, I suppose it would be all right. Will there be many others beside myself who can see you? My parents don't like to draw attention to themselves. They would be very upset if the television news arrived in our backyard to interview a troop of fairies."

"I was told it was just about impossible for any big people to see us. Unfortunately, it appears my companion and I have very out of date information about conditions here. I can't make any promises."

"Where is your friend? Is there anything I can do to help him?"

"He's still very weak. I left him sleeping in a small shelter I made for us under the juniper bush."

An awful thought struck me. "We have a cat!" I exclaimed. "This is his territory and he is out on the prowl. I've got to get you and your friend out of here, now."

"I'm not afraid of a cat. I can move very fast if I must."

"Well, you should be afraid. He might be able to see you and he's a very skilled hunter. You and your friend will look like tasty snacks to him. Let me take you both somewhere safe."

The fear in my voice must have convinced him for he jumped off the planter and raced toward the juniper bush in the far corner of our yard. I had no trouble keeping up with him and out of the corner of my eye I saw our cat, Churchill, drifting silently through the grass near the fence. I felt relieved I was there to protect Connal.

Our cat Churchill is part Persian and part Russian blue. The fluffy soft grey fur makes him almost invisible at night. It was lucky I had spotted him.

Churchill appeared on our doorstep one morning as my mother was leaving for work. He was injured, starving, and pitiful. My mother couldn't help herself. She fed him a couple of defrosted frozen fish sticks and he never left. My brother Gordon said he resembled the cat in the movie *Pet Cemetery* and suggested we name him Churchill. Since he was near death when he came, the name seemed appropriate.

"What's your friend's name?" I asked as I knelt down beside the juniper.

"You can call him Max. His real name is much longer and I'd rather he told you himself."

"We have a problem, Connal."

"We have a lot of problems. We have to find a safe place for us to stay, obtain more supplies, and get some help for Max. Do you have any suggestions?"

"Yes, I do, but you won't like it. We need to talk to a grownup and I think I know the right person. My grandpa, Duncan Owen, lives very near here. If anyone can help you, he can."

"Are you sure he can be trusted?"

Somehow I convinced Connal that Grandpa was our best hope. I think it helped that our cat's curiosity got the better of him and he walked up and peered under the juniper. It was quite obvious he could see Connal.

Max never awakened when I picked him up. I couldn't believe how heavy he was. Connal climbed up and rode on my shoulder. He was also extremely heavy for his small size.

"I thought fairies were supposed to be light and airy," I grumbled as I walked back to the house."

"So did I," snorted Connal. "That's another thing we weren't expecting. The only good thing is I'm much stronger than I expected to be."

When we reached the house, I stood in the shadows and called to my mom through the door. I wasn't taking the chance she could also see the fairies.

"Mom, I want to run over to Grandpa's house for a while. I'll phone back as soon as I get there."

"Oh good, your father and I have to go out for a while. Do you want to stay over since it's the weekend?"

This was a piece of good luck. Now I would be able to explain everything to Grandpa and get Max and Connal settled before coming home again.

My Grandpa lives four doors down the street. During the walk I again noticed Churchill following us at discrete distance. As I rang the doorbell, he joined us on the front step. Somehow I felt oddly comforted by his presence.

When Grandpa opened his door, Churchill pushed past me into the house. Grandpa smiled down at Churchill and said, "Hello, cat. Back for more tuna?"

Then he squinted at me and tilted his head back and forth. "What are those two misty patches? There's one in your hands and another near your head."

"They're supposed to be fairies and I'll explain everything once I tell Mom I'm here."

The first thing we did was look after Max.

Connal told us that, in general, the care and treatment of fairies should be reasonably similar to that of humans. Using this as our guide we made Max as comfortable as possible and cleaned and treated his wounds. He groaned and thrashed around a little but seemed to be sleeping easier once we tucked him into the makeshift bed Grandfather set up on his desk in the living room.

Connal ate a late supper of honey, tiny chunks of bread, and small bits of apple. He washed it down with lots of milk and water. For such a small being he consumed a large amount of food. We even managed to get a little honey and water into Max when he woke up for a minute or so.

While this was going on, Grandpa was bustling around the house. He was intrigued to learn that fairies were allergic to most metals and didn't enjoy direct sunlight. He rummaged around in an old box and brought out several pieces of transparent plastic which he referred to as "solar control film". It's used on windows to screen out some of the sun's harmful rays, particularly ultra-violet. There was a selection of different colors and he held each one up and looked through it at Connal.

"Aha," he chortled. "I thought something like this might help. Connal and Max are still fuzzy, but I can see them not too badly. For some reason the blue piece seems to work best. I'll find an old pair of glasses and apply some to the surface."

"Not someone else who can see us," complained Connal.

"Hearing you is much harder, if that's any consolation," said Grandpa. "However, that could be because you're very small and I'm at an age when my hearing level is dropping. Still, I can hear you well enough when the room is quiet, and I think you owe us an explanation if you want us to continue helping you."

"You're right," said Connal. "Make yourselves comfortable. This is going to take a while. Remember a lot of it I don't really understand myself."

This is Connal's story as nearly as I can remember it.

"I am going to start at the beginning when fairies and men both shared the Earth and most definitely common ancestors. The old tales of fairies and men all mention marriage between the two groups and halfling children. That's a sure sign we are more alike than fairies want to admit.

In our usual shape we're often slightly taller than humans. The stories about wee folk arose from times when a fairy returned to your world from what became known as Fairyland. It takes a lot less energy to send a tiny wisp of matter across than a full sized fairy. Max and I came here on a quest for help and information.

When men and fairies were both limited to the earth, there was not much to tell them apart. The first change appeared in our eyes. We developed the ability to see a wider range of the spectrum and our night vision improved. Gradually, we became night hunters while humans preferred the day.

A side effect of this ability was seeing things that apparently weren't there. Most humans and animals will walk right through these apparitions. Cats and other night hunters usually do not.

As the ages passed we slowly discovered the truth about our visions. They came from another place that was somehow in contact with the Earth, not another world, but a place of endless possibilities. Through much trial and error we learned how to travel there and still return to our homes here. Later we began to feel more at home in Fairyland and rarely returned to Earth.

This Fairyland was a magical place where things could spring into being with almost no effort on our part. We named it the Undying-lands because, as far as we could tell, living there allowed you to live almost forever unless killed by accident. There were always dangers but we learned to avoid most of them. Sadly, everything has a price and now some of us don't want to continue paying it.

While in Fairyland it was dangerous to have children, so we often returned to Earth if we wanted to raise a family. At first we could return anywhere on the planet, but over time whole areas became blocked off. Later even those portals became smaller and smaller. It became extremely difficult for us to transfer at our normal size and hope to come back. This is when fairies began to be described as very small.

Because of our problems bearing children, our numbers grew slowly here on Earth and later in Fairyland where there was an added risk. This land was really not ours, so large numbers of mutations appeared. Some might have sacrificed those children who were not perfect, but our beliefs and laws teach us that all life is sacred and there should be compelling reasons for any killing. As a result, we developed a system for isolating our misbegotten children. We created a land apart where they could live out their lives. As you may have learned, segregation does not work.

The outcasts were not grateful for being spared. They felt they were looked down upon unjustly. This was true. It turned out many of the mutations were nature's way of adapting our species to a different environment. Many of the Misbegotten were actually better suited to living Fairyland than those of the pure blood.

Through trial and error my people once again began to bear mostly normal children and now we keep all our sons and daughters. However, the damage had been done. We must share our beautiful Fairyland with a group of dangerous beings who have sworn to hate us forever. The dominant mutation has changed them so much that the differences between us are truly profound. We both live in a state of eternal war.

When Max and I traveled here, we each sacrificed a tiny portion of our true selves and created the small beings you see before you. We are supposed to be airy wisps and in close contact with our true selves in Fairyland. Something must have gone terribly wrong. We are both very heavy and contact with the Undying Lands has been lost. Others consider me very brave, but I have never been so frightened in my life.

Fairyland has other problems as well. The world we have created seems to be under increasing attack from some evil force. The best way to describe it is a lack of stability. Things seem to appear and disappear for no reason we can fathom. This can be very dangerous. You can be lost forever just stepping out of your own front door.

Max and I belong to a small group that feels it is time to forswear our almost eternal life spans and the radiant beauty of Fairyland and try to return to Earth. There have always been a few fairies who have chosen to do this. For a long time it was possible to keep in contact with them, but for the past hundred years or so even this has become extremely difficult.

Max is a wizard which is something like a scientist. I am the warrior who was sent to protect him. We hope to be able to open a proper portal by working from both sides. Our quest is, to find one of the last fairies to come back, and ask if he could help us open a way large enough for a few of us to pass through at our normal size.

Max is very cautious and did a great deal of research before we came. He discovered people, who spoke English, could be found almost anywhere on the planet and he made sure both of us were fluent in its use. The plan was for us to enter through the closest suitable portal, hopefully in Ireland, and report back on present conditions. Next we would establish a base here so the dozen or so others who wished to return would be able to do so. With any luck our small number should be virtually unnoticed.

Bad luck, or someone's evil intentions, has been our lot ever since we arrived. This country is not Ireland. We could tell right away from the plants and animals. We were attacked almost immediately after we arrived by something that looked like a raven, but its actions were far too deliberate.

The first thing it did was throw all our supplies into the nearby creek. Then it attacked Max and dropped him in the creek as well. I was surprised to see him sink like a stone, so I immediately jumped into the water to rescue him.

I am a good swimmer but I found myself so heavy it was almost as if the water wasn't there. As soon as I hit bottom, I opened my eyes and tried to lift Max. Even with the buoyancy provided by the water, he was very hard to move. I had to drag him along as I walked and crawled across the muddy bottom and onto the bank. By the time we were out my head was spinning and my lungs felt as if they would burst. Max only survived because he was able to put himself into a trance that suspended all his life functions for a while.

I'm ashamed to admit it but I lost consciousness for a while. We were lucky the raven left while we were still underwater. When I came to, I dragged Max up the bank, across the field, through a break in the fence, and into the relative safety of James's garden.

I hid Max as best I could and went in search of food and water. The strain of the journey to Earth and our violent arrival had drained most of my strength and I lost consciousness again. I slept for hours before James found me trapped by the pumpkin vine. When I think of it now, I wonder if the pumpkin vine was an accident. I'm not weak and should have been able to break free on my own."

Here Connal stopped and shrugged his shoulders.

"Now what do we do?"

The peace of ordinary life seemed to fill the room and made an interesting contrast to Connal's strange story. Churchill had climbed onto my lap and was purring softly. Grandpa was sitting in his favorite chair with his feet up on the shabby leather-covered footstool. His blue tinted glasses made him look alien and strange. Connal and I settled back and waited for his answer.

There was a long pause before he spoke. "There are a lot of gaps in your story. I feel James and I have more questions than answers. However, it is possible fairies did share the earth with us in relative peace for a long, long time. Also, it does appear that you and your friend are in real peril and this must be our first consideration. We will do what we can to help you."

Connal sighed and placed his hand over his heart, "With all my heart I swear to you we mean no harm and will always try to avoid trouble when we can. The danger we face is real and Max and I have both sworn to complete our quest or die. We cannot afford to fail."

"This quest is your first priority, then?"

"Definitely," replied Connal. "We have already sacrificed much to get this far."

"Do you know the name of the fairy you are looking for and do you have any idea of where he lives? I don't suppose you have the name he is currently using or his address and phone number. That would be too easy."

"I don't think it would help if I gave you his real name. In the first place it would be a grave insult. It is also unlikely he would be using it here because it is different from the names you use and would draw attention to him. We know he intended to live quietly among you."

"Do you have any information that might help us?"

Connal closed his eyes and bit his lower lip.

"I think Max mentioned him living in county Kerry, Ireland. He said something about using the word "Kerry" as a name or reference. Also, Sean might be the first name."

Grandpa thought for a moment.

"A close friend of mine moved back to Ireland four or five years ago when he retired. He was a librarian and is used to doing research. I could ask him to see if he can locate a Mr. Sean Kerry who lives in county Kerry. However, first I will have to calculate the time difference between here and Ireland."

"Time difference," said Connal, "what time difference?"

I had been quiet for a long while, but now I had a question. "Connal, you said you knew you weren't in Ireland, but do you have any idea of where you are?"

"I thought perhaps this might be England."

"Not even close," I laughed. "Welcome to Winnipeg! You are on the other side of the Atlantic ocean in a country called Canada."

Connal looked absolutely stricken. "It will take months to reach him and we are running out of time."

"You don't know about telephones or e-mail, do you? They're a kind of human magic and they work just fine. We can talk to Grandpa's friend instantly, but we don't want to wake him out of a sound sleep. That's why we need to find out the time difference between here and Ireland."

"I could send him an e-mail message right now, but it would be easier to talk to him on the telephone," said Grandfather as he rummaged around in one of his bookshelves and brought out an old atlas. "Ireland is in a time zone six hours away from us. I will try to reach him before he leaves home for the day. I'll set my alarm for 1:30 a.m. and call him then."

"Will you need to tell your friend about Max and me? We don't want to attract any more attention than we have to."

"I don't think that would be a good idea either," agreed Grandpa. "I'll say an old friend of mine and his son just learned that a long lost uncle may be living in Ireland, possibly under the name Sean Kerry. They would like to make contact with him and see if he wants to come to Canada for a visit. Can you think of a code word to identify you? I could give it as your last name?"

"What about Max and Connal Fairyland?" I piped up. "If he asks you how to spell it, you can make it 'F E R R Y L A N D'. The sound tells you exactly what it is but the spelling suggests bringing something across on a ferry."

"That's not a bad idea," said Grandpa. "It should be obvious enough for him to contact us if he is willing to help."

I took Churchill into the spare bedroom with me and tied the door shut. Our cat has been known to open closed doors by swinging on the handles and I was taking no chances. Connal made up a pallet beside Max on the desk in the living room and Grandpa set his alarm clock and settled into his own bed.

I was sure I would hear the alarm but I overslept. I awoke to find Grandpa drinking his mid-morning coffee at the desk in the living room. I was surprised to see Max was now awake and engaged in a spirited conversation with Grandpa. Even more surprising was Connal. He was bounding about on the carpet doing what had to be some kind of martial arts exercises. He looked very fierce and experienced. At his full size he would have be a formidable warrior indeed.

Churchill glided into the room and I went over to pick him up.

"Leave him be!" cried Connal. "He'll make a good opponent."

I watched fascinated as Churchill and Connal rolled about the room. Churchill loves to play fight with me or my friends. He was famous for his ability to wrestle energetically with your arm, leg, or hand without leaving a mark. If he did get too rough, all you had to say was, "Ouch, or Churchill, no!", and he would ease up instantly. Somehow he seemed to realize Connal was a 'playmate' not food and entered enthusiastically into the game. After a short while I declared it a draw and separated them. I lifted Connal onto the desk and pulled up a chair beside it. Churchill jumped onto my lap.

I was pleased to see Max appeared much better this morning. He was still resting in his makeshift bed, but his color was good and his eyes twinkled merrily when he smiled at me.

"So this is the young fellow who rescued us from his garden. Your assistance is greatly appreciated. Perhaps, someday Connal and I will be able to return the favor."

"I'm glad to see you looking so much better this morning, sir. I can't believe I slept so long. What time is it? Has anything happened while I was sleeping?"

"It's now nine-thirty," said Grandpa. "That will be about three-thirty in the afternoon in Ireland. If my friend managed to find your colleague, someone should be in contact with us soon."

"Your grandfather and I spent an interesting morning exchanging confidences. You humans have made an incredible amount of scientific progress in the last hundred years or so. It's absolutely magical. In comparison Fairyland has changed very little."

There were all sorts of questions bubbling up inside of me, but at that moment the phone rang.

Grandpa picked it up.

"Hello, Randall. Did you manage to find Sean Kerry? That's great news! He's what? That's fast work. Do you have the name of the airline and flight number?"

The rest of the conversation lasted for several minutes but was only personal exchanges between Grandpa and his friend. I concluded that someone, possibly Sean Kerry, was flying over from Ireland and I whispered the news to Max and Connal. They were both startled and happy with this rapid turn of events.

When he got off the phone, Grandpa told us Mr. Sean Kerry would arrive sometime after lunch tomorrow with the intention of taking Max and Connal off our hands.

"This is almost too easy," marveled Connal. He turned out to be prophetic. It was too easy.

Max and Grandpa spent the day and evening talking about everything under the sun and I went outside with Connal. We located a tube of heavy sun screen and Connal rubbed it all over himself. When he stepped out into the sunlight, he was very pleased with its effect.

"This will make it so much easier to move around in the daylight."

Together we checked out the garden and near-by yards to make sure he knew his surroundings well enough to be able to defend it if necessary. He took his role as Max's guardian very seriously and was still uneasy because of all the troubles that greeted their arrival. We chatted away as we toured the neighborhood and I found him very easy to talk to.

"Do you really live forever in Fairyland?"

"No, we don't. "However, we do live for a long, long time. Max told me the first fairies appeared around the end of the last ice age. In addition to our night vision we had a fairly long life span of about one hundred to one hundred and fifty years. Through time this gradually increased to between two hundred and three hundred years, if you spent all your time on Earth. In Fairyland this would more than double again. It's not eternal life but, when you live in a world where little ever changes, six hundred years can seem like it."

"How old are you and Max?"

"I'm not sure how it would work in Earth years but I was born around two hundred years ago. That would be about one hundred years ago on Earth. Max was born about fifty Earth years before I was."

I was a little disappointed that Max and Connal would soon be leaving. It would have been fun to join in their grand and glorious quest.

I needn't have worried.

I was annoyed with Grandpa when he insisted I return home before lunch the next day to set up our small blue nylon tent out in the backyard. Then he brought Max and Connal over and asked me to fairy-sit while he drove to the airport to pick up Mr. Kerry.

Grandpa sometimes takes notions. He said he was uneasy about leaving us alone in the house while he was gone.

It turned out to be a pleasant afternoon. Max, Connal, and Churchill, because they were night hunters, spent the afternoon dozing in the warm, flower-scented air that drifted in through the mesh door. I had a good book to read and my mom provided lots of tasty snacks. I shared these with my companions whenever they woke up for a few moments. They both remarked on how hungry they felt and continued to eat a lot for their small size.

Everything was warm and peaceful when the silence was shattered by a loud clap of what sounded like thunder. The atmosphere thrummed with static electricity and I could feel the hair on my arms and the back of my neck stand straight up.

"What was that?" I cried.

"Something out of a nightmare, Gaia help us," whispered Max.

"Don't move," hissed Connal as he and Churchill peered warily into the yard. "The decoys seem to have worked, at least for the moment. It is a blessing we were not at the house."

Max smiled somewhat bitterly. "The best thing is the attack used up a tremendous amount of energy. Our enemies will have to try something a little less forceful the next time."

"Shall we stay here or make a run for it? Either course is very risky," said Connal. "The only weapon I have is this strange sword James's grandfather fashioned for me. It has a good edge and is not painful to hold but I'm still uneasy being near anything made out of iron." He waggled the small shard of stainless steel my grandfather had turned into a weapon for him. Because of my mother's metal allergy, Grandpa knew she could tolerate stainless steel and thought Connal might be able to as well. It turned out he was right.

"First, we must find a way to hide," said Max. "Our enemies will want to make absolutely sure we are not here."

There was a long pause while Max pressed the fingers of his hands to his temples and thought furiously.

"I can only think of one thing we can do, but I don't like it. We can use a tiny amount of another being's life-force as a shield. It's easy, painless, but morally questionable. James, I wouldn't ask you this except I am desperate. If you will share a very small amount of your life force with me, then the searchers will only sense one being here as long as I remain very close to you. I could take it without your consent but it would rest easier on my mind if you agreed to it." "I guess so. It doesn't seem much different than donating blood and my mom and dad donate all the time." I wasn't sure about the procedure. Would it hurt? Would I feel sick? I wished I could ask my mom and dad before we did anything.

There was no time to change my mind. Max reached out and touched my hand. I felt a brief tingling and that was it. I only noticed one change. I was aware of wherever Max was, even with my eyes closed.

Max turned his head and stared balefully at Connal. "Touch the cat, Connal. Quickly, we're running out of time."

"Bond with the cat!" yelped Connal. "I gave my oath to serve you faithfully even unto death. There was nothing about bonding with a cat. The disgrace will stay with me as long as I live. Can't I just die? It would be easier."

"Do it now!" Max's voice rang out with the finality of a judge pronouncing a sentence of doom.

Connal covered his eyes with one hand and gently touched Churchill on the tip of his nose. Then he slumped to the floor with his head between his hands.

"You could do worse," said Max. "Churchill is a very interesting cat. I do believe he knew his life would be linked to yours even before we did. Animals often seem to be aware of events in the near future. You may even find there are definite advantages to the bond."

Connal just shook his head.

Max turned to me. "Our enemies will no longer be able to sense us as long as we stay near enough to touch you, however, they can still see us. It is essential we stay out of sight until Duncan and Sean Kerry return from the airport. Have you any ideas?"

I felt myself half-raising my hand almost as if I were in school. "You have to stay close to me, Max, and Connal must stay near Churchill. Is that right??"

"Yes, go on," said Max, frowning.

"You and Connal are very heavy, but I might be able to carry you and Churchill all rolled up in a blanket. Unfortunately, I think Churchill would object. If you don't mind riding in my backpack, Max, we can make a quick trip into the house and get the cat carrier for Connal and Churchill. Then when it's safe, I can walk back to Grandpa's with all three of you and nothing should look suspicious."

Connal wasn't happy about being left behind with the cat. However, when we returned, we found him nestled snugly against a purring Churchill. I thought being so relaxed showed poor judgment on his part. It was only later I realized he knew how to take advantage of any lull in a battle so he would be fresh when the next attack came.

"Will there be trouble when my Grandpa and Sean Kerry return from the airport? Is it safe for them to go into the house?"

Max thought about this for a minute. "I believe they should be fine. By now our enemies will have checked out the house. It will take a while longer for them to check out the neighborhood. I'll try to warn you when they are coming close. Connal and I will hide. They won't be able to sense us and if they can't see us we should be fine."

Connal spoke up from his spot on the floor, "Max and I know Sean very well. He is very wise and very careful. He will be able to tell the house was under attack and will make sure everything is safe before they enter. He might even decide to come straight here."

After a few minutes of silence, Max and Connal both dived for cover. I didn't have any time to become frightened, so my startled look could have been caused by the sudden appearance of a man's figure outside the tent door.

"My dog ran away from me in the park. You haven't seen him, have you?" I could see his eyes were checking out everything in the tent.

"No," was all I said. My father once told me those with something to hide usually give it away by talking too much. I wasn't going to make that mistake.

The man continued to stare at me with the brightest blue eyes I had ever seen. "If you do see him, let me know," he continued. Then he straightened up and left the yard.

I noted he didn't even bother to describe the dog or tell me how to contact him. My Dad was right. If you're lying, don't keep on talking or you're sure to give something away.

After that time stood still. We seemed to wait for an eternity, but it was only fifteen or twenty minutes later we heard a car crunching along the gravel driveway and my grandpa's weathered face with its blue tinted glasses appeared at the door of the tent.

"Sean said it wouldn't be safe to stop at my house, so we came straight here to collect all of you and take you to somewhere a little more secure."

Somehow Grandpa sold Mom on me going camping with himself and his visitor from Ireland who wanted to see some of the Canadian wilderness. I was surprised she let me go because it was only June twentieth and there was still a week or so of school left. However, end of school tests were finished and I wouldn't really miss anything important.

Grandpa and Mr. Kerry rode in the front seat and Max, Connal, Churchill, and I were in the back. After we were out of the city I fixed up a spot under the back window so Max could look out. I know you're supposed to use your seat belts but they simply wouldn't work on tiny fairies and I decided Max and Connal might as well enjoy the ride.

My intentions were good, but I don't think it worked. Connal climbed up beside Max and they spent a long time talking in a language I didn't recognize. From the look on their faces they were really worried about something.

Grandpa said we were going to a place near Bissett, so I took out the Manitoba map and located the tiny town. I found it on the edge of the true wilderness that makes up most of the Canadian Shield. It was on the far end of a loop of road that penetrated a long way into this largely unpopulated area.

"What's in Bissett, Grandpa?"

"There is an old gold mine there, but it's been closed and not very much is left of the town. Mr. Kerry believes there is someone there who can help us."

"I hope so," I replied. "Are we still in danger?"

Mr. Kerry twisted around in his seat so he could look at me. He had penetrating pale blue eyes reminded me of someone. It was a shock when I realized they were very similar to those of the man who came into the backyard looking for his lost dog. I hoped my face didn't give anything away.

"I'm not sure," said Mr. Kerry in his soft Irish accent, "but I do believe the person I hope to contact will know what to do."

"Can Grandpa ever return to his house?"

"Well, apart from his plants and any other living thing inside the house being dead, he should have the most sanitary house in the neighborhood. He could even eat any food in his refrigerator. It would be just fine. I wouldn't eat it myself because I'm not too enthusiastic about eating commercially irradiated food which is not harmful either. I prefer things to be in a more natural state."

Mr. Kerry turned away and I looked out the window and watched the brilliant greens of the Manitoba countryside flow past the car window. I had a lot to think about. Some things made sense and some did not. One of the things that did not make sense was the way they spoke.

I twisted myself around so I could see Connal and Max.

"Why does Mr. Kerry have an Irish accent and you don't. You said you hoped to reach Ireland."

"You are very clever to have noticed," said Max with a smile. "Our accent is modeled after Mid-Western standard which was the accent used by U.S. movie studios in early movies and television.

We hoped that, when we reached Ireland, the people would think we were Americans. This would explain any mistakes we made in usage and custom."

"I rather pride myself on my mastery of colloquial phrases and slang," added Connal.

Max rolled his eyes, "I only hope his puns are funnier in English."

"You're just jealous," concluded Connal with a self-satisfied smile.

I always liked the idea of living in Canada. We have lots of space and not too many people, but now I wasn't so sure. I looked again at the map and discovered we would drive past the Newago Indian Reservation. I had never been there but one of my mother's friends lived there. I don't know why, but this made me feel a little better.

After we crossed the Winnipeg River, we had a fifty kilometer stretch of road where there was nothing but rocks and muskeg until we reached Maniggan and the Newago First Nation. We drove for a long while along the east side of Lake Winnipeg without ever seeing the lake. Mother's friend had told me there were wonderful golden sand beaches in the area. Sadly, we would not be able to enjoy them.

Lake Winnipeg is a truly enormous lake. The early explorers who came here expected to find the Pacific Ocean because the aboriginal people told them how the lake water went up and down during reasonably short periods of time, like the tides on the ocean. They were right about the water but it wasn't the ocean. What they observed were wind tides caused by strong winds pushing the water up on the shores of the shallow southern basin.

When we reached Maniggan, we turned east and drove along the forty kilometer stretch that would take us into Bissett. The road went up and down and around sharp curves. There were lots of swampy areas and occasional rock outcrops. There was very little traffic. We met only a couple of cars and a logging truck which came careening around one of the curves. It missed our car by inches. I was glad it was high summer and the sun wouldn't set until well after nine-thirty. At least Grandpa was able to see where we were going.

There are only a few people who still live in Bissett, the remnant who chose to stay after the mine closed. Every so often someone does reopen the mine when the price of gold rises but when profits become too small it closes again.

It struck me, if someone was going to kidnap or kill us, this wouldn't be a very smart place to do it. In a big city no one pays much attention to other people, but in such a small place it is likely someone would notice our arrival and departure.

We drove out past the edge of town and parked by the Wanipigow River. Everyone got out of the car and walked down to the water. I carried Max in my backpack and Connal and Churchill in the cat carrier. I muttered under my breath about how the grown-ups had left the kid to do all the heavy stuff. Both the backpack and carrier were extremely heavy. It was a relief to set everything down by a thicket of willow bushes where I opened the top of the carrier. Churchill got out and stretched and Max and Connal took cover in the brush.

Sean Kerry and my Grandpa walked down to the water's edge. Mr. Kerry took a small object out of his pocket and threw it into the water. He said it would let others know we were here. Then they both walked back to the car and began to set out a picnic supper on a blanket close to the backpack and carrier.

It was a very simple meal of fresh buns, cold cuts, and cream cheese. There was an assortment of fruit and a package of cookies for desert along with some cans of soda pop to drink. Hunger made it one of the best meals I'd ever tasted.

After we cleaned up, we sat and waited. I walked up and down by the river's edge for a while then I joined the rest in their silent vigil. The sun was just about to slip behind the now dark and mysterious trees when a battered pickup truck drove up.

A tall man climbed out. He had a tanned angular face, black hair sprinkled with a little silver at the temples, and the darkest eyes I've ever seen, eyes so dark it was hard to distinguish the iris from the pupil. He did not look pleased to see us.

"I hope you have a good reason for coming here," declared the stranger. "I should probably blast you all on the spot, but I try to avoid rash acts that may cause problems later."

Sean Kerry stood up and walked toward him.

"Evan Hunter, I presume. I am Sean Kerry, also known as mmmph."

Here Mr. Kerry said something I could not make out.

The stranger looked surprised.

"Your real name, no less! This must be something extremely interesting and dangerous."

"There is an evil approaching that affects everyone. I believe there is no time left to debate. It will destroy us all, fairy and human alike, if we don't act now. I give you my word we come in peace." Here Sean Kerry dropped to one knee and bowed his head. "We await your decision."

The stranger's eyes widened and he shook his head. "Tomorrow is mid-summer and we're very busy. This is not a good time. Oh well, get into your car and follow me."

We followed him back to the highway and then off onto a rutted, nearly impassible side road. I was glad it was getting dark because I couldn't see where we were going and that gave me one less thing to worry about.

We reached what appeared to be a long, low house hemmed in by scrubby pine trees. There were no visible lights. When the door was opened, all I could see was a slightly lighter gray rectangle where we entered. It never got brighter than this as we groped our way along a hallway, through another door, and down several flights of stairs.

Suddenly a door opened and we walked into a brightly lit rather utilitarian corridor which seemed endless but was probably less than half a kilometer long. There was a space along the top of the right hand wall containing some kind of recessed lighting. The effect was very bright but not too hard on the eyes once they became accustomed to it. There were doors set into recesses at fairly regular intervals along the corridor.

The door nearest to us looked more like an airlock than a regular door. Something you might see in a fancy high tech laboratory. On the other side was a space that served as a kind of reception area. Evan told us to wait and we sat on a padded bench fastened to the nearest wall. Our group reminded me of naughty children waiting to see the principal.

I let Churchill and Connal out of the cat carrier and placed Max on my backpack which I scrunched up so he would have a kind of back rest.

Max gave a long sigh. "Well, the bright side is we've made contact much, much faster than I would have thought possible. Now, if we just live long enough to see sunrise tomorrow."

Grandpa Duncan turned and gave him a sharp look. "You mean that, don't you? Do you feel any responsibility for getting James and I involved in this perilous adventure?"

"Not really," Max replied. "James was in danger from the moment he found Connal in the strawberry patch. There was nothing I could do to change that."

Before a real argument could begin Evan returned with a much older man. He was tall and slender with the same bright blue eyes as Sean Kerry and the stranger in the back yard. He was dressed in an old t-shirt and faded jeans but I knew we were meeting someone important. An aura of power radiated from him. He stared long and hard at Max and Connal. I had the feeling he was very exasperated.

"It is instructive to see our old enemies brought so low. I have no sense of triumph though because I am sure you bring bad tidings for all of us."

At this point the new arrival switched into a language I didn't recognize and he, Mr. Kerry, Connal, and Max left through one door while Evan Hunter took Grandpa, Churchill and me through another.

He ushered us into a room containing eight bunk beds and a few assorted chairs and tables.

"It's mid-summer and everyone is really busy but you can all sleep here for the night. I believe you had supper so we won't have to worry about feeding you until morning. There are showers and toilets through the other door."

He didn't wait for any questions just went quickly out the door and I heard the lock click. Grandpa looked troubled. "I don't like this one bit, James. It is cold comfort, but I suspect Max is right and we are safer here than back in Winnipeg."

"It's all right, Grandpa. I don't think we had any choice."

"On the bright side, the beds look reasonably comfortable, and I'm glad of a chance to sit with my feet up for a while. Let's gather up some of the extra pillows and make a cozy spot on one of the bottom bunks. It's time to do some serious thinking. Hopefully, we will relax enough to be able to fall asleep later."

We sat together, propped up by pillows against the end of the bunk. Churchill joined us and promptly fell asleep.

I could tell Grandpa didn't want to talk. I suspected he was going over everything he and Max talked about to identify any nuggets of helpful information. I decided I would try to follow his example.

One thing he didn't know about was sharing my life force with Max. There hadn't been an opportunity to tell anyone and I wasn't sure I wanted to talk about it anyway. I had noticed certain changes. Being aware of Max's presence wasn't the only thing that was different.

My memories were all intact and whatever made up my personal identity felt the same, but I seemed to have acquired a whole new set of skills. It was something like upgrading a computer. All the old files were intact but something new had been added.

I felt as if I had a program running inside my head that was focused on integrating these new skills and absorbing an enormous amount of strange information. Whenever I focused on this change, my head began to spin and my stomach became queasy. I don't know what would have happened if I wasn't so good at blocking things from my mind.

When I was a toddler, my legs were badly burned and the ability to block at least some of the pain was a matter of survival. It was a pleasant surprise to discover I could control this runaway flood of information in much the same way as I could control the sensation of pain. Necessary information could still flow into my mind but only in comfortable amounts. For example, it wasn't as if I could read minds or anything, but my new ability allowed me to know what people were likely to do next and make a very good guess at the reasons why. My mom always said I was mature for my age and dad refers to me as long headed, but this went way beyond that. I decided to think of this new talent as my 'computer program'.

As I sat curled up next to Grandpa, I found myself wide awake and calmly analyzing our present situation and speculating on our chances for survival. I knew Grandpa was really worried and I kept thinking, "I'm only a kid and I should be scared but I'm not." I was more interested in sorting out all this new and alien information.

It was reasonably certain these new mental skills were an unintended side effect of bonding with Max. Also, I was completely sure that at the moment of bonding Max intended no harm and did as much as he could to neutralize its effects. When the bond took place, there was an instant when I got a glimpse of his inner being and knew he was a person who was truly good and kind. There was also a secret so well hidden I suspected even he didn't know about it.

Someday I would have to make a decision regarding this secret information, but not now.

Two possible reasons for my new skills were; first, Max was rushed and desperate and second, Max's physical condition was not normal after coming to Earth. It was obvious he weighed much more than he should and that was likely only a small part of other unexpected physical changes.

Eventually Grandpa, Churchill and I fell asleep and wakened only when the door opened and Evan Hunter returned.

"Its morning," he said wearily. "If you come with me we'll find some breakfast for you."

"You've been up all night talking to Max, Connal, and Mr. Kerry."

Evan gave me a sharp look. "Yes," he answered curtly.

A little red flag waved inside my head and I realized I should hide my new abilities as much as possible. It would be safer that way.

"What do you plan to do with us," asked Grandpa.

"As little as possible," answered Evan.

Breakfast was unremarkable. It was a buffet much like you would find in a medium priced motel. Except that we were underground in some kind of subterranean complex and possibly awaiting a fate worse than death, everything was just so ordinary.

Evan seemed determined to ignore us as he sat and moodily crunched through a bowl of flakes with a few strawberries sprinkled on top. I wondered if they had been picked locally. We had a very early spring but it was very early for local fruit. I sprinkled lots and lots of them over my bowl of cereal. If this was to be my last meal, I was going to enjoy it as much as possible. I poured some milk into a paper plate for Churchill. I know milk isn't good for cats, but I felt it would do until I could find some proper cat food.

The silence began to bother Grandpa so he began to talk to me.

"This place was built quite a while ago. Judging from the furniture and fittings, I'd say sometime in the nineteen-fifties. They did quite a bit of bunker building back then."

"Why was that?"

"A lot of people were worried about atomic bombs and the possibility of having a world war. Many shelters were built by the government but it's likely some big companies might have done something similar."

I guess the long silence was bothering Evan as well because he suddenly decided to join our conversation.

"Actually, construction was started by the federal government as some kind of research laboratory. After a while they decided it was too remote and concentrated their efforts in Pinawa at the atomic energy research facility there. Michael, the man you saw earlier, found out they were going to abandon the project and managed to purchase it. His company has been maintaining and expanding this site ever since."

"How did he keep it a secret?" asked Grandpa.

"He didn't even bother. All of the local people know it's here. Many of them have worked down here from time to time. The activity level has always been kept low key and people pretty much forget it's here. The best way to hide anything is out in plain sight."

"You said everyone was busy because of mid-summer. Are there many other people here?" I asked.

"A group of us who still follow the old religion decided to hold our celebration here this year."

"That's right," said Grandpa. "Today is June twenty-first. It's the summer solstice, the longest day of the year."

One of the side doors opened and a group of new people straggled in and proceeded to have breakfast. I didn't recognize any of them, but they seemed ordinary enough. A second group came in through another door and I saw Sean Kerry and Michael but not Max or Connal. When Sean saw us, he brought his breakfast over and sat down. He looked exhausted.

"Where are Max and Connal?" Grandpa asked.

"They are still being checked out. Their extra weight is very strange and we are attempting to solve that problem before we do anything else." Mr. Kerry looked worried. "This is not the way the process is supposed to work."

Michael, the person who seemed to be the leader here, also came over and sat at our table. He looked very tired and worried, too.

"It's been a long, long night," he said as he smiled wearily at us.

I felt that here was another person who could be trusted to do the right thing even though I sensed a strong underlying current of irritation and frustration. I somehow knew he was a man who had just taken up a terrible burden.

"What will happen now?" said Grandpa Duncan.

"Evan owns a cottage on a nearby lake and for the moment you and the rest of your party can stay with him," continued Michael. "It's probably fortunate you came at this time because we have a lot of people here who can work on the problem starting today. You can return to Winnipeg if you like but I believe you will be safer if you remain here for a day or two."

Grandpa nodded his head. "That sounds reasonable. "We can go whenever Evan is ready."

CHAPTER TWO
Evan's Cottage

Evan had a well maintained cottage high on a rocky bluff overlooking a very large lake. There was a well-worn wooden stairway down to the lake shore and a fair sized boat house and dock.

"The cottage looks a little lonely with all the trees cleared back from it," I remarked.

Evan smiled. "I thought it might be safer that way for several reasons. First, we live in a cold climate and I want my solar panels to get as much light as possible. Second, this allows the summer wind to blow away the mosquitoes. Third, open space gives me the chance to create a fire break if there's a forest fire. Fourth, it makes it difficult for intruders to get close without me noticing them. Are those enough reasons for you?"

This long speech reminded me of something my father had once said about Queen Victoria. She had just finished a book and was asked what it was like. Her reply was, "This book told me more about penguins than I wished to know."

I felt, if Evan decided to tell you something, you might get a lot more information than you were expecting. I also suspected he would be very good at not telling you anything he didn't want you to know. The extra information was really a kind of camouflage.

That's why I just smiled and said, "Yes, thanks."

Grandpa, Churchill, and I followed Evan into the cottage where he proceeded to go into a lot of detail about where to find blankets, beds, food, firewood, and much, much more. He evidently expected us to fend for ourselves because he was returning to the underground shelter as soon as we were settled.

"I'm expecting my two grandsons here for the next week or so. They should arrive sometime this afternoon. If you have other questions, just ask them."

As he was leaving he turned to grandpa and said, "Did your people come from Wales? I was born there myself."

"My father, David Owen, came from a small village near Cardiff," replied Grandpa. "He worked in the mines when he was young, but he worked for the railway when he came to Canada."

"You look like your father," said Evan, leaving grandpa and I surprised and confused.

After he left, Grandpa found some fishing tackle and went down to the dock. I sat with him for a short while but it was boring so I started to wander off.

"Don't go into the woods even for a short distance. The last thing we need it to have to organize a search party for you."

I went back to the cleared area around the cabin and picked a few strawberries growing at the edge of the trees. Strawberries from a garden can never compare with the wild sweet sun-warmed taste of nature's unaltered creation. The strawberries I had for breakfast could have been local after all.

Next I wandered through the cottage and checked out Evan's well stocked workshop. I didn't touch anything but I did amuse myself by trying to identify as many of the tools as possible. My grandfather's workshop is one of my very favorite places and it was comforting to be surrounded by such familiar objects.

It had been hot and dry for the past few weeks and everything smelled powdery and dangerous. A thirsty wind was pouring up from the south. The leaves rustled and seemed to be sharing dangerous secrets with the pines who answered with faint sad whispers.

I had noticed a fire alert warning near one of the campgrounds on our way here and I hoped no one was breaking the rules by building open fires. Fire is an ever present danger in Manitoba's boreal forests in a dry season. A single spark can transform thousands of acres into an awesome firestorm.

I tried to read one of the books I found inside the cottage but by lunch time I was getting really bored. I was very happy when a car drove up and unloaded Evan's grandsons. They were both older and taller than I was. I wondered if they would let me tag along with them.

"Hey, kid! What's your name?" said the taller one.

"Where's Uncle Evan?" said the other with a grin.

"My name's James. Evan said he had some work to do. He told my Grandpa and me you would be coming. We're staying with him for a few days. My Grandpa's down fishing off the dock."

"I'm Clifford," said the older boy, "and this is Kelsey. Would you like to go for a boat ride? We know a place where we might find lots of early strawberries."

"That would be great!" I was eager for anything to break the monotony.

"Are you sure Uncle Evan wants us to use his boat?" asked Kelsey.

"I think he would want us to do something to entertain his guests and a boat ride is as good as anything," replied Clifford, firmly ending the debate.

I must have looked uncertain because Kelsey smiled and gave me a playful shove. "Don't worry, kid. The only reason I wondered about the boat is because it has a very powerful motor and you can get into trouble quickly if you don't know what you are doing. Fortunately, Clifford and I have had tons of experience driving motor boats. There are very few roads around here and we all use boats a lot."

The three of us went into the cottage and packed a lunch. Then we walked down to find Grandpa at the dock. I was surprised when he decided not to come with us because he said he was feeling tired and wanted to take a nap. The second surprise was when Churchill jumped into the boat.

"Do you live in Bissett?" I asked once the boat was underway.

"No, we live near Maniggan on the Newago reservation. It's on the shore of Lake Winnipeg. We have a great sandy beach there. It's really nice. Not like the rocks and swamp around here, though this is pretty, too. Maybe we can go down to the beach sometime before you leave."

It was wonderful out on the water on this brilliant sunny day. The sky was a clear bright blue with an odd fluffy cloud here and there for contrast. Clifford kept the boat purring along about fifty feet from shore. You could smell the pine trees and enjoy the play of light and shadow as the light breeze made the leaves on the shore shiver and shake. Summer green on the Manitoba prairie is dazzling. Visitors have said it reminds them of the green in Ireland. Here in the Laurentian shield the green is much darker.

When my family toured the Black Hills, we were told the 'black' in the name was because that's what the pine trees made the hills look like in the distance. In the Laurentian Shield there are many dark green pine trees while the vivid green of the poplar and birch trees provide a pleasant contrast.

I had a wonderful time as we glided effortlessly over the water. It came as a surprise when the boat turned toward the shore and Kelsey jumped out so he could fasten a line securely to the nearby trees. We had arrived at our destination. It was evident my new companions were very familiar with the area.

Clifford, Churchill, and I climbed out and we all clambered up a rugged path to the top of a rock outcrop that overlooked the lake.

"Will your cat get lost?" asked Kelsey.

"I don't think so. He's not like a dog because he doesn't walk beside me, but when I go for walks at home he likes to come along and stays close enough that he's never been lost yet. My Mom says she had quite a few cats when she was little and they would all follow her on walks, even over the narrow plank bridge that crossed a small river."

First we walked to a place where there were wild strawberries. They were little and wonderfully sweet but there weren't very many. Then we found another place and picked enough to bring back for supper. Mostly we just sat around in the warm sunshine and talked while Churchill either napped or prowled around the perimeter of the clearing.

I didn't want to say anything about why we were here but it wasn't necessary. We talked about TV shows we liked and TV shows we hated, teachers we liked and teachers we hated. I told them about where I lived in Winnipeg and they told me about where they lived in Newago. By the time we got ready to leave, I felt I had known them forever.

There was definite a family resemblance between Clifford, Kelsey, and Evan but they had very different personalities.

Evan was a very dangerous man. He could be a trusted neighbor and a true friend, but you must be cautious. It would be unwise to accidentally place yourself in the line of fire between him and his enemies. He was on a lifelong search for a kind of truth and justice he might never find.

Kelsey was quiet but he had a warm smile. He tended to think carefully before he spoke and what he did say was usually helpful. His large store of physical energy allowed him to arrive anywhere just ahead of everyone else.

Clifford was sunny natured and very capable. He was like a warm sun-drenched rock, open and comforting but solid granite underneath.

We had just settled into the boat and Kelsey was untying the last line when Churchill, who had curled up in my lap, suddenly stood up with his tail and fur all fluffed out. He stared intently across the water at a small boat that was rapidly approaching our little harbor.

"Look at Churchill!" I exclaimed. "He doesn't like whatever is coming in that boat. Can we get out of here, please? And make it fast."

"No problem," said Clifford. "Uncle Evan's boat is faster than anything on the lake."

The motor roared into life. Gone was the sedate purr that had brought us here. With the motor howling Clifford headed straight for the middle of the lake on a trajectory that would bring us quite close to the strange boat.

Clifford saw how frightened I looked. "Don't worry!" he shouted. "I want to be in the middle of the lake when we're going this fast. I don't want to wreck Uncle Evan's boat on the underwater rocks close to shore."

There was spray everywhere but I still got a good look at the people in the boat as we shot by. I was quite sure one of the three men was the same one who had come into our back yard looking for his 'lost' dog. Worse than that, I was sure he'd recognized me.

Evan's boat was very fast so it wasn't much of a chase. However, the other boat did keep us in sight. Clifford deftly maneuvered our boat next to the dock and Kelsey jumped out to tie us to the dock. I looked back over the lake and saw our pursuers had stopped well out from shore and were sitting watching us.

Down the wooden stairs came Grandpa, Evan, and two small children. I wondered what the children were doing here when things were so dangerous. A shock ran through me as

I recognized they weren't children at all but Max and Connal now almost two feet tall.

"Who are the guys out on the lake, Uncle Evan?" asked Clifford. "Are they what you told us to look out for when you phoned?"

"I do believe they are," said Evan with a grim smile. "Now we know for certain some of our suspicions are correct."

I wanted to know what those suspicions were but I was too intimidated by the look on his face to ask, and he didn't offer any explanations. Maybe later I would ask Clifford or Kelsey.

I couldn't help blurting out, though, "Max, Connal, you're bigger!"

My Grandpa shot me a look and I didn't dare to ask about that either.

Evan looked quickly around the immediate area and said, "Let's get back to the cottage and decide what, if anything, we should do now. Everything is pretty much in place here, so we should be safe for the moment."

Kelsey retrieved the strawberries from the boat and we climbed the weathered wooden steps to the clearing around the cottage.

Inside we found food had been laid out for us and I realized how hungry I was. The strawberries were particularly delicious. I took comfort in that. At least something good remained from our excursion on the lake.

The whole meal was very quiet. No one seemed ready to talk.

Someone had piled books on two chairs so Max and Connal could reach the table. Now they were bigger I could see their faces more clearly. I was surprised at how similar they looked. They could have been brothers. If Max was a hundred years older than Connal, he certainly didn't look it.

We were nearly finished our meal when Connal suddenly started to speak.

"My but we're a silent lot. You'd think the end of the world was near and we're all under immediate threat of death or worse. We should be rejoicing."

"Don't be an idiot!" snapped Max.

"Oh, but I'm not," replied Connal rather too sweetly. "Just think. When things can't get any worse, they've got to get better."

There was another short pause and I decided I had to know what was happening.

"Listen, I don't understand any of this. Can't you tell me what is going on?"

"You probably won't be able to understand a lot of it," said Max.

"I don't care! Tell me as much as you can."

It was like a cork popping out of a bottle. Everyone began speaking at once which was just as bad as the quiet had been.

Then Evan raised his voice and called for silence. He said that, since we were all in his home, he would tell the story as he saw fit. He knew others would argue with parts of it because of the longstanding feud between them, but he would try to be as fair as possible.

Evan's story was similar to the one Connal had told us earlier but there were differences. Here is part of Evan's story.

"In the old tales elves were often called the White Court and the Black Court. Among themselves they spoke of the High Court and the Deep Court. Max, Sean Kerry, and Connal belong to the High Court and Michael, the people at the underground shelter, and I belong to the Deep Court.

Both the Deep Court and High Court began as a single group of people who were very skilled in metal work. This ability was much in demand and they became very rich and powerful. Then several people in the group developed an allergy to metal. At first this seemed to be a terrible problem until they discovered this sensitivity to metal allowed them to find new sources of ore. Through time the clan became divided into two groups. Those who mined the metal became the Deep Court, and those who could find it became the High Court.

The Deep Court continued to specialize in metal working while the High Court concentrated on studying plants and animals. Otherwise their language and social customs remained the same and they considered themselves related to one another. They moved from one area to another looking for metals to work and tried to blend into whatever society dominated that location while secretly maintaining their own identity. If their neighbors began to resent their presence, it was important to have extra supplies of food and weapons to draw on so they could leave quickly and safely. Their survival often depended of on the goodwill of brave individuals within the local group. Because of this, elves worked hard to maintain networks of friends who would give them temporary shelter while they searched for a new home.

Gold and other precious metals were durable and highly portable and they quickly realized how important it was to build up some kind of treasure trove for protection. Early on they developed a sophisticated financial system. Credit was given for both material goods and for good deeds. Consequently, most elves believed it was important to keep careful track of your debts and obligations.

Both the Deep Court and the High Court have different versions of why the feud began. The sanitized version says the difference was philosophical. The High Court believed man should search for perfection in a unified society while the Deep Court believed the earth was perfect the way it is, diversity is to be enjoyed, and one's loyalty should only be given to your freely chosen group. The more realistic version says it was a struggle over who controlled the mineral wealth. Both groups tell stories of slavery and oppression by the other Court.

During the last cycle of internecine violence the High Court was defeated by the Deep. The old stories say the king of the High Court led his people down into the ground and they were seen no more. The High Court's history tells of making a mass exodus into Fairyland through a secret portal in one of the mines.

The Deep Court remained on the Earth's surface where they systematically acquired more and more wealth and power. Through time the words Deep Court have joined into one and we now call ourselves The Core.

The Core exists as a loosely knit system of small independent groups. Membership in a successful group, while highly prized, is still a matter of absolute free choice for the individuals involved.

Centuries of practice has made us very good at escaping general notice. We are particularly skilled at creating new identities for those whose long life spans would draw attention to our existence. We also have extremely effective ways of keeping our existence secret.

Here Evan paused for a moment as if to emphasize this last fact. The expression on his face was particularly bleak. I began to wonder about what methods they might use and I suspected they would be quite deadly. No wonder Connal and Max had been so worried.

Evan finished by saying he believed this single minded search for perfection and uniformity was in large part responsible for the problems in Undying-Lands and the problems now being experienced on Earth.

Sean Kerry sprang to his feet his face flushed.

"I thought you were going to be fair. None of us have enough information to jump to any conclusions."

"I stand corrected," agreed Evan grimly. "You are right. We must remain open to all the possibilities if we are to have any hope of success."

"It well may be our troubles are caused by the Misbegotten," continued Sean. "However, if that is so, why do they insist we are responsible for the instability affecting everyone?"

"The three people we saw out on the lake suggest a rather different source of our present problems," added Max.

"Just what are those problems?" I cried feeling completely exasperated. All the adults seemed to know what was happening and were prepared to keep talking in circles while giving out as little information as possible.

Connal must have agreed with me because he jumped up on the table and began pacing nimbly up and down among the cups and plates and platters. He ticked off the various problem items on his fingers.

"First, something is very wrong in the Undying Lands. There is an evil force growing there and no one seems to be able to stop it.

Second, the portals which we used to travel back and forth between Fairyland and Earth are being systematically sealed off.

Third, we have no idea of who is responsible for this or if it is a good outcome or a bad one.

Fourth, there appears to be a third group involved, mostly here on Earth. We have identified at least one of its members and that suggests it has something to do with mind-control. Several members of the Core have already been seized and a few have been killed.

Have I left anything out?"

"You forgot to thank Evan and his people for the truly amazing feat they accomplished today," said Sean Kerry. "At great personal risk they set up the process which will shortly allow both you and Max to return to your normal size. They have also set up another process that will permit our friends and colleagues to return to Earth as well, even if most of their substance must remain in Fairyland for some time yet. It's a small price to pay for a gallant rescue."

"Connal," I cried. "Is this true?"

"Yes, James, it's true. Your parents may end up with a troop of tiny fairies in their garden after all." Then he drew his sword walked across the table and knelt before Evan. "I owe you and yours a great debt, Evan Hunter. I hope with all my heart that someday I may be able to repay you."

"I don't like you very much Connal. Old quarrels die hard, but I will say this, your reputation for bravery is well founded. I would not have believed anyone would risk what you did today to save Max and your friends. You faced complete destruction and never turned a hair."

"It's amazing how brave you can be when you know you don't have a choice," laughed Connal with an impish little bow to his audience. "Now let's talk about what we will do next."

When Connal started walking up and down the table, Churchill had begun to prowl around the room. I watched him stop in front of the patio doors and peer intently into the yard. Suddenly, his fur started to rise and he began to hiss and snarl at something outside in the yard.

"Look at the cat!" cried Grandpa.

Everyone rushed over to look. The twilight sky had a warm orange glow to it and it took us a second or so to realize some of the glow came from a fire in the woods.

Evan displayed a fine grasp of Anglo-Saxon swear words and bolted out the door followed by the rest of us.

The woods seemed to be filled with people rushing toward the fire. This surprised me but not as much as all the water that was now in the air. Evidently, Evan had a large underground sprinkler system which was now turned on. This would help to divert the fire if the wind blew it this way. My opinion of Evan Hunter's resourcefulness went up another notch.

I started to follow the others when I felt something tugging on my pant leg.

"You'll just get in the way," hissed Connal. "Evan has the woods filled with his friends and any number of them has fought fires before."

"This may be just a diversion," added Max. "I think we three should take cover and protect their backs. If our enemies show up, we may be able to do something to stop them or at least delay them until help comes."

I wondered if there was anything we could use for protection in Evan's workshop and turned and raced into the house. Connal and Max followed me. The only thing I could see, which might look threatening, was a nail gun. I didn't even know if it was loaded but at least I had something in my hand. Connal and Max grabbed two stout pieces of wood.

"This will have to do," grumbled Connal. "If all else fails we can bite them on the ankles." He seemed to find this amusing and I found myself smiling.

Max, Connal, and I crouched beside the cottage in the darkest shadow we could find.

"If they have your night vision, this isn't going to do much good, is it?" I muttered.

"Hush," said Max. "At the very least we are now a somewhat smaller target."

We didn't have long to wait.

Three shadowy figures crept silently toward the cottage.

"Three big men against three wee folk," muttered Connal. "At least we're not outnumbered." I was learning Connal had a flair for gallows humor.

"Can you keep them occupied for a moment or two?" whispered Max.

"I'll do my best," I said softly. I got the nail gun ready. Then I stepped out of the shadows and smiled as pleasantly as I could. "Can I help you? The others are down at the fire on the other side of the cottage."

"Get back in the house, kid. You shouldn't be out here," growled the biggest one of the three strangers.

"Neither should you," I said politely. "I have a gun and I'm prepared to use it." I was bluffing and I hoped they didn't know it.

Suddenly, the largest intruder doubled over and clutched his foot. Then a second stranger let out a yelp. The third man danced nimbly out of reach and tried to grab one of the two small shapes capering around them.

The three large bodies and two small ones created quite a scuffle. Max and Connal were very fast and the whole scene reminded me of a visit to a farm when several baby pigs had escaped their pen and we had a hard time trying to catch them. You needed more than one person to catch each little piglet and Max and Connal were a lot smarter and more agile than baby pigs. The whole venture turned into a kind of slapstick comedy. Luckily for me, they were so distracted I was left standing on my own and feeling rather stupid and helpless. But, I didn't have to be quiet. I started calling, "Fire! Fire!"

I remembered reading somewhere if you were in trouble yell fire, not help, because people respond faster to that demand. Also, the people on the other side of the cottage were already fighting a fire so it might seem logical for them to assume there was a fire somewhere else.

I was right. In a matter of seconds a large group of smoky figures pounded around the corner of the cottage and joined in the fray. It was over very quickly. The three intruders were subdued and snugly secured with duct tape. Max and Connal had disappeared into some low bushes to the left of me. I could still sense where Max was but this ability seemed a little fainter. I hoped with time it would disappear.

My grandpa walked over to me and scowled at the nail gun. He loves to build things and recognized it instantly. "Here, give me that fool thing before you injure someone." He sounded tired and cross. I guess he felt responsible for my safety and it bothered him there was so little he could do. Even the right choices were dangerous.

We all crowded into the cottage and 'crowded' is the operative word. Evan had been expecting trouble and had made one phone call to a friend in Bissett and one to another friend in Maniggan. He told them he felt there might be a little trouble at his cottage tonight and asked if they'd mind patrolling the nearby woods. He suggested they could bring someone with them to help pass the time.

It must have been a slow night on television because it looked like half the adult population of both places had showed up, liberally smeared with mosquito repellant and fortified with a case or two of beer. The whole area around the cottage had been crammed full of people having a remarkably quiet party. There was even an off-duty Mountie who came along to join in the fun.

The fire and the capture of the intruders seemed to be a perfect ending to an exciting evening. Everyone was smeared, smoky, and jubilant.

"We all pitched in," said Grandpa his eyes glittering gleefully behind his blue glasses. "Whatever was used to start the fire landed in a small clearing almost within reach of Evan's sprinkler system. Also the wind was in the right direction to help us steer the fire toward the water. They'll have to patrol the area for a while to make sure it doesn't start again, but everyone seems sure we've killed the sucker. It was touch and go for a while."

"What do you want me to do with them," said a stocky young man in a grimy T-shirt. "Do you want to press charges? The Royal Canadian Mounted Police is always ready to be of service," he added with a grin.

"We don't have any eye-witnesses who saw them start the fire, so I don't think it would be worthwhile until we have more evidence," said Evan. "If you would take down their names and addresses and escort them out of the area that would be enough for now. We'll fill you in with what we know sometime tomorrow."

"Fair enough," said the Mountie. "I will take down their particulars and walk them back to their vehicle.

"I'd offer you all something to eat and drink if you're willing to go back to the bunker where there's more room," said Evan. "I'm very grateful for everyone's help. You've always been good neighbors and friends to me."

"That's what friends are for," said an elderly man from the back of the room. "We'll have a party to celebrate another time. Right now, it's late and most of us are pretty tired and looking for our beds."

After everyone left Connal and Max appeared outside knocking on the patio doors. Connal was still carrying his stout stick of wood.

"You let them go, did you?" asked Max.

"Yes," replied Evan. "George Miller heard a thump of something landing on the ground near him that burst into flames. He didn't see what it was or even which direction it came from."

"But, they threatened me," I said. "Can't you get them for that?"

"The only people who heard were Max and Connal and we wouldn't want them appearing in court in their present state. Besides they could always claim they saw the fire and came over to help. We're probably lucky they don't want publicity either or we might find ourselves being sued for assault."

"They are more valuable to us moving around freely," said Sean Kerry. "I managed to get close enough to each of them during the melee outside to mark them. Now there is a way to locate them wherever they go. I believe it would be impossible to get any information out of them. Protecting their master means more to them than their own lives. This way they may lead us to whoever is causing our problems."

"How can we do that?" I asked.

"We can sniff them out, just like Churchill already does," he replied with a chuckle. "He seems very sensitive to their presence. A dog might be better though and I will recommend using dogs to others."

I still wasn't sure what he was talking about but I was so tired I didn't care anymore. I felt confident the few people who were still out patrolling the area would be able to look after us and I fell into a dreamless sleep as soon as I lay down.

I thought I would sleep all day but I was up around 8:30. The wonderful smell of bacon and eggs frying on the stove completely revived me. Clifford was doing the cooking and Evan had just finished eating and was going out the door with Max and Connal in tow.

"Are they going back to the bunker?" I asked Clifford.

"Yes. They've still got a lot of work to do. Uncle Evan said if all goes well, you might be able to return to Winnipeg shortly. He asked your Grandpa to drive down to the nearest RCMP detachment and answer any questions they might have. He's already left. How do you like your eggs?"

"I like them scrambled, thank you."

I've never been a big eater but since Max and Connal showed up I'd been wolfing down enormous amounts of food. I was beginning to wonder about that.

Clifford deftly scooped up some scrambled eggs and dumped them on my plate.

"As soon as you've eaten we're going down to look at what the fire did. Do you want to walk down with us?"

I agreed to go with them but I was feeling rather cross. On one hand I knew I would be bored silly going down with Grandpa while he answered a lot of questions, but I still felt that once again I was being left out and had no way of finding out what was really going on. It was very frustrating. I decided to begin solving small mysteries and perhaps the big ones would be clearer.

As we left the cottage I turned to Kelsey and said, "Evan said you were his grandchildren, but you call him Uncle Evan."

"Yeah, he is our grandfather. Our grandmother was killed in a car accident and our mother was raised by her grandparents. Our dad was killed in a boating accident and when mom remarried, she and her new husband moved out to Alberta to be near his people. Clifford and I went to live with mom's parents. It's a very traditional way of doing things."

"It can be a little confusing," added Clifford. "I think we began calling our grandfather Uncle Evan to distinguish him from the grandparents who were raising us."

"I don't know about that," said Kelsey. "It may have been our Grandpa and Grandma who started calling him Uncle Evan. As you heard last night Evan's people live very long lives and they may have done this to protect him and us. Evan is over one hundred years old now but he doesn't look it. 'Evan Hunter' is at least the second identity he's had. People from around here like Evan and probably suspect a lot of things about him, but they don't believe in talking out of turn."

"Do you need protecting, too?"

"It's unusual for the longevity gene to be passed on," continued Kelsey. "It does happen and Evan's people always keep an eye out for children who inherit it. Evan was quite amazed when they discovered both Clifford and I have it. I know he spent a long time talking with our grandparents. Together they decided another one of our recent ancestors must have had the gene and they think they know which one."

"Evan always stayed close to our mom and us and lately we've started to spend more time with him here at the cottage. There's lots of things he wants us to know," added Clifford.

We stopped at the edge of the burned out area. It made a fairly narrow corridor down to the water's edge. I noticed some of the brush and trees had been cut from the edge to help contain the fire. I walked over to examine some of the blackened stumps that remained.

"It looks like they came prepared," I said as I shot a questioning look at Kelsey.

"When our friends were getting ready to come down last night, my grandpa came and told them there might be a fire," he replied. "He often knows ahead of time when something is going to happen, so everybody brought tools and even some fire extinguishers just in case."

"My Grandpa Duncan is like that sometimes."

We heard someone tooting a horn back at the cottage. It was Evan. He had returned to collect Churchill and me and take us back to the bunker with him. They wanted to run tests on us. I was not looking forward to these so called tests.

I keep calling it a bunker because that's what it started out as, but it was a lot more than just a shelter. Through the years Michael's company had maintained it and improved both its size and function. Beside the living quarters, where we had been before, there was a control center with continually updated computer systems, a state of the art laboratory, a fully-equipped workshop where you could make almost anything, a huge storage area, and even a small silver mine. They had run across a pretty fair vein of silver while they were building and decided to mine some of it. It was handy because over the years they had developed a lot of sophisticated uses for silver.

On the drive to the bunker, I decided to keep solving small mysteries and remembered something strange I'd seen the evening we arrived in Bissett.

"How did you know we were by the river? I saw Sean Kerry throw something in the water. Was that a kind of signal?"

"You are very observant, James. Yes, Sean did let us know you were here. It's a very old method of summoning that was widely used by both our peoples for centuries.

We were all drawn to water and fascinated by its beauty. We studied it extensively and learned to respect its wonderful versatility. Indeed, we often built our strongholds right under lakes or out in the ocean. It is the best hiding place you can imagine, and the main source of what others called our magic. What you would call technology."

"Did you come to live in Manitoba because of all the water?"

"No, I didn't. I fled here under an assumed name one step ahead of the law. That's when I became friends with your great-grandfather. He helped me escape detection and establish my new identity."

Actually, Michael Flynn is here because of all the water. His Core group did some studies in the late forties early fifties that suggested water would become much more valuable than oil. That's when his group purchased the bunker and began extending it.

I was the only Core associate in the area at the time, so he asked me to represent their interests here. He is a good leader and I can respect his decisions. Over the last fifty years the number of our people living here has increased dramatically because now they realize he was right."

"Did you ever want to go back to Wales?"

"I miss the magic sometimes. The damp and the mists do strange things to sound and electricity. You can often find 'thin' places there. Those are places were where the Celtic people claim the veil between the worlds is thin.

Strangely enough, there are lots of 'thin' places in Manitoba, probably because of all the lakes and rivers. The aboriginal people will tell you many strange stories if they trust you.

I've always wondered what prompted the early settlers to come up with the name Manitoba for this province. Gitchee Manitou is the native word for the Great Spirit. Was it planned we should invoke one of the names of God whenever we speak about our home?"

This whole conversation was quite fascinating and I was really sorry when we reached the bunker and I had to go inside.

When Michael discovered Max had bonded with me and Connal with the cat, he was very angry.

"I don't know what you are worried about," I said. "It didn't hurt me."

"I'll believe that when we run enough tests. You have no idea how dangerous bonding is. My people often refer to the High Court as 'soul stealers'. That isn't true but it gives you some idea of how much we hate the whole idea. I am convinced bonding lies at the root of the troubles both here and in Fairyland."

"What's wrong with it?"

"Think of it as a kind of brainwashing taken to the highest degree. You are bound completely to someone or something and it lasts forever. Long ago it was simpler and not so powerful. The Core was bound to the High Court and was forced to serve them for years and years. Finally we broke free but we cannot forgive them for what they did. Our battle for freedom was incredibly bloody and cruel and the scars have lasted to this day. What is terrifying is that lately there appears to be an even more powerful kind of mind control someone is using. We agreed to help Max and Connal because they know a lot more about mind control than we do."

"Why is that?"

"When we broke free, we forbade the practice under penalty of death. Consequently, what we know is centuries out of date. However, it is still used extensively within the High Court. Ask Max when you get a chance. It makes me so angry I can't even talk about it."

Both Churchill and I went through any number of tests. Most were quite simple and physical. They also tested our brain waves and I spent a lot of time doing both oral and written exams.

After about five hours, Michael walked up to me shaking his head. "Max is good. I wouldn't have believed he could cause so little damage and his trick of bonding Connal to the cat is not only very clever but it gives us a clue of how to counteract some of the effects of bonding. It's fascinating!"

It was my turn to become exasperated. "Do you realize no one has told me what bonding is? It would be really helpful if someone explained."

"You're right," said Michael. "Bonding is just what it sounds like. You are tied or bound to someone or something. You cannot do anything to free yourself except under very special circumstances. The most powerful person in the bond has some responsibilities and all of the control. Also, the more people you can bind to you the stronger you become."

"What kind of special circumstances would let you become free again?" I asked.

"It appears this can only happen if the one in control does not fulfill all of his responsibilities. It's the seriousness of the failure that does it. Small failures won't cause the breakdown of the bond even if there are many, many small failures over a long period of time. We hope by working with Max and Connal we can find an easier and more efficient way of freeing people."

"I don't think I'm bonded to Max. Am I?"

Michael sighed. "I am not sure about that. You said you could sense his presence. Is this continuing to fade or is it staying about the same?

"About the same."

"I find it really interesting that you appear to have the ability to block off parts of your brain to unwanted stimuli. Some adults, who practice deep meditation, can do this but it's unusual for someone of your age. The early physical trauma you endured seems to have given you some protection from the force of the bond. You seem to be relatively untouched."

"What's wrong with bonding?"

"We find it morally offensive even though it has become part of the survival skills needed to exist in Fairyland. I also suspect it is presently Max's chief worry, whether he realizes it or not. There is evidence to suggest the bonding system they use may be at the heart of the problems here and in Fairyland. Beliefs, thoughts and wishes seem to have a power over actual physical events they don't here. 'Be careful what you wish for,' is far from an empty phrase in Elfland."

"Can you tell me about the bonding system they use?"

"It has a lot of similarities to the feudal system. There is a king who controls all the power. He delegates some of his power to his lords, but they have to swear they will be faithful to him forever. All of the lesser citizens belong to one lord or another and each must swear allegiance to their lord and the king. The only exception is the free clans. Their members adamantly refuse any kind of bond though they will offer temporary allegiance to various lords if they feel it is required.

I will grant that, in the system used in Fairyland, a lot is expected of the king and his lords in return. Moreover the penalties for any failure on their part are severe. Because conditions in Fairyland were always a little unstable, bonding was generally thought necessary. It was better to avoid any disagreements that might cause real physical problems.

I can't tell you much about the process they use to insure this. They could use electricity, chemicals, or just plain magic, magic being another word for an unknown technology.

Max understands bonding better than anyone and he's offered to explain, but that's like someone offering to explain the theory of quantum mechanics to your grade school class. What we really need is an outstanding mathematician."

"You could ask my dad. I guess you could say advanced math is his hobby."

"What are you talking about?" said Michael sharply. "Is he really very good?"

"My grandpa says he's some kind of wizard when it comes to math. You can ask him about it."

Michael suddenly became thoughtful. "I wonder, I wonder if that's why Connal and Max appeared so near your home."

I had a lot to think about as I sat in the bunker reception area waiting for Grandpa Duncan to pick me up. I was glad I had told Michael about my new abilities. If he felt I was all right, there was good reason to believe him. Churchill was curled up on the bench beside me and he certainly seemed fine. I wish I had asked Michael what was so important about Churchill's bond with Connal. Connal certainly hadn't seemed pleased about it.

On the drive back to the cottage I asked Grandpa about Dad.

"Dad's really good with numbers, isn't he?"

"He has a rare and wonderful gift," said Grandpa with a rueful smile. "I just wish he could have attended university and studied advanced mathematics. His father had died just before he graduated and I hired him for a summer job. There was no money for him to go on to university but, when I realized how talented he was, I helped him get a degree in accounting. After he met your mother, there was no way he was going anywhere without her. He's a good accountant and I soon made him a partner. Now that I've retired the whole business is his. It's a very successful firm and he has a happy life, but I always think he's ignoring his real gift."

"Michael said they needed a mathematician and I told him about dad. I hope I didn't do anything wrong."

"I don't think it will be a problem. Your dad is a very smart man and he can look after himself. I wonder if we should have told your parents everything right from the start. Unfortunately, it would have taken much too long to convince them and we needed to find a refuge right away.

Whether you knew it or not, there was a good chance you and I might be killed. We already knew too much and the Core isn't the only group good at keeping secrets. Max told me it was possible he could protect us because he and Connal have skills the Core desperately needs. Unfortunately, you and I do not. If Evan Hunter had not spoken up for us, it is likely we would have been killed."

"I think I know why he did that."

I explained how Evan was grateful for great-grandfather's help when he fled to Canada.

"I never knew any of this," said Grandpa. "I'm going to phone my father the first chance I get. I'll try to get the whole story from him. I wonder if Evan realizes he's still alive."

My great-grandfather is ninety-two and lives on the West Coast. His health is starting to fail but his mind is very keen. If he ever knew Evan, he would remember him.

The sun was still blazing in the sky when we left the bunker. During the car ride we kept the windows open and only the breeze pouring in made the oppressive heat bearable. When we stopped, the heat became intolerable. It seemed the forest might burst into flame spontaneously and I tried to put that thought out of my mind. Last night was as close as I wanted to come to a real fire.

Sounds of laughter and splashing water drifted up to the clearing. I walked to the top of the wooden stairs to the lake and saw Clifford and Kelsey skylarking about in the water.

"Come on down and join us," shouted Clifford.

I was about to say I hadn't brought a bathing suit when I saw they weren't wearing them. The thought of all that cool water was irresistible. I ran down the steps and left my clothing in an untidy pile on the worn wooden boards of the dock and jumped in.

They had an old blue beach ball with them and we played a game of catch without any rules except just being silly and treasuring the silky feel of the water on our skins. The whole world seemed to be filled with light, joy and sparkling water.

When the sun went under a cloud, we noticed the change at once.

"That looks like a bad storm coming up," said Kelsey squinting up towards the clouds boiling up from the southwest. "I just saw a big lightning flash. We better get up to the cottage."

We climbed onto the dock and gathered our clothes. I saw Kelsey's eyes widen. He had noticed the scaring that covered my feet and my legs below my knees.

"What happened to you?" he asked.

"There was an accident in our basement when I was just a little kid. My dad was painting a sealing compound on the floor and a spark or something caused the fumes to burn. It was lucky the flames didn't burn very high."

I'm glad they didn't ask any more questions. The scars are beginning to fade but the memory of the pain is still very strong.

We were still walking across the clearing when the first heavy drops of rain began to fall and we all stood on the small porch for a few minutes watching a curtain of rain hide the lake. When the hail stones started, we ducked inside the cottage. The first bits of hail to fall were tiny, more like sleet pellets in a winter storm. Then they became larger and more dangerous. Soon the ground was covered with them.

"Will there be broken windows?" I asked. "I really like storms so I'd like to sit beside the patio doors and watch if that's all right?"

"I don't think any windows will break, "said Clifford. "I believe Evan installed Plexiglas a while back."

The three of us grabbed some cushions and piled them in front of the doors and sat back to enjoy the show.

The scent of a summer storm had a kind of perilous sweetness. The relentless intensity of the rain made my long and trying day melt away. The formerly drab and dusty world became almost too vivid and overwhelming.

It seemed as if the ancient gods of the sky were putting on a magical show just for us. The sound of the hail striking the cottage gave me goose bumps of pure pleasure. The flashes of lightening filled me with excitement. The sound of the wind whipping the trees to and fro was like music. I was sorry when it settled into an ordinary rain.

The smell of food finally lured Clifford, Kelsey, and me away from the patio doors. Grandpa had been busy while we were watching the storm. He'd cooked a big bowl of spaghetti and defrosted some little meat balls. There was a thick and spicy tomato sauce and lots of grated cheese. Once again I found myself ravenously hungry.

We were about to dig in when we heard Evan's truck drive up, so we waited a few minutes longer until Evan and Connal could join us. Max and Mr. Kerry were too involved with something at the bunker to leave.

Again tonight, Grandpa piled books on a chair for Connal to sit on at the table and I was startled to realize the pile of books was smaller.

"Connal, are you bigger again today?"

"Yes, I am and it's a great relief. The process is working very smoothly and it won't be long before I'm back to my normal size. It's nice to know I'm not going to explode any minute."

"Why would you explode?"

"You noticed right away how heavy Max and I are. That's because our substance is pouring through a very tiny hole between here and Fairyland. The pressure for all of our mass to come across is enormous and what did arrive here was denser than normal matter. What Evan and his friends did yesterday was allow the hole to become somewhat larger to relieve the pressure on both sides. The real trick was to allow this small body to grow fast enough to absorb what was coming across. We're lucky Max and I didn't explode when we first arrived. Once the process is finished everything should be relatively normal again."

"You mean we've just avoided a disaster."

"Yes, but another one could be on the way."

"What's that?

"We have something of an immigration problem on our hands. We thought there were only twelve more fairies who wanted to come with us. The plan was for them to send over a tiny portion of themselves to be checked out by Michael and his group before the rest of their bodies came over. However, when Michael and Sean opened the portal, at least thirty small beings popped up all demanding to cross over. Sean was very upset and both Michael and Evan were furious."

"There's lots of room in Canada. Thirty more people shouldn't be a problem."

"Ah, but they are. The original twelve we knew and could safely vouch for them. The others could be anyone or anything. There are evils abroad in Fairyland no one wants to come here.

To make things more confusing some of these beings appear to be duplicates."

"You mean someone sent two beings."

"No. I mean there are two beings claiming to be my old friend Cormac. The only thing we can do is proceed very slowly and finish the transfer one individual at a time. This will take much longer because we will need to run tests on each one to make sure they are who they claim to be and mean no harm. The imposters we will just send back."

Connal had a wolfish smile when he said this. I had the feeling being sent back was not a good thing.

"Is there any danger of these fairies exploding?"

"They're all quite light and airy so it shouldn't be a problem."

"It's still raining out," interrupted Evan. "Would you boys like to hear a story? Let's get the dishes cleared away and we'll gather round the fireplace."

We boys cleared the dishes and Evan and Grandpa washed up. Connal and Churchill stepped out on the porch to watch the rain until we were finished.

"Uncle Evan is a good storyteller," said Clifford, "but, I think this is going to be a teaching story. My grandparents also tell stories. Some are just for fun but most are supposed to teach you something."

After Evan got a fire burning briskly, we all found comfortable spots around the fireplace. The warmth from the fire made a nice contrast with the cool air wafting in through the patio doors. It was pleasant to watch the flickering flames and the shadows dancing on the walls. The fire last night had been so dangerous yet tonight our fire only enhanced the spirit of safety and peace filling the room.

"Max isn't here tonight so I can feel free to tell you his story. It isn't polite to tell a story like this when the person is present. Connal, you can interrupt if I get something wrong, but it is important for Duncan, James, Clifford and Kelsey to know certain facts that now affect their lives."

"I agree," replied Connal gravely. "If you don't know what came before, it is hard to prepare for what happens next."

Evan cleared his throat and paused for a long moment to make sure he had everyone's attention before he began.

"There is one distinction I want to make clear. A fairy in the old sense of the word meant a full sized person with special abilities or powers. Nowadays a fairy is generally thought of as a tiny being. I find it saves confusion if I use the term fairy to refer to very tiny beings and elves to indicate a size resembling normal humankind. As you now realize a fairy is a kind of avatar that was, and is, part of the life force of an elf."

"What is an avatar?" whispered Kelsey.

"It's a kind of model the Hindu gods create when they visit Earth," I whispered back.

There was another pause. Then Evan cleared his throat once more and the story began.

"There was a time when the crown prince of Elfland was seeking a wife. Many young women were presented to him but he always found something wrong with them. One day, while he was riding on the borders of his father's kingdom, he saw a girl picking strawberries near the edge of the forest. Even from a distance he realized there was something special about her that drew him across the meadow. He had seen much prettier young women but this girl was truly gifted with charm and he fell in love with her the instant she looked at him.

The tragedy was that, when she looked at him, she also fell in love. This was a fate her parents had tried hard to avoid. They had been warned if she ever married the king's son it would be her death. This is why they sent her far away from the royal city.

When the prince learned of the danger, he tried to leave her but he could not and she was just as bound. They were wed with great ceremony and lived happily together in a beautiful white and gold castle the prince had built specially for her.

One of the duties of a royal prince is fathering children to preserve the imperial blood line. However, having a child in

Elfland was perilous for the mother and the child. To avoid this, the king sent out his servants and they found an active portal so the prince and princess could return to Earth and start a family. The prince wanted to stay in their beautiful castle and remain childless, but the princess said they had to go. If she was going to die she wanted him to have a child to remember her by.

The time they spent on Earth was a very happy one. After they had a baby son, the princess begged to stay longer. She knew something the prince didn't. Returning to Elfland would signal the end of her life. When the little boy was five years old, they prepared to return but the princess discovered she was again with child. After this son was born, they stayed another four years and wanted to stay longer.

It was not to be. The king had been injured in battle and was dying. Sadly they left their cozy cottage and returned to the perilous beauty of Elfland.

What no one knew was the princess was again with child. In all the sorrow and confusion surrounding the Elfking's death and the prince's coronation the princess, now queen, was able to hide her condition. It was several months before it became apparent the princess was carrying a third child.

Even on Earth it had always been difficult for female elves to bear children. This is one of the reasons there never have been many of elvenkind. Under the best of circumstances having a child was often a death sentence for the woman. It became traditional for the women to live somewhat apart to protect them. A woman of pure elfish blood was always treated with the greatest respect. Forcing a woman to be your wife was punishable by death. Great love was considered to be the only reason worthy of taking such a risk.

The new king knew he was fortunate to have two healthy sons and wanted to avoid having his beloved queen bear this third child. Especially, since the instability of Elfland routinely produced defective children. Many didn't survive birth and those who did were often malformed and only considered fit to be servants to the others.

The queen was determined to have the child no matter the difficulty. She knew of a wise woman who claimed to be able to protect the unborn and see them safe into the world. She searched the kingdom to find her and stayed with her until the baby was born.

Everyone was amazed when the third little prince came into the world whole and perfect. Even the wisest of the elf lords could find no fault in him.

The queen was not so fortunate. Immediately after the birth she began to wither. She lingered for three years before she died.

The king went a little mad from grief. He spent most of his time away from the castle because he could not bear to watch his adored wife dying. It was left to the eldest son to stay by her side and offer her what comfort he could. This sad experience changed him forever.

The middle son spent most of his time with his absent father on his travels. He learned much about the craft of being a king. The third son was well liked and well cared for but he felt in some way responsible for his mother's doom. At an early age he began to search for answers to the causes of her death and the other ills that beset Elfland.

Time passed and the elves noticed the eldest son was becoming more remote and preoccupied. It was not a great shock when he declared it would be wrong for him to remain heir to the throne of Elfland. His middle brother was much more suited for the job. He decided to return to Earth where he had been so happy as a child.

Perhaps this is just as well, for soon after he left, the King died and the middle brother ascended to the white throne. Finn learned his father's lessons well and has been a brave and true king in this dangerous time. He knows his sworn duty and will sustain all those who remain in Elfland until the end.

Sic transit gloria mundi." *(So passes the glory of the world)*

We were all silent for a short while then Evan sighed and smiled at us.

"Two of the characters in the story are people you have recently met. Do you know whom I'm talking about?"

"Connal and Max," ventured Clifford.

"I may be well born but I'm no prince," said Connal with a grin.

"Then it has to be Max and Sean Kerry. They're the third son and the first son. Wow! Mr. Kerry could have been King of Elfland," I crowed.

"You'd be well not to mention that in his presence," warned Connal. "He'll never regret the loss of the crown, but he won't want to be reminded he didn't fulfill his hereditary duty. It's a heavy burden carried by all the royal blood."

Grandpa Duncan stirred restlessly on the over-stuffed brown leather couch. I was surprised to see he wasn't wearing his blue glasses but I realized Connal and Max were now large enough to be visible to normal people.

"Evan, I have a question. Was it only the fairies, excuse me elves, of the High Court that were unable to have many children? Did The Core have this problem as well?"

"Only in the beginning," said Evan rather smugly. "After we broke free from the High Court we did not want to subject our children to such genetic flaws as extreme sensitivity to sunlight and metal allergies. Marriage outside of our group, if not encouraged, was very acceptable, particularly if the person had some beneficial physical or mental trait. In return we offered them a chance at improved vision and a longer life. The majority of my people have dark hair and eyes. However, there are many of those, like Michael, who look as if they were close kin to Connal, Sean, and Max."

"Sometime, when Connal isn't here, can you tell us a story about him," asked Kelsey.

"It would be better to hear the story from someone who actually likes him. There is too much bad blood between us for me to do a good job of it," replied Evan with a bitter smile.

I was watching Connal and he looked more puzzled than offended by this remark.

Grandpa Duncan jumped up before anything got nasty. "I will now sing "The Ballad of the Frozen Logger" for you while Evan makes us some popcorn.

Evan hurried out the kitchen. He seemed to take his duties as our host very seriously and must have realized he'd gone too far.

After Grandpa finished making the logger into axe heads, Connal sang a comic ballad about a young man looking for a wife. Kelsey and Clifford each told a non-traditional story about Nanabosho and I recited "Scots Wae Hae", which I had memorized one rainy Sunday afternoon after watching "Brave Heart". Then Grandpa found some dice and he and I taught everyone how to play "Farkle". The evening ended on a very pleasant note.

CHAPTER THREE

Going Home

The next day Grandpa took Clifford, Kelsey and me further west to Wallace Lake for a little fishing. When I heard the name of the lake, I got goose bumps. The poem I'd recited last night was about William Wallace. Since I'd never heard of the lake before, it was a little spooky.

I think I may be a little like my Grandpa and have a feeling about certain things before they happen. It may be a special talent or just coincidence. It's possible I noticed the name Wallace Lake when I was looking at the Manitoba map on the drive here though I had no memory of it. Seeing the word Wallace could have triggered my memory of the poem. Who knows?

I decided to keep Grandpa company while he fished off the campsite dock. Clifford and Kelsey took off for a ramble around the area. They said they'd be sure to come back for lunch.

The wind was coming in from behind us so the water near the dock was calm, but the water further out was alive with tiny sparkles of light from the ripples stirred up by the breeze.

Grandpa and I were both enjoying the warm sunshine and the peaceful scene when we heard light footsteps approaching along the dock. An elderly man was coming toward us with a gentle smile on his face. There was something familiar about him and I wondered why.

"I believe you must be Duncan Owen. I'm Clifford and Kelsey's grandfather William Wallace."

I blinked my eyes. I'd just been thinking about William Wallace and we were at Wallace Lake talking to a William Wallace. It was a very spooky coincidence.

"I'm very pleased to meet you, Mr. Wallace. The boys speak about you often and I feel I know you already," said my Grandpa as he started to stand up.

"No, stay where you are. I'll join you and we can talk."

The three of us sat in companionable silence on the warm dock for a while before Mr. Wallace began to speak.

"There was a time when everyone believed some dreams warned us of things to come. People who had these dreams were respected and their advice was heeded. Today few people believe and those who have dreams often don't believe in them either until it is too late."

Here there was a long pause until my grandfather spoke up.

"You are right. I've known such people and once in a long while I have dreams like that myself. It is not good to ignore either the people or your own dreams," sighed Grandpa.

"I thought you might be another dreamer. That's why I want to tell you about one of my dreams. Kelsey and Clifford have always been in danger because they are just a little different from you and me. Evan, my wife, and myself have always worked together to keep them safe.

A week ago I had a strange dream. I saw my grandsons walking ahead of me. I knew they were Clifford and Kelsey but I couldn't tell which was which. Also, I couldn't tell where they were. One moment they seemed to be near our home and the next somewhere in Winnipeg. The location kept switching back and forth. The one thing that was always there was a shadowy black hand that kept reaching out for them. Suddenly, one of my grandsons disappeared. I could hear him calling for his family. Then there was nothing but silence. It was as if he had died.

My heart was broken because I knew we were going to lose one of them. Every night after that, I went to sleep praying I would find a way to save my grandson. Three nights ago I saw your grandson James in my dream. The grandson who was left was sitting on the ground weeping. James walked up and laid his hand on his shoulder. He said, "If we look together, I know we can find your brother."

"Will this put James in more danger?" asked Grandpa.

"It doesn't matter, Grandpa. You once told me, 'Evil can only win if good people do nothing.' Doing nothing won't make our problems go away."

"I truly believed James should be warned," said Mr. Wallace. "Why else would I see him in my dream? I have already told my grandsons about the dream and asked them to be careful."

"Who would want to threaten Clifford or Kelsey?"

"I'm not sure," said Mr. Wallace. "Evan suspects it has something to do with water. The world is very short of fresh water and this area has a great deal of it. Evan's friend Michael once told me he came here years and years ago because of all the water. Some people think fresh water will be more valuable than oil."

My Grandpa sighed, stood up, and started to pack the fishing gear away.

"Clifford and Kelsey will be back soon for lunch. Will you stay and share our meal?"

Mr. Wallace agreed to stay and the three of us set out the food on one of the weather-beaten picnic tables near the lake.

When the boys returned, we settled around the table and had a pleasant meal together. Everyone seemed very relaxed but I noticed we only talked about neutral subjects like the weather. I found myself taking a liking to Mr. Wallace and I finally got brave enough to ask him about something Kelsey had said the night of the fire.

"Mr. Wallace did you warn everyone about the fire because of a dream?"

"No, I didn't. I heard Evan had asked for some help because there might be trouble. This made me think about different kinds of trouble and what I would do if I wanted to cause trouble. It occurred to me, because the woods were so dry, the simplest thing would be to start a fire. Then I walked over to where everyone was getting ready to leave and mentioned there might be a fire. It was a logical idea and the others decided to be prepared."

Kelsey and Clifford found a stout rope tied to a branch that hung over the water. They asked me if I wanted to go for another swim. None of us had swim suits but it didn't matter because the spot wasn't visible from the road and there was no one else around the campsite that day.

We had such a good time it wasn't until we were driving back to Evan's cottage that I began to worry over what Mr. Wallace had told Grandpa and me. I was getting very upset because one of them might be in peril. Then I thought about what Connal would do. I knew he must have been in all kinds of risky situations in his life. I remembered seeing him curled up beside Churchill that day in the tent and I realized if no one was in immediate danger I should relax. Enjoy life and save your strength for the real battle.

When Grandpa, the boys, and I returned to the cottage there was no one there. Only Sean Kerry showed up before we were going to sit down to eat. The meal was very quiet and the conversation low key. After the dishes were washed and put away, Sean gathered us all in the living room.

"The good news is Max and Connal should be returned to their full size in a few weeks and the fairy situation is somewhat under control. We have had no new arrivals for the past day, so we can assume everyone who wanted to return to Earth is now here. Also, Max and I have been able to provide a lot of information about bonding. Michael's people should be able to stay ahead of this unknown group who seem to have developed a new and very dangerous technique. We suspect the reason, for their attacks on Connal and Max, was to prevent the Core from gaining any knowledge that might stop them.

You will also be glad to learn Max and Connal will be able to return to Winnipeg tomorrow and Mr. Owen and James can go with them. It is necessary for me to stay here and work with Michael.

Thirty-two fairies in one place present quite a problem. We decided to divide the group in two and send fifteen fairies away to Winnipeg. Max and Connal have agreed to take responsibility for them and Evan and I will look after the others here at the bunker.

I apologize to both Mr. Owen and James for the imposition, but this was the best solution we could come up with."

There is an old Chinese curse that goes, 'May you live in interesting times'. Interesting times being such things as wars, famines, floods, and the like. It occurred to me that living near fifteen fairies might also qualify as interesting times.

Shortly after lunch we left for Winnipeg. I felt sad I didn't get to swim at the lovely sand beaches on the Newago First Nation. Kelsey and Clifford promised me, if I ever returned, they would take me to visit their home and meet their grandmother.

Grandpa and I sat in the front seat and Max, Connal, Churchill, and the cat carrier full of fairies were crammed into the back. Grandpa's car is rather small and Max and Connal were now about my size. The fairies were proper fairies. They were the size of small action figures and weighed almost nothing. I could see them, but to most other people they were blurs of light. We wanted to keep them out of sight during the drive and the cat carrier was quite large enough for that.

This did not mean the fairies were happy about it. They wanted to be free to explore the car, look out the windows, and ask lots and lots of questions. I know Grandpa was relieved when they were all ordered into the carrier. Driving is easier and safer if you don't have a fairy flitting about your head. Churchill slept on the seat between Max and Connal.

We stopped at Grandpa's house first and everyone went inside. We released the fairies and warned them not to go outside. It was a bright sunny day and I don't think any of them wanted to do it anyway. Then Grandpa, Connal, and Churchill walked over to my house. Max and I remained to fairy-sit. Grandpa said he wanted to tell my Mom and Dad everything that had happened. If they were angry with anyone, let it be him.

"I hope I won't be in too much trouble when I get home," I confessed to Max.

"I think they'll be so happy to have you home safe you won't have a problem. I'm more worried to how they'll accept Connal, fifteen fairies, and myself. Tell me about your parents."

"My dad owns a small accounting firm and my mom is an office manager for a big government department."

"That's what they do," said Max. "Tell me what they are like."

"They love each other very much," I blurted out. I was surprised I said that because it had never occurred to me before. However, it was one of the things that made my family different from the families of my friends. Most of them came from happy families and I'm sure their parents loved each other, but at my home it was much more intense. It was a like a kind of electricity in the air.

"My mother is very beautiful and my dad is handsome." I felt on safer ground if I returned to simple physical descriptions. "They are both dark haired. My mom has brown eyes and my father's eyes are blue. They don't tan easily but they rarely sunburn either. They are both average height." Here I paused.

"What do they like to do," prompted Max.

"Mom loves music and plays several instruments. She has a wonderful alto voice. Dad likes to run for exercise and he has a gift for solving number problems. He calls it his hobby. Several years ago he found a chat room on the internet devoted to advanced mathematics. He spends a lot of spare time there. He made several good friends on line who are interested in the same kind of problems."

Max looked thoughtful.

"Michael thinks your father's ability may have been what brought me here instead of somewhere near my brother where I had planned to go. Someone must have known what Connal and I were doing. There's been interference all along the line."

"Your right," said one of the nearby fairies. "After you left, I went over all your preparations and found many subtle things had been altered."

"James I'd like you to meet my old teacher Cian," said Max. This name is pronounced with the hard Celtic 'c' just like in the name Connal.

Cian didn't look old to me but who can tell with fairies.

Max and Cian began to discuss what changes had been made so I wandered over to the window to look outside. I was glad to stop talking about my parents. To me they are just Mom and Dad and that's all there is to it.

As I stood gazing out toward the front street a different fairy bounded up and landed neatly on the edge of a sun catcher my Grandpa had stuck to the window. These real fairies were quite strong and very light. This enabled them to bound high into the air which gave the illusion they were flying. They did not have tiny wings.

The fairy balanced expertly on the edge of the sun catcher where he was level with my eyes.

"My name is Cormac," he said using another hard 'c'.

"I'm pleased to meet you," I replied, all the while wondering if he was the real Cormac. "Do the other fairies speak English?"

"Only Cian and I studied with Max and Connal. The others will have to learn it as quickly as possible.

I understand you befriended Connal and Max when they first arrived. I've known Connal since he was born and I've always tried to protect him. I hope you will continue to be his friend. Don't judge him too harshly. It is hard to keep your honor spotless when your life is filled with sorrow and battle. He is the most feared warrior among the elves, but believe me when I tell you his heart is kind and pure. I hope you will always come to his aid in time of trouble."

"I'll try to do my best," I replied. Secretly I wondered what a twelve year old could do to protect a fierce warrior elf. Oh well, I'd do whatever I could because that's what you do when you like someone and I liked Connal.

Max gathered all the fairies around him and began to explain what life was like in the world of today. At least that's what he said he was going to do because he switched into a language I didn't know. I wished him good luck. He would need it. Our world is a pretty crazy place sometimes.

I was bored so I went over and switched on the television. That was the end of Max's formal lesson. The whole group bounded over to my side of the room and began firing a steady stream of questions at Max. At least I assume they were questions. They all seemed wildly excited. Max gave up and came and sat on the sofa with me. For the next hour or so the fairies watched television with us. They seemed to be having a wonderful time. I was glad they did not have loud voices because all fifteen of them kept chattering away to each other and Max. It felt like a big party.

I was so interested watching them I lost track of time and was quite startled when Grandpa and Connal walked through the door.

"It's safe for you to go home now," laughed Connal with a mischievous grin. "At least it's as safe as anything is going to be for a while."

"Thanks a lot," I sighed. I said good-bye to Max and wished him luck explaining 'commercials' to his small unruly students.

I was so glad to escape I didn't have time to worry about what my parents would say when I walked through the door.

I needn't have worried. I don't know what Grandpa and Connal told them, but my parents just gave me a big hug and sent out for Chinese food.

During supper I filled out some of the blanks in what they already knew. Mom and Dad are good listeners. It felt good to be able to talk about the strange things that had happened, particularly bonding with Max and all the food I'd been eating lately.

"Your increased appetite could be explained by a very natural growth spurt. You're not a teenager yet, but there's no fixed time line for the onset of adolescence. That's when most young people eat a great deal because they are growing so fast." said Mom trying hard to be reassuring.

"The important question about bonding with Max is do you think it helped or hurt you?" continued my Dad. "It's important to be honest with yourself when you answer this question. In fact it's probably all that really matters."

"I believe I've gained more than I've lost. I understand a lot of things I wasn't able to before. The one thing that bothers me is I feel closer to Max than to my best friend or my own brother and I suspect I always will."

"Do you feel any less close to your friend or your brother now than before this happened?" said Dad.

"No, of course not."

"Then it shouldn't be a problem. A feeling of closeness is a gift. A lot of people go through life unable to feel close to anything. How do you think Max feels about you?"

I thought about it for a moment while my new ability went into overdrive.

"Max will always do whatever he can to help and protect me. I have become his responsibility even though I'm not truly one of his own people."

"I think you are very lucky then," said Mom.

Sitting around the table in our warm peaceful kitchen felt wonderful. I realized how fortunate I was and I got out of my chair and gave each of my parents a big hug.

A small voice inside me kept quoting Dorothy from the 'Wizard of Oz', "There's no place like home. There's no place like home."

CHAPTER FOUR

July

The beginning of July seemed almost normal. Grandpa's house has three bedrooms, a master bedroom and two smaller ones. Max and Connal were now sleeping in the two extra bedrooms until they could find other suitable accommodations. The fairies were given free run of the basement.

They liked this arrangement because, before they moved to Fairyland, the people of the High Court traditionally lived underground because of their sun allergy. Grandpa fashioned one of the basement windows into a fairy door so they could go out and about after sundown. We kept them supplied with sun screen for emergency daylight trips and they spent a lot of time watching television.

I was surprised when Churchill settled back into his usual routine at our house. It did keep him away from the fairies. His hunting instincts could make it dangerous for them. Both Connal and Max spent most of the day with us as well.

My Dad was really enjoying himself. He and Max would spend hours going over data from various tests and experiments Max had carried out both in Fairyland and in Bissett. Then my Father would go on line and he and his friends would try to describe what happened in a mathematical equation, which really puzzled me.

"Why would you use an equation to describe something? Why not just use words?"

This made him pause for a moment before he replied. "The way our universe really seems to work doesn't make sense to our limited earth-bound brains. Maybe we don't have the right words. The closest we can come is to describe the true universal constants with numbers."

"Are you sure you're not saying that because you like number puzzles?"

"Perhaps, I am, but there are a lot of very smart people who agree with me."

He found a book called *Quantum Mechanics for Dummies* and suggested I read it. I'm pretty good at math and I understood some of what I read but most of it was beyond me. Even the simple idea of light being both a particle and a wave was frustrating. How can something change because of the observer?

I'm not sure why Connal decided he would spend most of his time with me and let Grandpa handle the fairies. Perhaps it was because the fairies kept pestering him with questions about everything. These small beings were important powerful people in Fairyland and were used to getting whatever they wanted when they wanted it. It was hard for them to adjust to this strange new world. Among other things they found the language barrier more difficult than they had expected.

Both Connal and Max had studied Earth a great deal before they came here, but Connal did not trust this information. His standard answer to most questions was, "I don't know." This irritated both him and the fairies.

He amused himself by introducing me to the basics of hand to hand combat. He said we were concentrating of the 'soft' version that stressed defense. I was suspicious of the word soft because I was collecting quite an assortment of bruises and scrapes. I would have fared worse except my grandfather allowed him to dig up a large area in his backyard and we hauled in sand to make what Connal called a training circle. I discovered Connal never backed away from anything. When you thought he was easing off, it was merely another feint. I soon learned to maintain my guard at all times.

I also wondered if Connal was developing a crush on my Mom. As soon as she was around, he would follow her from room to room with a dreamy look on his face. She baked him cookies and brewed the kinds of herbal teas he liked. He flirted shamelessly with her and she flirted right back. I thought it was rather weird.

I actually mentioned this to my parents and they told me everything was just fine. They had been told things about Connal I did not know. He had never known his own mother and had fallen in love with the idea of home and family. For him our big old house was more magical than any enchanted castle.

Our family's house does have a real charm. Visitors and friends are always talking about how much they like our house. It's three stories high, made out of local yellow brick and is about one hundred years old. A wonderful wide verandah curves around two sides and most of the windows on the main floor have leaded glass panes across the top. On sunny days there are always a few rainbows floating across the rooms.

It sits in the middle of a very big lot that is one hundred feet wide by almost three hundred feet deep. Grandpa Duncan says it is almost an acre of land. Where my Grandpa lives the lot is half as wide so that would make it half an acre. Both lots back onto a lovely park with a creek running through it. My brother and his friends used to go fishing in the Assiniboine River which is less than a thousand feet to the south. The whole area is filled with flowers and lovely old trees.

If that weren't enough, we are also half a block away from Portage Avenue which is a major thoroughfare with excellent bus service. I can't imagine anywhere else I'd rather live.

I wondered how Winnipeg compared with Elfland. When I asked Connal if he was homesick, he said the only thing he really missed was his friends.

"Everywhere is beautiful if you take the time to look. 'There is a world of wonder in a single rose leaf.'"

For someone who appreciated lovely things and took such good care of his body, it puzzled me how he always seemed to wear the most faded and ragged clothes he could find.

One day I asked Max about it.

"Oh, that's Connal's way of hiding out in plain sight. During his youth it was a survival skill, particularly when he was living with his father. He did not have an easy childhood and it was safer for him if he could disappear into a crowd. I think he's rather good at blending into his surroundings. When he wants your attention, he can get it soon enough."

Another odd thing I noticed about both Connal and Max was the way they usually had a scrap of paper and a pencil tucked away somewhere on their persons. When I asked Connal about this, he told me, while his people's language and customs were close to those of the Celts, one of the differences between the two groups was that the High Court's wise men and women believed in the power of the written word.

Celtic Druids believed their chief strength was the power of their minds. They developed a system which produced amazing analytical skills and powerful memory retention. They did write but usually just messages and these were often in code. They were afraid, if knowledge was written down, it might fall into the wrong hands.

Connal's people believed hard won knowledge was too precious to be lost just because someone died before he could teach others what he had discovered. As soon as an elf learns to write, he keeps a journal. These journals were his people's greatest treasures and Connal was delighted when he discovered I also kept a journal. I did it because I'd had the same teacher in both grade two and grade three and she'd insisted the whole class keep a short daily log. After two years of this many of my classmates and me still keep them out of habit.

About a week after we came home, on a day when Connal and Max were busy with my Dad, Grandpa appeared at our back door. He was carrying a scoop net, rake, shovel, and metal detector stuffed into an old golf bag. Even stranger were the two fairies seated on his shoulders. One was Cormac and the other was a woman named Kelda. I hoped they had used lots of sunscreen lotion because it was another bright sunny day.

"Come on, James," said Cormac. "We're going to hunt for sunken treasure."

He'd startled me and all I could say was, "What treasure?"

"Your Grandpa thinks it's high time we found the articles the crow dropped in the creek. If they were heavy like Connal and Max, it would take a strong current to move them very far."

"I know where Connal climbed out on the bank. He showed me the day after he arrived when we walked around the neighborhood," I volunteered.

"That should save us a lot of time," said Grandpa. "I hope Cormac and Kelda will also save us a lot of effort. They say they are very sensitive to many substances as well as metal."

When we reached the creek, Grandpa and I took off our shoes and socks. Then we waded into the water each carrying a fairy. We started out about fifty feet downstream from where Connal said the crow had tossed their gear in the water. We each held a fairy close enough to the water so they could keep their hands in the flow of the current.

I carried Kelda and she tried to explain what she was doing.

"Like colors in water. Hands smell like nose."

I took that to mean her skin was sensitive to what was in the water.

87

The creek was running at its normal summer level so the water didn't come much beyond mid-calf. It was pleasantly clear and cool with a gentle golden brown tint that leaches out of the leaves and grasses settled on the bottom. The tall old trees overshadowed the water and created dancing shadows on the banks and glittering spots on the water.

When Kelda or Cormac noticed something different, they would select a likely spot and Grandpa and I would grope around on the bottom while they watched from the shore. We found drink cans, bottle tops, broken glass, bits of wire, and old milk cartons. We fished everything out and put the trash in a garbage bag. We also located most of the things Connal and Max had lost. These we cleaned up as best we could and placed them in a small wooden box. The whole process took about an hour. We never did need Grandpa's metal detector.

It was a very happy group that walked through the back gate into Grandpa's yard.

We found Max reading in Grandpa's kitchen while he waited for his casserole to bake. He had decided he would help out by cooking. "It isn't much different from mixing magic potions," he'd remarked with a wry grin.

I placed the box on the table in front of him.

"Look inside," I told him.

Max placed his hands on the box and smiled at us.

"You've brought me a present. Whatever can it be?"

When he lifted the lid, there was dead silence and Max's eyes opened wide in happy surprise. He ran his fingers lovingly over the tiny objects inside. Then he gave a gasp of delight.

"You even found my book! This is truly a treasure beyond price. I was sure it was lost forever. What it contains will allow me to repay Michael and his people for all their efforts. Even better, I can now help those who came with us to start a new life. You have no idea how valuable this is."

"It wasn't damaged by being underwater?" I asked.

"It was packed in such a way that very little could harm it. Certainly not water."

"May I ask what makes it so valuable," said Grandpa.

"Because the people of the High Court had difficulty with metals, they became experts in what used to be called magic potions but you would call organic chemistry. The results of over ten thousand years of investigation and study are encoded in this tiny book.

I planned to make some of the most useful and safe essences and thus earn enough money to support myself and the rest of our group. When the book was lost, I was very worried. A lot of what is in there I can do of my own knowledge. However, the best formulas are very intricate and can be dangerous if not done exactly right. I know Michael will be very interested in what I have to offer."

We were standing around the table admiring the tiny tools in the box when Connal sauntered into the room.

"What have you got there?" He leaned over to look in the box and picked up something that looked like a twig or oversized toothpick. "This is a miracle!"

Max shrugged his shoulders. "Connal's reclaimed his staff and all's right with the world."

"Please, Max. Don't tease. Can you return it to its proper size?"

"We really don't have time at the moment and it will create any number of small explosions. That might attract unwanted attention. I'm sorry. I know how much it means to you."

"Yes, but we can enjoy all the colored lights and have a celebration tonight. I think we should offer thanks that something has gone right." A sly smile crept over his face and he continued, "Besides you'll be able to restore your precious book."

In the end Connal got his way. That evening at twilight we had a small gathering out in Grandpa's garden.

There were Max, Connal, Grandpa, Mom, Dad, myself, and the fifteen fairies. We brought out a radio and the fairies danced to the music on a rock station while we big people enjoyed the floor show. Connal had found an old mandolin that once belonged to my Grandmother. He played and sang a song in his own language that seemed very exciting. "War music," he said by way of explanation. Mom, Dad, and I sang "I Gave My Love a Cherry" a capella in three part harmony. I sang the tune, my dad the tenor line, and my mother's beautiful alto voice flowed under and around the wistful music. Everyone was drinking ginger beer and nibbling on small crackers.

The fairies could manage crumb sized pieces of cracker, but finding small drinking containers with handles was a problem. They could use their food bowls but we didn't have a ladle. We decided to fill a small saucer with ginger beer and I trimmed plastic coffee stirrers so they could use them as straws. If you've ever looked closely at coffee stirrers you'll notice a tiny hollow center. The fairies thought the straws were great fun. Especially, when someone realized they could spray the others using the straw. Everyone was in high spirits.

Max and Grandpa set up the picnic table out on the back lawn. They were careful to keep it well out in the open to avoid any overhanging trees. They ran out a long extension cord and plugged it into a rather crude looking machine they had made in the workshop. They assured everyone it would produce some sort of alternating magnetic field which would be able to restore the staff to its former size. It would also work on Max's book. These were the only two items they brought with them that had been compressed before being sent to Earth.

Max and Grandpa Duncan's light show came off without a hitch. The working parts of the machine produced a hazy green glow, but there were also lots of sparkly bits, many different flashes of colored light, and every so often a small ball of fire would shoot high in the air like a roman candle. Because there were just two items to enlarge, it only took half an hour from start to finish.

When it was all over everyone cheered.

My mom brought over a bottle of her homemade wine and we were gathered around to toast our success when two faces peered over the fence from our neighbor's yard. Instantly the fairies disappeared under the picnic table.

"Hello, folks. Is everything all right here?"

Grandpa's back yard is fenced and there are lots of trees and low bushes. It is not easy to see into it even in the daytime. We thought we were safe but one of our neighbors must have noticed the flashing lights and notified the police.

Grandpa strolled over to the fence and smiled at the officers.

"Good evening, officers. Is there a problem?"

"Do you have a permit for those fireworks?"

"Yes I do. I went down to the city offices late this afternoon. I was assured that as long as the display took place on private property under adult supervision there would not be a problem."

"In any event you're too late. We've just finished," said my Dad who had come up to stand beside Grandpa. "Our friends, who are here on a visit from Ireland, just had some very good news and we've been celebrating.

I could tell the policemen were a little upset. Not so much with us but because they were scratched and tousled from trying to find a way to get close to the yard. They had come up the back way from the creek through a lot of shrubs and bushes. Thank heavens, they'd been too distracted to notice the fairies.

After they left, we opened the wine and I filled a saucer for the fairies. We were a little giddy from our narrow escape and we quickly emptied the bottle. Mother asked if she should fetch another one but Max said it wasn't necessary. I think he was a little annoyed with the fairies, who continued to have a great time spraying wine around. He picked up the saucer and moved it some distance away from the picnic table.

"There! Keep your nonsense away from those who choose to stay sober. We have some important matters to discuss."

After the fairies moved out onto the grass, Max smiled indulgently at them. "It makes me happy to see them enjoying themselves. Their lives have been grim for a long while."

"What did you want to discuss?" asked my father.

"I am going to phone both Michael and Sean. They should know about the recovery of my book. I imagine they will want to come here as soon as possible tomorrow. Would you and your wife be willing to have them as guests for a night or two?"

"Certainly," said my Mom. "It's a big house and we can always throw a little more water in the soup. They'll be very welcome."

Grandpa touched Max on the arm to get his attention.

"When you talk to Sean, tell him I may have an idea about why you appeared here rather than Ireland."

"You know why that happened?" asked Max.

"Not really. But, James showed me the general area where you appeared and, when I thought about it, I realized it was where James's father and I had tried out a gadget I built for one of his internet buddies. At the time we didn't think anything had worked, but maybe it did."

"Wow!" said my Dad. "It's only power was a single triple A battery. Mind you, my friend said he thought it could create a very tiny wobble in the space-time continuum. He will be so excited."

"I'll definitely tell Sean and Michael" said Max.

Connal hadn't said anything for a while which was unusual for him. When I glanced at him, I noticed he was cradling his staff, now at full size. The fingers of one hand were tenderly stroking its surface. I realized this plain stick of wood must hold some special memories for him.

"Your staff means a lot to you?"

"More than anyone can ever know," he said in a gentle voice that was hardly above a whisper. "It's the hair's breadth between life and death, the strength to struggle onward and never give up, and the recollection of a lost love."

Max had come up behind me and now he laid a hand on my shoulder.

"Ask me another time and I'll tell you the story about it. There are things you don't say when the person is present."

CHAPTER FIVE

Triumph And Disaster

Sean and Michael arrived in time for coffee the next morning. Evan Hunter arrived about ten minutes later bringing along Clifford and Kelsey. Grandpa, Max, and Connal arrived almost at the same time. Because it was daylight, most of the fairies would be in their beds. I suspected more than a few of them would be sleeping off the effects of Mom's homemade wine. They had stayed out in the garden long after the rest of us had left.

Mom made a small pot of coffee, but it turned out she never used it. Everyone wanted tea which shouldn't have surprised me. Among our close friends and immediate family coffee drinkers are always outnumbered. I took this as a good omen and got out our big pottery tea urn. I prepared a huge amount of tea and balanced the urn on its ceramic stand over a burner on the stove that was turned down low. I felt they might be talking for a long while.

Clifford and Kelsey helped me with my tea preparations but, instead of going in to listen to the adults talking, they asked if they could go swimming. I must have looked startled.

"Don't worry. We've got our bathing suits," said Clifford with a sly grin.

"Come right this way," I replied. "You can change upstairs in my room."

They both trooped after me up the stairs.

"When you said 'stairs' you meant it!" exclaimed Kelsey as we reached the third floor which is where I sleep. "Hey, you've got a neat view of the city skyline."

"It used to be better before they built the apartment building on the other side of the green space. I like to sit on the window seat at night and watch all the city lights."

"You've got a lot of room up here," said Clifford.

"It used to be my brother's space. He's about ten years older than me and lives down in Fargo now. He's studying to be a doctor."

I took three fluffy towels from the linen cupboard on the second floor and we walked out to the pool.

"My mom always asks people to leave their towels up on the deck. That way they should still be dry when you come out. It's amazing how much water gets splashed about at ground level."

I laughed when I saw my friends' faces as they walked down the steps into the water. My mother insists we keep the pool warm. It's usually somewhere above eighty-five degrees. Once in a while it's been over ninety when the thermostat got stuck. It's very different from swimming in our usually chilly Manitoba lakes.

The three of us did a lot of splashing for the first while. Later the warmth of the water made us so relaxed we just sat together on the steps with the water up to our necks exchanging confidences.

"Did they tell you they figured out who the extra 'Cormac' is?" asked Clifford.

"No. Who is he?"

"Cormac isn't his real name. He finally confessed he believes he's Cormac's grandson. That's why he looks just like him. They ran some tests and everything backed up his story. His name is Garridan. It's a name that means 'he hid'. The strange thing is he doesn't know for sure who his parents are. His mother is probably one of Cormac's daughters but he hasn't any idea who his father is."

"He's spent his whole life searching for his family," Kelsey chimed in. "Cormac was the only one he located and when he saw him, even though it was from a distance, he was sure it was true. The physical resemblance is so strong it was like looking in a mirror. He never had a chance to speak to him because this was while Cormac was working with Max at his castle and no one was allowed in or out.

Just before they opened the portal to let the elves through, Max's servants offered to include any others who wished to join them. There was a big rush to accommodate the extra bodies. Garridan put on some sort of disguise and they sent him right along with the others. His disguise disappeared when he came across so he was in really big trouble when he got here. It must be sad to have no family," concluded Clifford.

"He's lucky the real Cormac acknowledged him and said he'd take responsibility for him," added Kelsey. "We left Garridan at your Grandfather's house before we came here. Cormac was waiting for him."

"You mean we now have sixteen fairies living in Grandpa Duncan's basement. It's going to take forever before they're all processed."

"Maybe not," said Clifford. They've found a way to speed up processing and the reason we're here today is to see if anyone wants to erect a building where this can be done in relative safety and privacy. The bunker at Bissett is too valuable to be kept at risk."

"Evan drove here today because he wants to check out some land north of the city. We came along for the ride to visit with you," added Kelsey.

"I'm glad you did," I said as stood up and stretched. My mother appeared on the deck and my stomach told me it was time for lunch.

The adults were talking and laughing all through the meal. The information in Max's book must have been really valuable. You'd think they had won the lottery. Perhaps they had. Time alone will prove that.

As soon as lunch was over Evan left with Connal to check out the parcel of land that was for sale somewhat southwest of the Sandycreek Reservation. I noticed Evan was treating Connal with an uneasy politeness. This was such a big improvement I wondered what had happened. Connal, however, seemed oblivious to the change and continued to be his usual exuberant self. They stopped together for a moment in the doorway to say something to my mother. It was the first time I'd taken a good look at the two of them together and I felt my jaw drop. They were carbon copies except one was so dark and the other was so light. There had to be a close family connection somewhere.

After lunch, Clifford, Kelsey, and I went for another short swim. Then we pulled the wooden picnic table into the shade and I brought out an old deck of cards and a container of plastic chips so we could play poker. We'd played a few games together while I was at Evan's cottage. We were just nicely started when Max came out and sat down at the table with us.

"Put down the cards, lads. I think it's necessary to be a storyteller today," he said softly and we all turned to look at him.

"There is a painful history between Connal and Evan. Neither of them knew the full story until yesterday. Parts of it are so terrible those who knew the tale could not bring themselves to tell it. Talking about it seemed wrong because it would only bring needless suffering to the innocent who have already endured so much. I only agreed to tell the three of you because it is too dangerous for you to remain in ignorance."

Max paused for a moment to make sure he had our full attention, and then he began...

"There was a time when a rich and powerful lord's wife gave birth to a beautiful baby boy. The father was very proud to have such a fine son and vowed his child would grow up to be the finest warrior in the kingdom. He would use his great wealth to hire the finest armorers, the best instructors, and fastest horses so no one could be his equal.

Legend has it that a rival lord heard this boast and became angry. He placed a curse upon both father and baby son. "Too much perfection shall be the ruin of all your house." And so it was.

The child's father believed that to be the best at anything, you should never be satisfied. The poor child grew up constantly being told whatever he did was never good enough. He did grow up to become the finest warrior in the kingdom but his father was never satisfied with his success. Worse still the young man was never satisfied either. Outside all looked perfect but inside he was maimed.

One day he fell desperately in love with a beautiful young woman. Those who knew her say she loved him as well. Remember he was both brave and very handsome. What he should have done was follow our customs, offer her some trinket like a few flowers or a pretty stone, and ask if he could share her bed. She would have told him, "Yes, no, or maybe," and that would have been the end of it.

Unfortunately, he could not face the possibility of failure and he did not have the self-confidence to believe she could love him for himself. Instead he went off to war and earned much honor and renown for his valor. When the king asked him what reward he wanted, he asked the king to give him the beautiful woman for his bride.

And so they were married, but they did not live happily ever after. His wife had been bound to him forever and could love no one else, but he never felt satisfied. He worried her love was not as good as love freely given. He became jealous of other men when there was no cause.

One day war broke out and the unhappy warrior went away to defend his king. He was distracted by his troubles and did not fully concentrate on the perils of the battle. The leader of the enemy force broke through his guard and gave him a terrible wound. He would have died if one of his warriors had not risked his own life and drove the enemy leader away.

The wound had damaged not only his body but his mind was scarred as well. When he returned home, he was never the same. He became more jealous and unreasonable than ever.

No matter what she did, his wife could not please him. You see, she was gifted with a special charm that caused everyone who met her to fall a little bit in love with her. This caused no end of problems even though the warrior knew it was impossible for her to be unfaithful to him.

One day she realized she was with child. Being a loving wife she was delighted to be carrying her lord's baby, however, she was also terrified. What if his jealousy turned him against the child and he decided to destroy it? Sadly, this is what happened.

The warrior sent his wife away with orders to kill the unborn baby. Since she was bound to him, he believed she could not do otherwise. What he had forgotten is the special bond between a mother and a child that can nullify all others. The wife fled through a portal to Earth and took refuge with her eldest sister and her husband.

The husband was a good man and a skilled doctor. The lord's wife believed his abilities would help her bring the baby safe into the world.

This was not to be. Somehow the warrior learned where his wife had fled and decided to follow her. His madness had grown much worse and he decided she must have been unfaithful to him and it was now his duty to kill her and whoever was her lover.

He took only one of his bondsmen with him and went through the portal.

When they came to the house, they realized there were three people inside. The warrior created some ruse that made third person leave on an errand. He wanted no witnesses to what he planned to do. His wife was near her time and the shock of seeing him started her labor pains. This infuriated him so, without saying a word, he struck her down and stood over her as her life slowly bled away into the uneven wooden floor.

The doctor was a brave and valiant man. He rushed over to push him away and help the woman. The warrior seized the doctor and commanded his horrified bondsman to help tie him to the heavy wooden table. The bondsman tried to reason with him but was silenced and ordered to help with the torture.

The phrase 'skinned alive' is just a starting place for what happened. Further description would only make a horrible crime worse.

The bondsman was a true hero in his own right. He was absolutely appalled at what he was being forced to do. He struggled so hard to break his bond with the warrior he lost consciousness and fell to the floor.

It was a terrible scene the sister saw when she returned, her husband dead and her sister dying in a room awash with blood. Her fury knew no bounds.

"You arrogant fool. Know that you have killed my husband and my sister and I curse you forever."

Immediately the madness cleared from the warrior's brain and he knew what a horrible thing he had done. He ran howling into the night.

The bondsman struggled to his feet and walked toward the sister. The tears flowing down his face washed small streaks in the bloody spatter.

"I am sorry. I was bound and forced to help him. But know this, when he wasn't watching, I did certain things to numb your mates pain and hasten his death."

"I know you did," said the sister softly. "Will you help me by carrying him out and laying him in the garden? I cannot bear to touch what remains of my love. I will see what I can do for my sister's child."

The bondsman wrapped the torn and broken body in a sheet and took it out to the garden. The indifferent stars and waning moon shone wearily down giving little comfort and less hope. With only these silent witnesses he knelt beside the shrouded corpse and offered prayers to ease the departing spirit on its journey into the darkness.

When he came back into the cottage, he found the wife standing beside a wicker basket on the table. The baby moved restlessly inside the encircling blankets and the women was gently stroking its small head. When she heard the bondsman's footsteps, she turned toward him.

"You are covered with my husband's blood. May I embrace you this once so I may feel something of him close to me for the last time?"

The man opened his arms and they held each other in a sorrowful embrace. The entire length of their bodies was pressed tight together and the man's eyes widened with sudden knowledge. At last they stepped apart.

"You are with child," he said gently.

"Yes," she answered, "and that is why you must take my sister's child and care for him. With no father it will be difficult enough to care for my own child, but it's more than that. This is the child of a man I will hate to the end of my life and beyond. As much as I loved my sister, I could never give her child the love all innocents deserve."

The man, who was a bondsman no longer, took the baby back with him to Fairyland. He found an old woman who would care for the baby. Then he went to the king and related all that had happened.

The king should have sent someone to kill the evil warrior, but he felt he owed him too much for his past bravery. The warrior was ordered to do penance for the rest of his life and forbidden to touch a sword or dagger ever again. The king believed this was enough, but it wasn't. Some things should never be forgiven."

My mother came out of the house with a pitcher of lemonade and a plate of warm oatmeal cookies.

Max poured himself a glass and took a bite out of a cookie.

"Who do you think the people in this story are? It may be a little difficult for you to figure this out so I shall tell you names and you will try to match them up. The names are Connal, Connal's father, Connal's mother, Evan's father, Evan's mother, and Cormac. There's even a brief reference to Evan."

"Connal's father is the evil warrior, Connal is the baby, and the Connal's mother is the lady who died giving birth," I said feeling pleased with myself.

"That's right," agreed Max.

Clifford frowned thoughtfully, "Evan's father must be the man who was tortured to death, Evan's mother is his wife, and Cormac is the bondsman." There was a brief pause and then Clifford's eyes lit up, "And Uncle Evan is the baby she was carrying."

Kelsey had been very quiet while Clifford and I were sorting out the cast of characters. He suddenly sat up straight.

"That makes Evan and Connal cousins and Clifford and I are third cousins, aren't we?"

"Yes, and now you understand why it is so important for you to know what happened in the past. Evan has just learned what I've told you. He hated Connal so much he couldn't think straight which is very dangerous. It was ironic because Connal's father, not Connal, was the real villain. Evan was angry with the one person who probably hated his old enemy more than he did."

"Why was that?" I asked.

"Because the story doesn't end there," said Max with a grim smile.

"The man, who saved the baby, Cormac, was famed for his ability to work with horses and other livestock. The king was delighted when he agreed to serve as part of his household even though he refused to give more than a simple spoken bond to obey the king's laws. The royal family was noted for the number of their servants who were free so this was no problem.

Connal spent seven years living happily with the members of a distant sept of Cormac's own clan. He was well liked and would have stayed longer except the old woman who cared for him died. The elders held a meeting to decide what to do about him. They knew who his father was and after much discussion decided to return him to his own family. This was a tragic mistake.

They realized how wrong they were the moment they saw the horror and disgust on the Lord Connal's face. He hated the child because his presence reminded him of the terrible crime he had committed. The village elders immediately offered to take the child back with them but the lord ordered them to leave at once.

They tried to contact Cormac but the king had sent him out with the army to help secure the northern borders. He was a most successful warrior and was named a hero by the bards, but it was three years before he returned and hurried to check on the young boy.

The scene that met Cormac in the castle courtyard was horrendous. Connal was near death. He had been severely beaten for some childish misdemeanor. In truth he was trying to protect his friend and half-brother who was the guilty one. His brother had also been beaten, but the whip they used on the Connal had been coated with iron. The pain must have been incredible. Then he had been locked in an iron cage. The allergic reaction to the iron was steadily draining the life from the pathetic little figure. They say, if there had been more time, Cormac might have killed Lord Connal right then, but the boy would not have lived. Cormac wrapped him in his cloak carried him away to help and safety.

After he recovered the boy was placed in training with the army. Here he excelled in all manner of military arts. He became an even more formidable warrior than either his father or grandfather and I believe they were both jealous of his success.

They waited patiently for a plausible excuse to kill him. The first opportunity came when they learned he had fallen in love with a beautiful young girl from a free clan. That in itself would not have been a problem but the girl became pregnant. This could allow a child, who would not be of pure noble blood, to have some claim on the family and this might disgrace the honor of the house. Connal's father also complained that he had not asked his permission to bond with the young woman. While both of these reasons were not supported by any law of the land, the father and grandfather arranged for servants to waylay Connal and beat him severely.

Cormac had long asked the king to do something about young Connal's situation and this is where I came into the story."

"Did you know Connal or Cormac before this?" asked Kelsey.

"Cormac taught me to ride when I was just a boy, but the first time I met Connal was when I found him bleeding to death in a ditch and rescued him. I was even riding a white horse," said Max with a grim smile.

"What does a white horse have to do with anything?" said Clifford.

"Don't you know? The brave knight in fairy stories usually arrives riding on a white horse," said Kelsey.

Clifford made a face at him.

"I'm afraid I wasn't much of a white knight. I was feeling grumpy and irritated. I felt my brother, the king, should have dealt with this problem long ago and now here I was wasting my precious time on a rather nasty errand.

As I rode up I noticed grey shapes hovering in the woodlands near the roadside and I wondered why the peasants were just standing around instead of working.

I discovered later the instructions had been very specific. "Make sure he bleeds for his sins," were the words told to me. Also, everyone was expressly forbidden to come to Connal's aid. All they could do was stand by helplessly and grieve while he bled to death. You may find it hard to believe but all of those bound to Lord Connal's honor adored young Connal and were horrified at how badly he was treated.

I gathered Connal into my arms and carried him off to the cottage of a woman skilled in healing. As soon as he was able to travel, I brought him before my father and demanded that I be allowed to take him for my bondsman because I was a prince of the royal blood and his father would not be able to touch him. It was the best solution I could think of at the time."

"And everyone lived happily ever after," I interjected.

"Only for a few short months.

I paid the bride price for the girl and brought her to live with Connal. They were wonderfully happy together. He would have married her in a minute but we all felt it would be too dangerous. In the end it didn't matter because both the girl and the baby were soon dead. Nothing could be proved but we felt certain Lord Connal was somehow responsible.

Connal was mad with grief and I became very worried about him. Fortunately, a beautiful woman friend of mine came to visit me and I asked her if she would try to, you know, cheer Connal up."

"Say what you mean," snorted Clifford. "You wanted her to have sex with him."

"That, too. But, this woman was far more skilled at pleasing men than just sex. She was very powerful in the women's circle and famed for her ability to heal shattered souls. One of the things she did to help him was encourage him to use the quarterstaff. She had discovered that, while Connal had lived with Cormac's people, he had met a man who was an expert, no a wizard, with the quarterstaff. This man spent a lot of time training Connal and the other boys in its use. Connal became his best pupil and he always remembered it as the happiest time in his childhood.

When it was time for her to leave, the woman gave Connal a present to remember her by. She had found someone who could make wood as hard as steel and had him fashion a special quarterstaff for Connal. It must have cost her a king's ransom, but she held high rank in the women's circle so was able to afford it. She challenged him to become even better than his old teacher. The staff was a clever way of giving him an avocation which allowed him to work through his grief and loss.

She drifted in and out of his life for many years. They always remained close but I never realized how close till I learned about Garridan. You see, the woman was Cormac's daughter by his first wife. Her name was Stara. She was very beautiful and very wise.

Both Cormac and I suspect that Garridan is Connal's son. Connal still doesn't know he has a son and he won't until the DNA results come back. There is no reason to trouble him with this until we are sure. Stara's death was another tragedy.

Somehow Lord Connal must have learned of the child. It was common knowledge he was the one who strangled Stara. This is why Cormac claimed a blood revenge for his daughter and killed him. What we never understood was why she had been tortured before she was killed. I am sure she died protecting Garridan. That he is still alive is proof she succeeded.

"That's so interesting," mused Kelsey. "Now we've got a tiny fairy for a fourth cousin."

"Kels, I swear you won't be satisfied until you find out the whole world's related to you," laughed Clifford.

Max stood up, stretched, and smiled down at us.

"That was a long sad story for such a wonderful sunny day. Your Uncle Max suggests you all relax and have another swim."

Kelsey and I went back into the water but Clifford followed Max into the house. We were still splashing around in the pool when Clifford returned.

He looked happy and amiable, almost mischievous.

"I'm off to see my friend, Wayne," he announced.

"And his very pretty sister," added Kelsey.

"That, too. I think I might need a little cheering up," said Clifford, echoing Max, as he turned away and started for the back gate that led into the park.

"Do you ask permission to leave? Remember what Evan said!" Kelsey warned.

"I spoke to Sean and the telephone number is written on the pad. It's broad daylight. Nothing is going to happen."

Kelsey and I exchanged worried looks. Then he shrugged.

We both knew we ought to do something but neither of us wanted to be the tattletale. Our shared guilt for what happened will always be with us.

CHAPTER SIX
A Narrow Escape

It was just before supper time when Evan and Connal returned from their expedition to the area between Netley Marsh and the tiny town of Libau. Connal sweet talked my Mother into making him a sandwich and took off for a run around Assiniboine Park. He was always very serious about keeping up some sort of fitness routine.

It wasn't until the rest of us sat down for supper that the others realized Clifford wasn't there.

Evan was furious with both Kelsey and me. Even with my father in the room to protect me, I was petrified about what he might do.

"He said he talked to Sean and had permission," stammered Kelsey.

Evan whirled around to confront Sean.

"Did you let him go?" he snarled.

Sean looked offended and got the look in his eyes people have when they are quoting from memory.

"Clifford said, 'Is it O.K. if I go outside and wander around for a while?' Then I said, 'Don't go far away from the house.' And he replied, 'I won't.' Since there are several fairies patrolling the area behind the house, I assumed it would be safe."

"Does anyone know where he was going?"

Kelsey was white as a sheet and looked as if he might throw up so I answered.

"He said he was going to see his friend, Wayne. He left the telephone number on the pad."

A quick phone call determined Clifford had never arrived. Wayne's family said they'd organize a search from their end and all of the adults, except my mother who remained behind to answer the phone, immediately left to look for him in our neighborhood and then work their way toward his intended destination. After everyone left, my mother telephoned the local police station and asked them to keep an eye out for Clifford. She also found out what we had to do if we needed to set up an Amber Alert because he was not yet eighteen. When she was finished, she stayed near the phone and Kelsey and I wandered out into the yard. We were sitting at the picnic table when Connal returned from his run.

I stood up and went to meet him. Kelsey stayed slumped over the table.

"Connal, something bad may have happened. Clifford is missing. Everyone is out looking for him."

"Do you know which way he went?"

"He left through the back gate and we saw him walking toward Portage Avenue."

Connal paused and looked thoughtful for moment. Then he said, "Oh yes, I thought I smelled something. Luckily, the marker Sean used during the incident at Evan's cottage is very long lasting. You boys stay right here." Then he went around our house and started walking toward Grandfather Duncan's house. On his way he picked up Churchill, who was curled up on the deck and I heard him whisper, "Come on cat. Let's go hunting."

I felt guilty I hadn't stopped Clifford earlier that day. Then I remembered what his grandfather told me.

I started to follow Connal when I noticed Kelsey was following me.

"Where are you going?" he demanded.

"I think Connal knows something about where Clifford is and I'm going to try and help him. When we were at Wallace Lake, your grandfather told me I would find one of his grandsons when they were lost."

"Then I'm coming with you. You can't stop me."

I saw the grim resolve in Kelsey's eyes and I knew it would be useless to argue. Besides, we'd have to hurry if we wanted to keep Connal in sight. He moves so quickly, he often seems to flow over the ground.

Even though we ran, we might have lost him if he hadn't ducked into Grandpa's workshop. He came out fastening some sort of glove on his hand and there was a small bundle strapped to his back. He reached back inside the door and brought out his quarterstaff. He was whistling softly to himself. As soon as he had everything adjusted to his satisfaction, he took off at an easy lope through the back gate and out into the park.

I was glad I often ran for exercise. I'm not as good as my father, but I can maintain a pretty steady pace when I want to. I think Kelsey, who was wearing rather heavy boots, found it harder to keep up, but he was so intent on finding his brother he scarcely noticed any discomfort.

We didn't want to get too close to Connal anyway because he might insist we go back. What I worried about most was our presence might be more troublesome than helpful. I'd had a belly full of guilt for one day.

It was still bright out when we started running through the park but the sky began to darken rapidly.

"There's a bad storm coming in from the west," said Kelsey.

"I know. It's getting really sticky and I'm sweating buckets," I agreed as I wiped the stinging salt perspiration out of my eyes.

Connal's route took him into the huge storm drain that runs under Portage into Truro Park on the other side. The creek was running low so we didn't get our feet wet. When we came out on the other side, I got a glimpse of Churchill who was running near Connal.

They seemed to be staying near the creek and when we next caught sight of them Connal was about twenty feet away from the water next to an old school calmly breaking a window and crawling inside.

I looked at Kelsey and we both shrugged ran up to the broken window. Churchill was sitting on the ground as if he was waiting for us. He meowed politely so I lifted him inside and then climbed in myself with Kelsey right behind me. I did remember to take the end of my T-shirt and try to wipe any fingerprints from the window sill.

Most of the windows were boarded up so it was quite dark. We had no idea where Connal was, but Churchill seemed to know so we followed the cat.

We found Connal standing where he could not be seen, beside the opening for a large double door. If I remembered the shape of the building correctly, the door would lead into the old school gym. When he saw us, the expression on his face did not change but he raised his finger to his lips. He seemed strangely relaxed and at peace. He smiled gently at us which scared me a lot more than anger or irritation.

"Well," he whispered, "since you've volunteered to help me, I might as well make use of you."

A howl of agony burst out from the gym and Kelsey jerked forward. Connal restrained him by putting a hand on his shoulder. The touch looked gentle but it was not. Connal's grip is made of steel. Kelsey winced.

"We can't go in there yet. They're almost finished and Clifford's life could be forfeit if we went in now."

He reached into his pocket and brought out his ever-present pencil and quickly sketched a rectangle on the wall beside us.

"There are more of them than I thought there would be. Clifford is tied to a table here. There are four men near him and there are another three people close to the south wall over here. There is a small table near the door. I want you two to distract the group by the south wall. You came without weapons but perhaps you can do something with the table. A clever person can turn almost anything into a weapon."

There was another cry even more agonizing than the first and then we heard the sound of sobbing.

"It's time," whispered Connal. "Move as fast as you can when I give the signal. Pure speed may save you when nothing else can."

He picked up his staff and his eyes blazed with excitement. He smiled and whispered one last word, "Kill," then he stepped into the doorway and we followed.

"Now!"

There was a brilliant flash of light, screams, shouts, and our enemies reached for their weapons. Kelsey and I did exactly what we were told. We never had time to plan anything. Actually, I don't think we could repeat what we did even if we practiced for months.

We rushed over and each of us grabbed a leg of the rectangular table on the near side. Then we tipped it over so it became part shield and part battering ram. We did this so quickly, it felt as if we hardly hesitated in our race across the room. The only slight problem was I had some difficulty keeping up with Kelsey. He may have found it hard to run from my house to the school, but he excelled over the short distance. I hadn't realized Kelsey was a natural sprinter.

Connal exploded into the room just ahead of us and the three men near the south wall were focused on him. This allowed Kelsey and me to ram into them before they could swing their weapons in our direction. I think they might have got at least one shot away but there was no time to aim at us. Fueled by adrenalin the momentum of our charge flattened all three. We were very lucky they were standing close together.

Kelsey and I never saw what Connal did to the four men standing near Clifford. When we looked over there, all four were motionless on the ground and Churchill was padding across the floor to the table where he jumped up on Clifford's chest and started to purr. That's his way of offering comfort to someone he likes when they aren't well. I supposed he must like Clifford.

I noticed the man lying near me was starting to stir so I kicked him. I was only wearing running shoes but he did stop moving. I didn't enjoy doing it but I've never regretted it either. The man nearest Kelsey began to reach for his gun and Kelsey stomped on his hand. He was wearing sturdy leather walking boots and I heard the bones crunch. Connal was walking toward us and I saw him nod approvingly. Kelsey and I understood what was meant when he'd said, "Kill". He told us later, the only rule that applies to a sensible man in a death struggle is to make sure you survive and your enemy doesn't.

Connal had his staff in his hand and systematically touched the heads of all three of our victims. Each time there was a brief glow.

"They won't be conscious for at least half an hour, perhaps longer," he explained.

"How did you make your staff do that?" I said. "I thought it was made out of wood and wood is a non-conductor." I remembered the big flash of light when we ran into the room and I wanted to ask about that, too.

"I'll explain later. Meanwhile we have to get Clifford back to your house as quickly as possible. Here, Kelsey, you carry my staff, I'll carry Clifford and James can carry the cat. Churchill won't go out into the pouring rain willingly and I don't want him left behind."

He leaned over Clifford brushed the sweat soaked hair back from his forehead. Before he picked him up I heard him murmur softly, "Don't worry cousin. I'm here and I'm going to bring you home."

Churchill does not like to be carried so I felt that I had the most difficult job of the three. I finally took off my T-shirt and wrapped him in it so I could avoid the worst of his scratching and biting. When we got home, Clifford and I were the two who looked as if we'd been in a fight.

It rained heavily all the way home and Connal set a punishing pace. I began to appreciate how strong he was when I realized he was traveling much slower than he had to so we could keep up.

Our house is less than a ten minute run away from the old school and our battle with Clifford's kidnappers took five minutes at the most. We were back home in well under an hour.

My poor mother had been frantic. When we arrived, she spent the first few minutes switching between being very angry and very grateful.

"Why didn't you tell me where you were going?" she fumed.

"Because you wouldn't have let us go."

"Not true," snapped my mother. "I would have insisted on going with you."

Suddenly I saw her in a whole new light. It's a shock to realize your mother might relish danger and battle. I remembered she'd really enjoyed the time she got to kick down a locked door. Mary Owen was fearless when faced with any kind of peril.

Connal was absolutely charmed.

"Dear lady," he chuckled. "If you should ever consider taking another lover, I hope you would consider my own poor self."

"I know that no one could take the place of my own dear husband, but I thank you for your flattering offer," replied my mother with a small curtsey. "Now I'd better get on the phone and let everyone know Clifford's home. Does he need to see a doctor?"

"I doubt it," said Connal. "I'm very good at treating all kinds of physical injuries and I can do as much for his body as anyone can. The worst injury is to his mind and he needs to see Max as soon as possible. For now it will help him to be near people who care about him, so let's make him comfortable on the sofa in the family room."

Under Connal's direction and with lots of advice from my mother, Kelsey and I scoured the house for bandages and other materials to equip our little field hospital. Connal's knowledge went far beyond first aid. I realized he could never have survived all his battles over two hundred years without becoming an expert in all kinds of emergency medical procedures.

When Evan and the others arrived, Clifford was resting comfortably and Connal was sitting in an over-stuffed blue chair in the far corner of the room petting Churchill. The last thing I'd heard him whisper to Clifford was, "I promise you cousin, when you're ready for it, you and I will go hunting and our enemies will learn what it is to be really afraid."

He knew Kelsey and I heard him. As he was walking over to the big blue chair, he smiled at us and said, "Sometimes, when you are in a lot of pain, the best medicine is to begin plotting your revenge."

The first people to come back to the house were Evan and Max. They took only a cursory look at Clifford before walking over to where Connal was sitting.

"What happened to him?" demanded Evan.

"If most people had seen the room, they would have assumed it was some kind of gang initiation gone wrong. However, I'm an old hand at this sort of thing and it had all the earmarks of a bonding ceremony based on pain and humiliation. It was crude and amateurish but very effective."

Connal stood up and carried Churchill over to the sofa and placed him beside Clifford. The cat promptly curled up and went to sleep. Connal, Max and Evan walked silently out of the room.

Kelsey was keeping vigil beside Clifford so I thought I would walk into the kitchen and take a short break. My grandfather was sitting at the table with a mug of tea in his hand and he motioned for me to come and sit beside him.

"So you and Kelsey decided to go looking for trouble with Connal tonight?"

"I remembered what Mr. Wallace told me about his dream and I felt I had to help."

"I believe you. Just don't make a habit of it. Always avoid trouble when you can."

"I will. I promise you. It was strange though. I knew I would be very scared because what we were doing was so dangerous. I was scared, terrified. Then it was like my mind was filled with a kind of unholy glee. All of the rules were thrown aside and anything was possible."

"That's a legacy left to you by all your ancestors who faced extreme danger and survived because they would not let anything stop them. Skeptics would call it an adrenalin rush, but those who have experienced it know it goes far beyond that. It is sometimes called 'the way of the warrior'."

Grandpa's eyes had a faraway look and I realized sometime in his life he, too, had walked down the warrior's path.

Grandpa made us a couple of slices of cinnamon toast. The relative safety of our bright warm kitchen seemed so real and comforting compared to the danger we had just overcome.

"I was surprised at how good Connal is at treating wounds," I told Grandpa.

"Didn't you realize Connal is also a wizard? Max has been training him for years and says he's very skilled."

I was surprised. It suddenly occurred to me perhaps his quarterstaff was more than that. Don't wizards have magic wands?

Suddenly the kitchen was filled with silent people all of whom looked very grim. Evan was the only one who spoke.

"We have decided the only way to save Clifford from permanent damage is to complete the bonding rite. Michael and I have given our permission for Connal to assume responsibility for Clifford's life. It was a hard choice because this is like sending my own flesh and blood into slavery, but it must be done or he could lose his sanity and possibly his life."

I noticed three strangers in the group, two women and a tall thin man with a prominent Adam's apple. I assumed they were friends of Evan and Michael and had been out with them looking for Clifford.

Our kitchen was getting crowded so most of the group went into the family room. Max, my mother, and the two women remained in the kitchen. I noticed Kelda tapping at the window so I opened it so she and two other fairies could come inside. They were all carrying large bundles. At least they were large for a tiny fairy.

I realized one of the first things Max had done was call in the fairies who were patrolling our yard. He sent them back to Grandpa's house to collect the various ingredients he needed. He had spent a lot of time gathering supplies and had set up a makeshift laboratory in Grandpa's kitchen.

With my mother's help he was able to create a concoction he felt was rather primitive but should work quite well. They stirred this mixture into a dish of ordinary cooking oil and set in on the counter.

Kelda had watched what Max was doing and seemed to be arguing with him about something. They were speaking their own language so I wasn't sure what was wrong.

Finally, Kelda jumped on my mother's shoulder and began speaking in her ear. My mom doesn't see fairies too well even with blue tinted glasses, but she can hear them. Soon all the women were in a huddled at one side of the room whispering furiously to each other.

The older woman turned to Max and demanded, "Is what Kelda says true?"

"Yes, it is," replied Max a little distractedly. "It may be uncomfortable but it will pass by morning."

The last thing I heard as I walked out into the family room was the younger woman saying, "Don't worry. If he's willing I'll look after everything."

When everyone was assembled in the family room, we formed a rough circle around the sofa where Clifford was lying in a semi-conscious state. The fairies were perched in a row along the back of the sofa. They were whispering and laughing among themselves until Sean glared at them. I was learning that fairies are a boisterous lot in almost any circumstances.

Michael turned to the strange young man and asked him to take notes. My dad got a pen and notepad from the telephone desk for him.

"You don't have to describe the process, Guy," said Michael. "Max will be able to do that for us. It's more important to record all the questions you have while you are watching."

Max assumed the role of narrator so we would all understand what they were doing and why.

"Connal told us they were using chemical enhancements to create a completely passive state which allows one person to take control of another's mind through hypnosis and then extend that control so it lasts for the rest of their life by various forms of post hypnotic suggestion. The first thing we will do is continue the process but using different ingredients whose properties I know. This should also neutralize whatever was done by our enemies.

Connal agreed he was the best person to do this. He has a lot of experience and he and Clifford share some of the same blood. Because our enemies used rather primitive methods to prepare Clifford, he will be using the Old Rite.

During the ritual, the dominant person will take control of the other. It could be described as deep hypnosis of an individual in a completely receptive state. This is not the best way to achieve bonding. It's certainly not the usual way we do things now. This ritual harks back to a much more primitive time. However, I feel it is appropriate for this situation."

We had removed Clifford's clothes when Connal was treating his many wounds and abrasions. Now Max folded back the sheet from his body so he and my mother could coat it with the mixture they had prepared in the kitchen.

Clifford had been resting quietly but now he seemed to relax even more. The ghost of a smile appeared on his lips. When his body was completely coated, Max and my mother stood up and Connal stepped forward and knelt beside Clifford. He placed his hand on Clifford's forehead and bowed his head for a moment of silent prayer. Then he sat back and let his eyes range over our little group.

"I have suffered much from the evils of bonding and for the last fifty years of my life I have worked to find a way to free myself and my people. It is my earnest hope this will be the last formal bonding of any of my family. Gaia help me!"

Connal then took Clifford's hand and helped him to stand. Clifford started to sway slightly and Connal gave him one of his mischievous grins and punched him on the arm.

"Stay with me cousin. This won't take long and we're all on your side."

Clifford returned the smile and Connal once again became deadly serious.

"Kneel before me fledgling and I will pronounce your fate."

Clifford knelt and Max handed Connal his staff which he struck three times on the floor like a judge bringing his court to order. Then he began to speak.

"You will be bound to my honor as an equal.

The children of your line will be of equal rank to my own.

You will be bound to battle.

You and I have been touched by evil and through battle we may hope for justice.

You will be bound to my quest.

My quest is a search for freedom both for my people and rest of mankind.

Your quest shall also be for the freedom of others and for yourself.

You must seek freedom in all things even from this bond."

I was standing directly across from Cormac and I'd been watching his face because I knew he hated anything to do with bonding. I wondered why he'd remained to watch the ceremony. I could tell he was grumpy and irritated, but now a delighted smile spread across his face and he began a slow rhythmic clap. Soon everyone but Guy, who was busy taking notes, was following suit.

Max looked very surprised and interested at the same time. Connal smiled at them both and continued.

"Now I will pronounce your sworn duties.

You will protect our children, the people of our clan, and through them all of mankind.

You will obey the commands of The Core unless you have certain knowledge that forces you to take a different path.

You will obey all of my commands for a period of ten years. That will give you time to pay back most of your debt to me and others. At the end of ten years there will be a reckoning before you can begin to seek your own freedom.

For my part I pledge to you my love and loyalty.

I will provide counsel and training so you may take your rightful place among the warriors of The Core.

Do you accept my bond?"

Clifford raised his face to meet Connal's eyes. He was smiling.

"I accept with all my heart."

Connal then reached over to the sofa and picked up Churchill and placed him in Clifford's arms.

"When you are in need of extra strength remember the cat. Let it become your totem. A cat does not need anyone's approval to be happy or to decide which is the right path. If you need counsel, the cat totem will come to your aid."

Connal then put Churchill back on the sofa where he promptly jumped off and left the room. I wondered why he'd stayed so long because he doesn't like to be around a lot of people. Maybe he knew Connal wanted him for the ceremony.

Connal struck his staff on the floor three more times and then touched Clifford lightly on the chest. Tiny blue electric sparks danced all over Clifford's skin and I heard his give a slight gasp.

"Now rise and be welcomed into your new life."

Clifford got up from the floor in one effortless movement. He was smiling and looked euphoric. Connal handed Max his staff then reached out and grasped both of Clifford's hands.

"Draw near and I will give you your secret name."

Connal whispered something in Clifford's ear that I could not hear gave him a big hug. Clifford's face lit up with a radiant smile as they stepped apart and everyone clapped and cheered.

Clifford suddenly realized he wasn't wearing any clothes but Max quickly handed him the sheet we'd used to cover him and he wrapped it around his middle. Everyone came over to shake his hand and congratulate him. The more exuberant gave him a hug and a kiss.

My mother, always practical, said, "Clifford, come with me. You need a good warm shower to get rid of all that oil."

She herded him out of the room and the two other women went with them. The older spoke to Michael as they were leaving.

"That turned out surprisingly well. It looks as if we've dodged a bullet, Michael. It will be interesting to see how effective Connal's bonding rite turns out to be. For the first time I am very hopeful. Now I will make sure our fledgling warrior goes right to bed."

Now it was Connal who looked white and shaky.

"That took a lot out of me," he muttered. "I think I need a shower, too." He quickly removed all his clothes and walked out of the patio door to stand naked in the pouring rain. I was surprised but no one else seemed to be paying any attention. I did notice the old scars that covered his back.

"Is Connal going to be alright?" I asked Max.

"He should be just fine, but that kind of bonding is very painful. Also, I understand he used his staff earlier tonight which also takes a physical toll."

"How did you know that?"

"You didn't see Cormac, but he followed you. He knew it was too risky for him to take any direct action, but he could tell us what happened."

"I go where I'm sent and do what I'm told," piped up Cormac. "Max said to keep an eye on you two imps and that's exactly what I did."

"Go where you're sent and do what you're told, in pig's eye!" snorted Max. "You always do whatever you choose."

"You must be proud of Connal," said Cormac changing the subject. "You said he was your best pupil and now I'm ready to believe it, a bonding that will free the bondsman. Who would have believed it? More to the point, do you think it will work?"

"What Connal did was of his own choosing. He never told me anything so I haven't had time to think things through, but I believe it should work. Connal, poor soul, has done more bonding than anyone I can think of besides my brother the king."

"Did you force Connal to return to his people and repair the damage his father had done?"

"No. I tried to talk him out of it. It took fifty years of sorrow and pain before he felt he could leave and return to my service."

At this point I totally lost any understanding of what they were talking about and decided to go outside and check on Connal. I found him and Evan and Kelsey all sitting around the picnic table in the pouring rain. As I drew closer I could hear Evan talking.

"You saved my grandchild tonight and I absolve you of all debts my family may claim."

"Don't give up your claim so quickly. Tell me again in twenty years when the fledgling is a free man. Don't forget who I am and what I am. You must stand ready to protect Clifford. On one hand I have saved his sanity and possibly his life at the cost of considerable pain. On the other hand, the act of bonding produces a strong feeling of euphoria that is highly addictive. Worse than that, part of me is gloating because I have just acquired another valuable possession.

In other circumstances you and I should be true friends, but I'm not going to allow you to come too close because it would be very perilous. Our friendship would cloud our vision and could be dangerous for Clifford. Let me alone to do the best I can to keep my pledge of freedom for your grandson. May I suggest you concentrate your efforts on Kelsey? It will be hard on him now I have taken ownership of his only brother."

"I have one favor to ask," said Evan. "Will you allow him to attend university?"

"Allow him? I'll order him. He will not have a choice. I intend he shall be as well trained as his strengths and talents allow. Life won't be easy for Clifford, but I hope it will be interesting."

I didn't feel reassured by the word 'interesting', but I kept silent and walked back into the house and so to bed.

CHAPTER SEVEN
A Brighter Day

When the sun rose the next morning, it seemed as if our perilous night had never happened. My family plus all our overnight guests made our home resemble an anthill that had been poked with a stick. Fortunately, everyone seemed to be in wonderful spirits. There were snatches of songs and much laughter everywhere.

Kelsey, Clifford, and I ate our breakfast outside on the deck beside the pool. Kelsey and I chattered away, but Clifford seemed to have something on his mind.

"Who was the fair haired girl at the ceremony last night," he said pensively.

"I have no idea," I replied. "I think she's a friend of Michael and Evan. You could ask my mom. She was talking to her in the kitchen. Why?"

"Well, it was kind of strange. She came into the bedroom last night and well, you know."

"We know what?" said Max as he joined us at the table.

Clifford was startled but he recovered quickly. The look he gave Max was a mixture of defiance and sly teasing.

"She cheered me up."

Kelsey and I exchanged quizzical looks then tried to keep our faces straight. Was Clifford talking about having sex? Max didn't seem to be disturbed in the least.

He smiled at Clifford and said, "That is very interesting. The lady's name is Erna and she's a very nice young woman. I'm not familiar with the practices of the women's circle of the Core. 'Cheering you up' may be their way of welcoming a new associate or they just decided you needed to relax and have a really good sleep. Some of the ingredients I used last night can act as a rather strong aphrodisiac. I hope you responded appropriately and everything went well."

Now Max was teasing Clifford, but the fledgling warrior refused to let his feathers get ruffled.

"So much happened to me yesterday I just wanted to make sure I wasn't delirious or something," continued Clifford. "The world's a lot stranger today than it was yesterday."

I could tell Kelsey would have pushed Clifford for more details but he didn't say anything in front of Max and me.

The two brothers quickly finished their cereal and went upstairs to pack. I imagine they had a lot to talk about. Max finished eating and we went inside together.

It didn't take long for the house to empty. Sean and Michael left for Bissett and Evan, Kelsey, and Clifford went back to Newago. My mother and father left for work and I was on my own except for Max. He'd come over early and spent quite a while talking to my parents before they left. While I finished clearing away the breakfast things, he poured himself a cup of tea and sat down at the kitchen table.

"James, you and I have to have a serious talk."

"Sure," I replied. "What about?"

"For reasons I don't yet understand, I believe you and I have accidentally formed a bond. I have been trying to remove my influence but it's not working. My family was highly skilled in this form of control and while I do know how to remove it, the process is very painful and can be dangerous. Your parents have agreed to leave things as they are with the understanding that when you are older I will give you a chance to free yourself."

Max seemed so sad and apologetic I immediately wanted to rush over and comfort him. Then my new talents took over and I wondered if I really wanted to do this or was it just the effect of the bond. I paused and thought this was ridiculous. If I doubt everything I want to do, I'll never do anything.

"The bonding took place when you touched me that day in the blue tent, right?"

"That's right," answered Max.

"Well, it saved us and that's what matters. I know you were only trying to hide from your enemies. Don't worry, things will work out. I remember being disappointed when I learned you would be leaving with Sean. I thought it would be such fun to join you and Connal on your quest. I guess I should have been more careful with my wishes."

"I didn't know that," said Max, "but you're right. Your wish didn't cause what happened but it probably added to the effect.

You are a kindly soul James, but I want you to understand what is involved. The ugly truth is I own you and I can't even try to set you free until you are much older and stronger. Look deep in your heart and you will know this is true. I hope you can forgive me."

I knew he was right and it felt like being hit in the stomach. He really did control me. If Max wanted me to do anything, I would have to do it. Think about that, anything. There was no escape. It was as if the solid ground I stood on had opened up right under my feet.

Everyone has different ways of coping with something intolerable. In my painful childhood I had often used a kind of chanting to get through the agony. I started to whisper over and over, "It hasn't killed me yet. It hasn't killed me yet."

I gradually became calm. Then I remembered what the book on quantum mechanics said about the form changing by being observed. I would try to look at my problem differently and create a different result. It was a weird idea but somehow I knew I was right.

So, I just smiled at Max and said, "You are also a kindly soul Max. I suspect your ownership will keep me out of more trouble than it might cause. You do take good care of your property don't you?"

"I will protect you with my own life if necessary."

"See! What's wrong with that? I intend to accept my bond cheerfully and I am looking forward to helping you and Connal in your quest. I am where I want to be at least for now. What more could I ask for?"

Max was delighted, smug.

"Among my people a lord is judged by how valuable the people he controls are. It is a great honor to be considered a valuable man. I do believe my honor has just acquired a treasure beyond price."

Max stood and I knelt before him. I accepted my bond and he pledged his loyalty. Then he whispered his true name in my ear and gave me my true name.

I sort of wished my parents had been there, but perhaps this was better.

Connal had been standing in the doorway for a while. He had a big grin when he came across the room. He punched Max on the arm and gave me a hug.

"Welcome to Max's honor, fledgling. I'm glad he finally told you. He's been fretting over his sins for days. It isn't like Max the Perfect to make mistakes and he gets all broody when he does."

"It's just that I feel so responsible..." That was as far as Max got before Connal interrupted him.

"Max, go back to work. Everything is just fine. I'm going to take James out and see if we can find a suitable branch in the caragana bush to make into a quarterstaff."

Our backyard is really pleasant. There is a huge lawn surrounded by an assortment of trees and bushes. There are evergreen trees, willows, lilac, caragana, a variety of fruit trees and a fair sized vegetable garden. There are lots and lots of pots filled with flowers because my mom says they're easier to weed than flower beds. Because of the pool, there is a high chain link fence all around and the gates are always kept locked. That day it felt especially private and safe.

Caragana is used a lot for hedges and is something like the yew tree. Yew trees were used to make bows because they are tough, flexible, and the branches are very straight. Our yard has several clumps of caragana that haven't been trimmed in ages and are now well over twelve feet high. It didn't take us long to find a good branch. Connal had brought a small saw with him and cut it off close to the ground. Then we walked over to Grandpa's workshop where Connal trimmed it so it was a hand span taller than I was. He then told me to trim off the leaves and peel the bark. While I was busy doing that, he started to dismantle the black box I'd seen him wear when he went to rescue Clifford.

"Is that what made the big flash of light last night?"

"Yes, it is. In Elfland we didn't make much use of electricity produced by sources such as steam turbines or hydro electric generators. We concentrated on developing very efficient chemically powered storage batteries. This little box is just a kind of storage battery. Long ago kings and wizards used similar gadgets to terrify the common folk. It looked like they were able to call down fire from the sky to destroy their enemies. Actually, that was just a variation of what you saw yesterday. My staff has been treated with a substance which allows it to conduct electricity along its surface. Did you notice the glove I was wearing? That was to insulate my arm from the charge."

"Do you think anyone was badly hurt?"

"I don't know." Connal shrugged and seemed very casual about the whole incident. "However, your grandfather said there was nothing about any disturbance on the news. Any damage to the old school would probably be considered ordinary vandalism if there were no bodies lying around."

I wondered if I'd ever learn what happened to the man I'd kicked. I was surprised I didn't feel more concerned about it.

Connal showed me how the battery was put together. It seemed quite harmless, but he assured me the chemicals he used could produce a very powerful surge of electricity. He said the real secret was in controlling the amount of electricity released.

Connal is always easy to talk to, so I decided to ask him about a word I didn't understand.

"What did you mean when you used the word 'honor'?"

"Honor is a word that can be used in several different ways. It can indicate respect, as in honoring your country. It can mean recognition of a special achievement. Do you have an honor roll at your school which lists students who have good grades? Another meaning is a kind of a reward for merit like being given a badge of honor. However, this time you heard it used in a very old meaning.

When a person did some outstanding service for his king and country, they would be honored with some kind of gift or payment, usually land or valuable property. This is how a person could become rich and powerful. A gift of land included everything that was on the land such as minerals, castles, peasants, and what have you. My own family's honor was very large and spread in part along the western border. It was beautiful and rich but dangerous. We were proud to have earned it by our skill in battle. The king was most generous to us because no other family was as good at protecting the country from the Misbegotten.

When I came into my inheritance, I actually owned more land and property than Max who was a royal prince. However, I'm sure his holdings were worth more than mine. You see, I belonged to Max just as you do. I was also part of Max's honor. We are very lucky because the honor Max maintains has rather few people in it and all of them are well loved and well treated.

Through time you will come to feel as close to them as to your own family."

I had a lot to think about as I smoothed out the worst bumps on my staff and Connal pottered around in the workshop. I hadn't realized how neat handed he was with all manner of tools. He soon finished whatever he was doing with the black box and ordered me into the yard to try out the staff.

This first session was mainly about very basic technique. He made a diagram of the twelve basic strikes on an old piece of cardboard. I began to practice them making sure I was using the correct footwork. After a while we switched to unarmed combat and I collected a few more bumps and scrapes. Connal complained about my concentration which I thought was unfair. It was hard to stay focused because several sunscreen-coated fairies came out to watch us. They kept bounding in and out of the training circle while offering an endless supply of advice, encouragement, and ribald comments. It was apparent a lot of them were also bound to Max and this was their way of welcoming me into his household. I kept feeling better and better about what had happened to me.

After lunch Max, Connal, and Grandpa went to inspect some property where Max could set up a proper laboratory. I spent the afternoon soaking my bruises in our warm pool and reading *The Universe in a Nutshell* while sprawled on a deck chair in the shade of our huge old elm tree. What I read about quantum mechanics made my finding Connal in our garden seem quite ordinary.

The time flew by and I was surprised when my mother came out and called me for supper. She and my dad were in a really good mood. Evidently, things had gone very well for them today, too.

Michael had asked them to help with the arrangements for setting up the lab and everything was going very smoothly.

"It's all happening so fast," declared my father. "Michael's group must be unbelievably rich and powerful. Any help I needed was provided, often within minutes. As well, Michael sent me a new assistant, Marc, who is exceptional. It's hard to believe but he and Mr. Piddie have formed a mutual admiration society."

I sat up when I heard that. Mr. Piddie works in my dad's office and is somewhat eccentric. Everyone who works for my dad can tell you lots of Mr. Piddie stories. Max's term 'a valuable man' came to my mind. Mr. Piddie is an elderly accountant who is an expert on income tax laws. On one hand he is a fanatic about never, ever breaking the law, but on the other hand he hates our current 'tax mess' as he calls it and gains inordinate pleasure from finding iron clad loopholes wherever he can. His battles with Revenue Canada have a certain epic quality and to date he's never lost a single one. I wondered what this Marc was like if Mr. Piddie considered him a kindred soul.

My mom opened another bottle of her homemade wine and poured each of us a glass. My parents allow me to have a glass of wine on special occasions and tonight seemed to be one of them.

"Here's to a wild ride!" said my mom and we all clinked our glasses and took a sip.

"What is Max going to do that is so important?" I asked.

"This is going to be a real adventure, James," replied my father, "but like all adventures there is danger involved. Last night, after you boys were in bed, the rest of us sat down and made some decisions. One of them was that you, Kelsey, and Clifford would not be told directly what this is all about. This is a safety precaution as much as anything else. The Core was very insistent about this and your mother and I intend to follow their wishes. I suspect you'll solve the mystery on your own but, for the present, you'll be able to say you have no direct knowledge."

"Max brought a great gift with him," continued my mother. "It could damage our whole society if it fell into the hands of any group who couldn't use in a way that will cause the least harm. Even before they came, Max and his people had decided to contact one of the independent groups of The Core to see if they could work together. They felt a group of anarchists might succeed where others would fail. The Core is a kind of syndicalist anarchy and we have just formed our own syndicate."

"Anarchy," I said. "Isn't it about people going around throwing bombs at each other?"

"Unfortunately, people like that gave anarchy a bad name and I have no intention of trying to explain anarchy myself. Even anarchists can't agree about how it should work. If they could, it probably wouldn't be anarchy anymore," he chuckled. Today they use another term, libertarians, to describe themselves.

"The sort of anarchy, libertarianism, practiced by The Core insists, while on one hand the freedom of the individual is imperative, on the other hand people live and work most effectively in small independent groups. The trick is to do both in the context of a larger society. If you want to know more, go down to the library and check out the memoirs of Prince Kropotkin."

The St. James Public Library is right at the end of the next street and my parents are always suggesting books for me to read. I suspect this began as a way to keep me occupied and out of trouble when my brother left for university and I was too old for a babysitter.

"We're in a sort of 'good news' 'bad news' situation," said my father with a somewhat rueful smile. The good news is I really like the people who are working with us and Max's gift should make everyone in the syndicate very, very rich. The bad news is there are some very evil and powerful people who are working against us and, if they ever realize what we are doing, they will be utterly ruthless in trying to take the gift for themselves."

My mother poured more wine into our glasses.

"I thought it was a little extreme Max had to bring a trained killer with him for protection," she laughed. "However, the more I learn about the whole situation the more I appreciate our friendly Warrior Wizard."

"Confusion to our enemies!" my father intoned.

We drank a second toast. Then we all pitched in and cleared away the supper. My mother had some work to do so Dad asked me to walk over to Grandpa Duncan's with him.

"I wonder if you noticed your mother and I never asked you to keep what we told you a secret."

"You know I'm good at keeping things to myself?" I ventured.

"Oh yes, we know. You've never tattled on your brother and his friends in the years they carted you everywhere with them. Did you?"

"No, I didn't." Then I hesitated because I hoped he wouldn't ask me about things my brother wouldn't want them to know. I wasn't going to start telling tales now.

"Keeping your own counsel is wonderful trait, James, and your mother and I respect you for it. Just keep in mind that you are almost an adult and there are times when good judgment should overrule loyalty. You don't want to be responsible for putting someone in danger. Let the incident with Clifford be a warning to you."

I didn't answer because I knew exactly what he meant. We walked up the steps to Grandpa Duncan's house in thoughtful silence.

Inside the house, things were starting to get lively. Most of the fairies were now awake and bounding about the living room. The television was turned on but it was muted and no one was really watching it. Max, Connal, and Grandpa were still sitting around the kitchen table sipping a fresh pot of tea.

Grandpa got up and brought out two more cups and Dad and I joined then at the table.

"I finally got through to Papa Owen today," he announced. "Evidently, he was away on some kind of senior's bus tour. He remembered Evan Hunter very well. Evidently, Evan and he traveled to Canada together. Evan was running from the law and Papa Owen helped him establish his new identity. 'Evan Hunter' isn't his real name. Papa wouldn't tell me why he was in trouble, but he insists he's a good man and a true friend. He asked for his phone number so he could call him."

"That's interesting," I broke in, "Clifford and Kelsey said he had changed identities."

"One thing I'm sure of," continued Grandpa, "Evan Hunter would be a very dangerous enemy."

We were all silent for a moment then my father shook his head and changed the subject.

"Duncan, do you remember young Romen Klimkiw? He joined the firm shortly before you retired."

"Most certainly," replied grandpa. "Wasn't he the fellow whose hobby was Ukrainian dancing?"

"That's the one. He's getting married at the end of July to a young lady who's a Celtic dancer, no less. I've bought several tickets to their social and I thought you and your friend Ellen would like to come with Mary, James and me. A large number of young people who are active in the Folklorama dance groups will be there. It sounds like it's going to be a lot of fun. The word is out around town and I had trouble getting enough tickets for all of us. It's the day after tomorrow, a Tuesday, which is an odd time, but the only day the hall was available."

If you don't live in Winnipeg, you probably won't know what a social is. It's a kind of party you pay to attend. The price of the ticket entitles you to listen to very, very loud music, dance, munch on free snacks, and later dine on potato chips, rye bread, cold cuts, cheese, and pickles. There is also a cash bar which serves both hard liquor and beer. While it is often used by community groups to raise money for various projects, most socials are held by young couples who use the money they make to help with wedding expenses.

I like the wedding socials because they involve the whole family and there are usually a few kids my age to fool around with. There's also a little underage drinking. This is sort of fun because it is a kind of forbidden fruit. The age limit in Manitoba is eighteen years, but kids are allowed to have a glass of wine with their parents when dining out at a restaurant so if you have a drink of something at a social it's sort of legal because your parents are there and presumably they said you could have it. They won't serve underage children liquor but you can usually coax an older relative to share. The mix is always free for everyone.

"I'll phone Ellen tonight," said Grandpa. I know she'll want to go. I'll come in any event."

"That's great. I've also got tickets for Connal and Max. I want you both to come with us."

Max looked dubious.

"I don't know if we should. There's such a lot of work to do."

"I think you need a break," said my father firmly. "You have been working steadily since you arrived and in three days the new lab should be up and running and Connal will be off to supervise the project near Libau. Once those two ventures begin, both of you will be lucky to see daylight for months.

It's going to be a great party. There'll be music and dancing, strong liquor, and lots of pretty women. Who could ask for more?"

It didn't take a lot of persuasion for Max and Connal to agree to come with us. They knew my father was right. It was time to have a little fun.

I was feeling uneasy though.

"Won't it be dangerous for us to go out? Look what happened to Clifford."

My grandfather smiled and shook his head.

"James, my boy, we're all living on borrowed time. We've never been safe since Connal and Max arrived. The truth is fate has involved our small family in a high stakes game with very ruthless enemies. Our best hope is to accept our lot with good grace. I plan to live my life to the fullest because I know my time may be brief. My shining hope is we could win and that's what makes it worthwhile."

"Your grandson is very brave," said Connal. "I saw him accept Max's bond with good cheer in the full knowledge of what he had lost. Even better than that, he's never given up hope. Have you James?"

I nodded my head.

Connal continued, "You're troubled because you think no one is doing anything to bring the battle to our enemies. What you do not know is The Core has been tireless behind the scenes.

Remember the tall young man named Guy who was here last night. He's a member of group devoted to using the knowledge Max and I brought with us. They are trying to neutralize the type of mind control that has already destroyed many of The Core. You have no idea how valuable it was for him to see how the Old Rite is used. A great good may come from Clifford's near disaster. Guy told me he is almost positive he will be able to free many of those now in our enemies' power."

Max reached over and rested his hand on my shoulder. Suddenly our bond was so strong I felt dizzy.

"There is much to be said for walking along the knife edge. When you realize how dangerous life really is, it frees you from worrying about those things that don't matter. Let's all go and have fun at the dance!"

As my father and I walked home down our dark tree-lined street under the gentle glow of the street lights, he put his arm around my shoulders and started to sing softly making up his own words to a familiar children's song.

"Momma's gonna take us to the dance tomorrow, dance tomorrow, dance tomorrow. Momma's gonna take us to the dance tomorrow and we can stay and play."

I knew the tune and joined in. I felt wonderfully happy as we went into our home.

The next morning I heard my Mother on the phone before she left for work. Somehow she had learned that one of my brother Gordon's close friends was working part time in a men's clothing store to help put him through university.

"We have these two friends who have just come to Canada and I'm going to send them to see you this afternoon. Gordon always admired your sense of style and I want you to help them choose something suitable to wear to a social where there's going to be a lot of vigorous dancing. Shirts, pants, socks, shoes, underwear, and whatever else you think necessary. I'll send James along with his credit card and you can put everything on that."

Both my parents work and they often find it hard to take me shopping. Last year on my birthday they presented me with my own credit card so I could go down to the nearby mall and buy certain specified items on my own. They did the same thing with my older brother when he turned fifteen and it worked so well they let me have a card when I turned twelve. Our family always expects its members to be reliable and so far there has never been a problem.

I hadn't realized how comfortable Connal and Max felt with my family until I had to chaperone them through the shopping expedition. I wondered if I should let them carry their own bus fares.

"Will these coins bother your allergies?"

Max looked a little startled. "No, we should be fine. Connal and I have coated our hands with a cream that will protect them."

When I counted out the correct amount of change, I felt like a midget parent handing out an allowance to giant children.

"Remember, you must use half for the trip to the mall and half for the trip back. You'll be fine if you follow me and do whatever I do."

We reached the mall without incident and I could tell both of them were beginning to enjoy themselves. Walking through the mall was interesting. Heads turned wherever we went. I suppose I had been so interested in how fast they had grown I had fixated on how tall they were rather than how they looked. They had more or less stopped growing when they were comfortably over six feet tall. I guessed they were around six two or six three at the moment.

Max had been surprised at how tall most people were today. Grandpa said that made sense when you remembered Max was familiar with the size of people who lived one hundred or more years ago when everyone was much smaller. The improvement in our diet had reduced the difference in height between elves and men.

I began to appreciate how strikingly handsome they were. In many ways they looked very much alike. You would assume they were brothers or at least very close kin. Their faces were modeled along the same lean angular lines as Evan Hunter, but both were very fair and had sky blue eyes. It was easy to tell them apart because Connal's curly hair was a dark honey color while Max's hair was a rather startling shade of golden red my mother calls strawberry blond. Its sedate waves made a glowing cap for his well shaped head. By contrast, Connal's hair seemed to have an untidy life of its own.

People might have been looking at them because of the color of Max's hair, but I didn't think so, and they certainly weren't doing anything that would call attention to themselves. I'd heard of the word charisma and I'm sure that's what everyone felt. It was like there was an aura around them that made you feel we could start the party now because the guests of honor had arrived.

When we reached the clothing store, I was relieved to find my brother's friend, Danny, was there and not on his coffee break or anything. I've always liked all of my brother's close friends because they were so good to me while I was recovering from the fire, but Danny was special. The word that comes to mind is urbane. When Danny did anything, there was always a touch of class to it. He and Max would get along splendidly and, if anything bizarre happened, his charm and good manners would never waver. You see I forgot to warn Connal about change rooms. I was alarmed he might suddenly burst into the store stark naked. The social rules of Elfland are somewhat different when it comes to appropriate places to wear clothes. For example, certain religious ceremonies were always performed without clothing. Most of the time Connal was a model of propriety but occasionally he would do something outlandish, like walking out into our backyard naked last night.

Danny was expecting us and was both charming, which I expected, and extremely organized, which I hadn't. He seemed to know exactly what he was doing and had such an air of confident authority that Max and Connal bought everything he suggested without a single objection.

We left most of our purchases at the store and took the pants away to be hemmed. This left us with a free hour before we could reclaim everything and leave for home.

"Would either of you like something to eat? I brought a little of my own money with me and if you let me choose we can all have a hot dog and an orange Julius."

"I didn't know you ate dog meat," said Connal.

"It's really pork or beef or chicken. Hot dog is only a name. Do you want to try it?"

"Thank you, very much," said Max. "We'd really enjoy some food right now. I never thought shopping would make me so hungry."

Our afternoon snack became very strange almost at once. I settled the two of them into the smooth plastic seats attached to the small plastic table and told them to wait right there until I returned with the food. They both looked happy and relaxed as they surveyed their surroundings with somewhat bemused smiles. It was mid-afternoon so the service was pretty fast. I didn't look back at the table until I had all the food on the tray so I was very surprised when I turned around. There was a woman with a young girl around eight or nine talking animatedly with my two charges. I hurried right over to see if they needed me to run interference for them.

"They're asking for something and I don't know what it is," said Connal.

"I'd like their autographs," pleaded the little girl.

"Are they famous for something?" cooed the mother.

"I guess so," I stammered, "but, not here. They're from far away."

In my mind I kept thinking I'd better get rid of them as fast as I can. I took the food bill and turned it over.

"Max and Connal write your names on the back of this paper and give it to the little girl."

They obligingly wrote Max Ferryman and Connal Ferryman with several extra flourishes. Connal even gave the little girl a light kiss on the forehead and smiled his most winning smile at the mother. They both sighed and seemed to float away from the table.

"What was all that about?" asked Max a little apprehensively.

"I have no idea but I hope it doesn't happen again," I muttered. It did though.

It took us a long time to eat those hot dogs and finish our drinks because every few minutes someone, usually female, would come over and start to talk to Max or Connal and even to me. I didn't want to alarm either of them so I just sat there and kept steering the conversations into neutral corners. Everyone seemed friendly, even a little shy, but that didn't stop them from coming over. As soon as we were finished, I got them out of there and we walked around the mall until it was time to collect our purchases and leave.

Connal seemed to think the whole thing was very funny and obligingly waved and smiled at everyone who waved and smiled at him. Max just looked resigned to it all. I was very relieved when we got home without anything really bad happening. I didn't know there was going to be a sequel.

When Tuesday, the day of the social, arrived, Mom, Dad, and I went in one car and Max, Connal, Grandpa, and his friend Ellen went in another. The community center we went to was still in our part of town but several kilometers west of our street, otherwise we might have walked because it was such a nice evening. Winnipeg is only something over 600,000 people but it is very spread out. There was a good sized parking lot which was filling rapidly when we arrived. Everyone seemed to be in high spirits as we all lined up to hand in our tickets and have our hands stamped. This was so we could leave for a few minutes during the social and still be able to come in again. There is usually some sort of security at these events, often an off-duty police officer.

Danny had done a good job and Max and Connal looked great in their new clothes. I just hoped they would blend in more easily at the social than they had at the mall.

We were early enough and were able to find space at one table for our entire group. Sometimes there is a live band, but at this social all the music was recorded because, in addition to the usual rock and roll, country, and pop, there was to be a variety of ethnic music. The couple, who were soon to be married, wanted to do something a little bit different. Since they met because of a mutual interest in folk dancing, they decided to include some of both forms for everyone to try. It seemed to be such a good idea several other friends who belonged to other dance groups asked to have their music and dances included. It promised to be a delightful evening.

Because the groom, Romen, works for my dad, all of dad's office staff was there, even Mr. Piddie. Mr. Piddie, it turned out, had volunteered to be the Master of Ceremonies. I was surprised at how easily he managed to get things going and keep everything orderly. I'd never realized what a droll sense of humor he had.

First, the DJ would play a set which is two or three pieces of regular dance music with a similar beat. Next, a small group of dancers would perform an ethnic specialty dance. Then, they would demonstrate a very simple dance routine and anyone who wanted to could go out on the floor and try it out. When that was finished, the DJ would play another set and so on. The other socials I'd been at all seemed to get off to a slow start and things don't get going until later in the evening. However, tonight it seemed most of the people attending really liked dancing, any kind of dancing, so the dance floor was already crowded.

"I'm not sure I know how to do this kind of dancing," Max whispered to my father.

Ellen must have overheard him because she took his hand and said, "Just follow my lead and you'll be fine. I'm a good teacher and I love to dance."

She must have been a good teacher and he was a very talented pupil because within a few moments they blended right in with everyone else, at least as much as Max can blend in anywhere.

One of the secretaries from dad's office was sitting with us. I noticed her listening to Max and Ellen and watching Connal. As soon as they left she touched Connal on the arm to get his attention.

"Don't you know how to dance either?"

"Not this kind of dancing. I do dance but it's different where we come from. Would you be willing to show me how?" He smiled his most charming smile and the two of them whirled away into the crowd.

Connal had been paying close attention to what Ellen and Max were doing and he learns as fast as Max does. I didn't think he needed any teaching at all.

I'd been around the fairies living in Grandpa's basement and I knew they all love music and dancing. They would burst into song or do a quick dance step almost anywhere or anytime. It shouldn't have surprised me that both full grown elves knew how to dance and were extremely good at it.

143

When I turned back to the table, I was surprised to find everyone else was up dancing. I sat there for a few moments wondering what to do next when a girl just a few years older than me walked by.

"You look a little lonely sitting there all by yourself. Would you like to dance?"

I was startled but I couldn't think of anything else to do so I replied, "Sure, why not? That would be fun." And off we went.

I hardly sat down after that. I danced every dance and, during the breaks, it was almost impossible for me to get near the table we had selected for our group. There was always a large number of people, mostly female, milling around there trying to dance with Connal or Max. They even hit on Grandpa Duncan, my dad, and myself. It was a lot of fun but I kept thinking about the mall and trying to figure out just what was going on. I knew Max and Connal were exceptionally handsome and good dancers, but there had to be more to it.

It was a really great party and everyone seemed to be having the time of their lives. The lights seemed brighter, the music gayer, the food tastier, and the dancing livelier. I hoped it wasn't some kind of mass hallucination.

Several times during the evening some of the young men, particularly the Ukrainian dancers, would clear a little space on the floor and put on an impromptu performance of some of their more athletic folk dance moves, and everyone would clap and cheer. Once Max and Connal joined in with some of the moves I'd seen the fairies perform. When done by a full grown person, they were quite spectacular.

Connal was at his charming best. He went out of his way to dance with as many women as possible, old and young. I don't think he danced with anyone twice. It seemed rather that he was determined to make as many women as possible fall just a little bit in love with him. Max was a little more restrained. While he danced gracefully with any number of strange women, he also danced with Ellen at least once more, twice with my

Mother, and twice with very beautiful dark haired girl. He was unfailingly polite and good humored but always a little distant. I noticed the raven haired girl because she was the only stranger who managed to have a second dance with either of them.

It was indeed a wonderful evening but I felt very relieved when it was all over.

The next morning the phone started ringing. I spent the morning fielding calls for both of our social butterflies as my dad called them. I dutifully wrote down numbers and promised to deliver them. Around lunch time I decided to take a break, turned off the answering machine, and went out to have lunch at Grandpa's. I took the sheaf of phone numbers with me.

I found grandpa puttering around in the kitchen making tuna sandwiches while Ellen and the social butterflies were sipping something that looked like lemonade and laughing over the idea that three or four girls had phoned there, looking for either Max or Connal. They were rather taken aback when I plunked down the fourteen messages we had received. Then both Connal and Max really began to laugh.

I grabbed a plate with a sandwich on it and sat down at the table with them.

"Will someone please tell me what the joke is?" I complained. "I think the whole thing is really weird."

"It's really very funny, even though it's also a little embarrassing." replied Max between giggles. "We tend to forget there are only the slightest of physical differences between us and the people we meet. We are really close kin."

"Kissing cousins or better," added Connal before he subsided into another gale of laughter. "We completely forgot how we smell when we're not careful."

"You don't smell," Ellen retorted. "At least I've never noticed anything."

"No, you probably wouldn't," replied Max. "But, tell me truthfully, do you find Connal and I attractive."

"Of course, I do. You're both totally gorgeous male animals."

"The reason why you've never noticed anything is you have a perfectly satisfying intimate relationship with Duncan, don't you?"

"Yes," said Ellen and she had the grace to blush.

This was interesting. I'd always wondered about her and Grandpa but they'd been very discrete.

"It's the same with James's mother. I doubt she's noticed anything either. It doesn't happen when your sense of smell is keyed into another male. However, if you are female and you don't have a mate or even if they've been absent for a long time, then you definitely would notice our pheromones. Among our own people it is customary to mask our scent to avoid any problems, but we completely forgot the females here might be affected."

Connal decided to explain further.

"A long time ago when everyone hunted for their food, it was very important to have a keen sense of smell. However, when people started to settle in one place in larger groups they relied less and less on this ability so this talent began to fade but it's still stronger than most people realize. For some reason my people prided themselves on their sense of smell and the talent remained strong. There was an interesting side effect to this.

Our women's choice of a mate became strongly influenced by scent. Males with an attractive odor had a better chance of having many children than those who did not. Over the centuries natural selection heightened the effect and, when we realized what the effects were, our men became very interested in further enhancing this outcome. In the beginning it was only simple things like bathing often and watching what we ate. Later we discovered other ways to increase the strength of the response. It became part of our culture and then it actually became part of our physical make-up.

When we could travel back to earth, there were many reports that our men were even more attractive to the women here than our own kind, especially in the period shortly after arrival, but it faded away if you stayed here for a long time. Many thought this was just a traveler's tale while many others swore it was true. It appears the travelers were not exaggerating."

Connal laughed when he saw the look on my face.

"Don't worry. It's very easy to mask the odor so there shouldn't be any more problems. Unless, of course, I spot a pretty girl and decide I want to court her," he added with a grin and a roguish wink.

That last remark didn't make me feel any easier, but I supposed it would have to do.

"What are you going to do about all the phone calls?" asked Grandpa.

"Tell the truth, or most of it. That's always the best and safest thing to do," said Max.

Max and Connal were extremely courteous and good-natured about the whole thing. They spent most of the afternoon answering every one of the phone calls. Max would patiently explain that he was a research chemist setting up a lab to verify certain experiments he had done. He would be working twenty-four hour days if he could. This would not leave him with any time for a social life. Connal's answer to all requests was that he was leaving the next morning to set up a research facility north of Winnipeg and had no idea when or if he would return to the city.

Their refusals were very gentle. They assured everyone they were flattered by the call and regretted not being able to comply with whatever was asked. They were equally gracious with the few male callers. It was an impressive performance. All the more so because I knew they really meant most of what they were saying.

When I walked home later that afternoon, Max came with me. Mom and Dad were having tea in the kitchen and Max pulled up a chair. I wandered out into the garden to see if I could find a few ripe raspberries. It was still too early, but I did pick a handful of snow peas and sat down by the planter filled with nicotina. I sat there for a while munching the crisp green pods and throwing the ends into the pot. I couldn't think of anything else to do and after a while I returned to the house. Max, Mother, and Dad were still drinking tea and talking. I had feeling they had been talking about me and I was right.

"I am going to be extremely busy at the lab for many weeks and your father will be working closely with me for at least two months. Moreover, your mother is shorthanded at her work because of vacations. All of us feel it would be a good idea if you went up to the construction site with Connal. There are a lot of things you could do there that would be very helpful," said Max.

I noticed he didn't say anything about having a relaxing vacation.

"We hope you will be safer up there with Connal to protect you," added my mother.

I didn't agree with her because I knew Connal's idea of safety left a lot to be desired. Still, I remembered telling Cormac I would do my best to help him, so I kept my worries to myself.

CHAPTER EIGHT
A Working Holiday

Connal and I were in high spirits as we started on the hour drive to Libau. We had his precious quarterstaff and my rather lumpy one securely bundled up in the back of the truck, Churchill was purring on the seat between us, and I knew Connal was excited about the bow and arrows my grandpa had brought over for him. It might be a great vacation after all.

Michael Flynn arrived at Grandpa's the day before with all the necessary identity papers for him and Max. Included were Irish passports and valid driver's licenses with photo ID. How they managed this I didn't know, but I was impressed.

"Maxwell Ferryman and Connal Ferryman," I read out loud. "These look very real."

"For all practical purposes they are real," replied Michael. "Our people have centuries of practice in creating new identities to shield those who live longer than normal. Those who do this work are enormously skilled."

It was one thing to create a driver's license, but I wondered how they would learn to drive. Michael also provided them with suitable transportation, a small car for Max and a serviceable half-ton truck for Connal.

I expected there would be driving lessons before turning them loose. It hadn't occurred to me they had been paying very close attention whenever they'd been driven anywhere and had continually asked questions about anything they didn't understand. Also, Grandpa had given them the driver education manual which covered the rules of the road. I was surprised to learn how easily they remembered everything in the book. After Michael left, Grandpa took them out on what he called a test drive. Later, he remarked he'd be willing to travel with them anywhere and that was that.

As we drove along Connal sang happily to himself in his own language and got me to join in on the choruses.

"It's time you started to learn our language," he declared. "Among our people you are now Max's foster son and as such you will be expected to speak fluently. Singing in another language is one of the very best ways to acquire the proper accent and intonation."

I wasn't sure I liked the idea of learning another language. I've been in French immersion since kindergarten and now I must become fluent in a third language. It was another unexpected hurdle for me to jump. However, singing was fun so I decided I'd worry about this later. I was discovering a lot of future problems never occur anyway.

"Are Max and my dad really going to be so very busy?"

"I don't think they'll have any free time for several months"

"Is it because of Dad's math that Max needs him?"

"Only partly. Basically, he's translating the science into terms that will be easily understood. Max thought it would go faster if the translator only had a moderate understanding of physical and biological science. That way they wouldn't split hairs all the time when he described his procedures. Your dad's been doing the preliminary work for several weeks now and Michael's people are very satisfied with the results. I only hope this project I'm working on will go as smoothly. We have even less time than we thought."

"Why is that?"

"Unlike Max and myself, the fairies here are still in close contact with their true selves in Fairyland and they report that several of them are now ailing. Max thought we had at least six months to a year to begin the transfer. It is my fear they may begin to die if they don't rejoin within the next month or so. We all knew the risks when we started, but it would be a tragedy to get this close to success and fail."

For a moment the whole atmosphere in the truck darkened as if a cloud had passed over the sun. Then Connal shook his head and squared his shoulders. He gave me a glittering sideways glance and an impish smile.

"Fate has thrown down the gauntlet, James. When we triumph over the odds, it will make victory even sweeter."

I noticed he said 'when' not 'if'. His determination and enthusiasm were catching and I found myself believing we really would succeed. Of course, I had no idea of what he wanted to do but it didn't matter. We were off on a fantastic quest and I was quite ready to do six impossible things before breakfast if that's what I needed to do.

We laughed and sang all the rest of the way to our destination.

Our route took us into an area quite close to Lake Winnipeg when Connal turned the truck into a gravel side lane and pulled up beside a small white clapboard house with the trim painted a rather aggressive peacock blue. The lawn was neatly mowed and the small garden that flourished in the sunshine had been laid out with military precision. A slender man with very erect bearing came out of the house. He was a little less than average height but somehow he seemed larger. He had no nonsense eyes and wore a small goatee. This was Evan's friend that Connal had met when the two of them drove up looking for land to use for the project. Kelsey told me he used to be a school principal and I felt sorry for the children who had been sent down to see him. It would have been a scary experience.

"Here we are Andy. We had a great ride up from Winnipeg!" exclaimed Connal as he bounded out of the car and strode through the gate in the neat picket fence. Churchill and I trailed warily after him.

"It's great to see you again," said Andy with a warm smile. "I've got everything ready and you can stay as long as you like."

"Wonderful! I'd like you to meet James, the young lad I told you about. James, this is Mr. Sawirski."

Mr. Sawirski gave me a cool, questioning look. Then a brief nod of his head indicated that I just might do and he turned his attention back to Connal. It wasn't the warmest of greetings but otherwise his hospitality was flawless. He was the sort of person who would easily forgive genuine mistakes but any willfully stupid behavior would attract instant wrath. I thought that, after the initial shock wore off, I would rather like to have him as a teacher.

We had homemade soup and sandwiches for lunch and I volunteered to help wash up afterwards. This earned me another brief nod of approval which I valued more than a lot of thank-yous.

After lunch the three of us piled into the truck and went to visit the construction site. The far end of the property was the shoreline of Lake Winnipeg, but the construction was to take place on the land nearest the road because it was somewhat higher ground. While most of the area was very marshy, there was some scrubby bush and scraggly trees up on the high ground. The place hadn't been chosen for its beauty but there were lots of excellent reasons for building here.

There was a well maintained four lane highway close by and the access roads were in good enough condition to take the large trucks delivering construction materials. The land was marginal for both farming and ranching so not terribly expensive which allowed the company to buy a large tract very quickly. Best of all was the fact that, while the town of Selkirk was only a short drive away, there were very few people living close by. This made it safer for everyone.

Connal and Mr. Sawirski were busy going over the preparations for the construction so I decided to wander around a little and explore my new home. When I saw all the marshy land, I wasn't too hopeful about being able to walk down to see Lake Winnipeg, so I was delighted when I discovered a faint trail which allowed me to pick my way down to the water. There was even a small sandy beach. I looked wistfully at the golden sand and sparkling water. I had found a beach, but it was doubtful if I would find any time to go for a swim. On that happy note I trudged back up the trail to find one of the trucks loaded with building material had arrived. Mr. Sawirski was standing beside it with a several sheets of paper in his hand.

"Here James, make yourself useful. Take these purchase orders and check them to make sure the whole shipment has arrived."

I immediately said, "Yes, sir," and began checking things off the lists. It occurred to me later that I was probably lucky I'd spent a lot of time around my Grandpa while he was building things. Mr. Sawirski was patience itself whenever I didn't understand anything, but he seemed pleased I was able to manage pretty well on my own. I do remember asking him what 'hoarding' was because I thought it was a spelling error. Actually, its plastic sheeting used to protect things from the weather.

The construction site was a beehive of activity all afternoon. It was getting dark by the time we washed up at Mr. Sawirski's house and started eating our dinner. I was very tired but Connal and Andy were in fine form. I discovered our new friend was very smart and had a wicked sense of humor. They shared a bottle of homemade wine and regaled each other with all sorts of tall tales. I was allowed just one glass which was just as well. I liked its flavor but it was very strong. I found myself asking Mr. Sawirski for his recipe for zucchini casserole so I could give it to my mother. The casserole was very good but I'm really not interested in recipes no matter how tasty.

"You need zucchini, onions, tomatoes, cheese, and bread crumbs. The amounts don't matter much because you use whatever you have at the moment. Partially cook the zucchini, onions, and tomatoes in a skillet, then fill the casserole with half the mixture, then the cheese and bread crumbs, then the rest of the vegetables, then more cheese and breadcrumbs. Cook for about half an hour. Repeat that back to me."

"Zucchini, onions, tomatoes, grated cheese, and bread crumbs. Fry veggies. Then wet stuff, dry stuff, wet stuff, dry stuff. Cook thirty minutes." 'Nailed it in one,' I thought to myself. I felt very, very happy.

Mr. Sawirski tilted his head to one side and gave a slight sly smile."

"You realize there will be a test on this tomorrow morning?"

"Oops!"

Connal took one long look at me and said, "Go to bed, now."

I fell asleep immediately.

The next morning it was Connal who grinned up at me from the breakfast table and said, "Do you remember the recipe from last night, James?"

"Zucchini, onions, tomatoes, cheese and bread crumbs. Fry veggies. Then wet stuff, dry stuff, wet stuff, dry stuff. Cook thirty minutes."

"It seems your wine didn't kill too many of his brain cells, Andy. Sometime soon I'm going to find out how you make it. It is definitely in a class by itself."

Before we left for the construction site, Mr. Sawirski sent me down into the basement to fetch a package of meat from his freezer. I had never seen a basement quite like the one under his house. I had thought the upstairs was extremely neat and clean, but the basement was far, far better. Everything was glaringly white, the ceiling, the floor, the walls, and the storage cupboards. There were black rubber treads on the stairs which provided the only contrast in the room.

"That is the whitest basement I've ever seen!" I exclaimed when I came upstairs.

"It is, isn't it? Evan Hunter is the person who did the work on it years ago. I got to know Evan when I was working near Bissett. My parents lived here then and they were having terrible problems with water in the basement because the land here is so low and marshy. Evan said he had some experience in dealing with underground seepage and, during one shutdown at the mine, he came up here and repaired the basement. I never knew what he did and I've never seen anything exactly like it either. My parents were delighted and Evan's been a close friend ever since. I never knew he had any family."

"Evan's a first cousin on my mother's side, but we lived so far apart I'd never met him before I came to Canada," replied Connal.

As we sat in the truck waiting for Mr. Sawirski to lock up, Connal turned to me and said, "When you get another chance, James, take a close look at the basement. It's a fine example of the traditional way my people build their underground homes and shelters. This one is just a room but you can imagine whole shining cities built underground."

I'd been told Evan and Connal's story and I knew it was true because Max wouldn't lie to me about something like that. Still, it wasn't till I saw the basement that I believed it in my heart.

We arrived at the construction site just minutes before the first workers arrived and I worked steadily all morning. We left Churchill at Mr. Sawirski's house where he seemed to be completely at home. At least one of us is going to have a good vacation I thought.

Just before lunch Connal and Andy had to make a run into Selkirk for some bricks they needed for a fire pit and I went along for the ride. While we were there, we decided to eat lunch in town and stopped at the local pizza franchise.

We were able to get a booth to ourselves and were starting to eat our food when Connal looked past my shoulder and remarked admiringly, "Now, there's a beautiful girl."

Mr. Sawirski turned to see who had attracted his attention.

"That's Ethne Eyolfson. She's a neighbor of yours. Would you like me to introduce you?"

"Yes, I certainly would." A small smile danced around Connal's mouth.

"She's also my god-daughter, so behave yourself."

Ethne obligingly brought her pizza order over and sat with us.

After introductions had been made, Ethne turned to Mr. Sawirski and said, "Is this the bad company you've taken up with? I hear you're building a grow-op."

"Grow-op?" said Connal. "What is a grow-op?"

"It's a place where criminal gangs grow a drug called marijuana," explained Mr. Sawirski. "It's very illegal but highly profitable."

"Well I hope our project is profitable. It's certainly not illegal. We're building a very, very large storage battery that will be used for research and development of better energy sources."

I thought to myself this was only half true. First we had to save the fairies. After that, Michael's associate, Guy, was just itching to get his hands on the battery once the rescue operation was complete. He and Michael believed there was a lot of money to be made from this particular power source. Guy was already building smaller prototype batteries from the information he already had. He would be making regular visits out to check on our progress with this super sized one. Michael considered him to be very talented.

I was watching Connal smiling at Ethne and alarm bells started to go off. He was attracted to Ethne and determined to make her like him. I couldn't smell anything but I imagined the air was suddenly full of pheromones. It was like watching a train wreck and not being able to do anything about it.

Connal was dazzling. He radiated charm. I was relieved when Mr. Sawirski stood up and said, "Time's up. We all have to get back to work."

The last thing Connal said was, "Why, don't you drive over and see what we are doing? I'll show you around."

Ethne just smiled but didn't reply and I hoped we were safe. I felt even more reassured when Mr. Sawirski remarked as we were walking back to the truck, "I don't think she'll ever show up. She's at the tail end of a very messy divorce and likely to have sworn off men forever."

"We'll see," was Connal's smug reply.

When we returned, I was given the job of unloading all the bricks and making them into a neat pile that was well away from the roiling anthill the construction project had become. That was why I signed for the package when it arrived by courier. The delivery van could not get any closer to the site and was in a hurry to return to Winnipeg. My brick pile was finished so I took the parcel and put it in the truck. I spent the rest of the afternoon as a gofer. James, go for the shovel; James, go for the nails; James, go for the coffee. I knew I was being useful but it all seemed rather trivial.

After supper, I remembered the parcel and brought it into the house. Inside the parcel was a sealed container and a note.

"What on earth is Max thinking?" complained Connal. "We're supposed to be attracting as little attention as possible and now this." He scrabbled around in his backpack for his cell phone and called Max. He must have been really upset because this was one of the few times he ever used his own language in front of anyone who didn't understand it. He didn't win the argument either.

He sat with his head in his hands for a moment then he smiled and sat up straight and pointed to the container.

"This is the sunscreen Max insists I start using. It's an old family recipe and I've no doubt it will be very effective. He doesn't think the ordinary sunscreen is strong enough for someone like me who is allergic. The bad news is that it turns you a bright green which gradually fades to a nice golden tan in about four or five days. How am I supposed to be inconspicuous and low key?"

"The best way to hide an elephant is in a herd of other elephants," said Mr. Sawirski. "Is this mixture really safe to use."

"I've never thought Max was particularly gifted when it came to tactics, but he's a true wizard when it comes to medical remedies."

"If your friend says it's safe, then I'll take some, too. Also, the weather network is giving UV warnings in the extreme range every day, so perhaps you'll have a few of the men at the site volunteer to try it as well."

"I'll phone Max and double check."

When he got off the phone he was definitely happier.

"You will be just fine. In fact, he wants James to take it as well."

We caused quite a sensation when the three of us arrived at the construction site the next morning. However, by the end of the next day there were six of us who looked like we had escaped from the Valley of the Jolly Green Giant. I think the three others were impressed because Connal had given the mixture to me. I heard one of them say, "It must be safe if they're giving it to the kid." When they finished their part of the work, Connal obligingly gave them some of the mixture to take with them. Luckily for them and us, it only turned you green the first time used it.

The only ripple of publicity the whole incident produced was a small article in the local paper headlined "Big Green Men Sighted Near Selkirk" explaining that a new sunscreen product was being tested locally. I was very happy when none of the big news services picked it up.

By Sunday, Connal, Mr. Sawirski, and I still looked moldy but the green was definitely fading. The mobile home, where Connal and I were to live for the summer, was ready for us. That morning we collected Churchill and our belongings and moved to the construction site. There was even a neat sign by the access road proclaiming this to be the future home of Nu-Tec Industries.

At that moment Nu-Tec Industries looked like an unfinished basement with a long low rectangular building attached to one side. The building was just a shell and the empty basement was where the storage battery was to be built.

There wasn't much we could do until Monday so Connal and I made another practice circle using the pile of sand that had been left over from some of the construction. We saved the turf we cut out and I carried the pieces over to our new residence and laid them out on the torn up soil around the mobile home. At least it gave us a start on growing some grass to cover the mud. I even found a discarded plastic container and threw some water over it.

It really didn't take long so there was time to practice some of the unarmed combat moves he'd taught me and I worked on the strokes for the quarterstaff. I even went for a short run down to the lake and Connal went for a much longer run along some of the access roads.

Andy and I had packed a food hamper before we left and Connal and I sat out on the deck to enjoy our lunch. We were both in a good mood, so I thought this would be the right time to ask him about Churchill.

"You were very upset when Max made you bond with Churchill. Don't you like cats?"

Connal looked at me intently and finally said, "That's a fair question, James. What bothered me had little to do with the cat. You are bound to Max, so you know what it feels like. What he ordered me to do dissolved our bond forever. The loss was shattering. It was only later I came to realize The Core is right. A freely given bond is much better and stronger.

Max said it best when he told me my friendship was even more valuable to him now because I could fight for him and with him."

After lunch, Connal decided to try out the bow and arrows. We set up a hay bale for a practice butt and made a rudimentary target from a piece of cardboard and some left over paint. He only shot a few arrows before he became restless.

"I've never been good with the bow," he complained. "I didn't have enough interest to do the amount of practice the skill requires. I appreciate Duncan's gift but I think I'll stay with the staff and the sword."

"What are you talking about? You haven't missed once."

"Hitting a stationary target is just the first step in using a bow. Moving targets are much more difficult and judging air currents more complicated. To make matters more confusing not only does time pass differently here but the force of gravity is not quite the same. My friend Cian would be able to account for all the differences, but I wouldn't want to rely on my level of ability.

Cian is very skilled. He was always annoyed with Max and me because we wouldn't practice more, but standing for hours holding a rock in your outstretched hand never appealed to either of us."

"Why would you do that?"

"It builds up the muscles in your arm so you can hold the bow absolutely steady.

You know, I still haven't walked down to the lake. Why don't we do that?"

It was another blazing July day and a hot dry wind was flowing up from the south. The rushes and tall grass did a rhythmic dance all around us. The marsh was alive with all number of small birds and animals. You just had to know where to look. Connal had keen eyes and kept pointing out things I would have missed.

The sky was vivid blue bowl fused to the shimmering earth by the intense heat. When we reached, the small beach we took off our shoes and waded along the edge in the waves that foamed around our feet. Connal looked with wonder at the long arc of water where no shore was visible and the lake merged almost magically with the sky.

"All this space and solitude, you feel as if you were standing on the very edge of the world. It makes me feel like singing a song or saying a prayer. Perhaps we are in a special place where the veil between this world and the next is very thin. Can you feel the magic all around us, James?"

Connal was still wearing the quiver of arrows and carrying his bow. I felt as if he was Robin Hood and at any moment the Merry Men would rise up from the marsh. Instead there were two dark figures coming towards us from the north. They were both carrying rifles.

Connal quickly knocked an arrow and turned on his charm at the same time. He also stepped slightly to one side so I was shielded. He does take his duties as a protector very seriously.

"Hello there! Where did you come from?"

The taller of the two figures scowled in our direction and said gruffly, "Our truck got stuck back there. What are you doing here? Are you the guys who are building the grow-op?"

"It's a storage battery," corrected Connal, "and James and I just came down to look at the lake."

"You guys look kind of green. You're not aliens or anything?"

"It's a new kind of sunscreen. Why are you carrying guns?"

"We didn't want to leave them in the truck in case they were stolen."

"Do you know how to use that thing?" asked the smaller figure looking pointedly at the bow and arrow.

"Well, enough," retorted Connal.

"I bet you can't hit that goose."

There was a large Canada goose flying overhead about fifty feet up and Connal in one fluid motion swept the tip of the arrow up, let it fly, reached back for another arrow, and nocked it into place.

The goose fell like a stone and I heard him mutter under his breath, "That was a lucky shot if there ever was one."

The two men looked impressed and a little apprehensive.

"You're sure you're not an alien." The larger man was still not convinced.

"I'm not alien but I do have a familiar." Connal gestured toward Churchill who had ventured out of the reeds.

Now the older man looked really confused but his younger companion's eyes lit up and he started to laugh.

"How wonderful, I've never met a wizard before."

I couldn't believe it. He'd been able to figure out Connal's obscure pun.

Connal turned up the charm another notch.

"By the way, I'm Connal Ferryman. Is there anything we can do to help you?"

The older of the two men finally smiled. "Not really. I think the axle's broken and we'll have to get some help back on the reserve. My name is Joe Nolen and this is my nephew Chris."

Everyone began to relax.

Connal smiled more than ever and continued, "If you come with us, I can drive you home. However, it's almost dinner time and if we can find the goose, let's have supper first."

There was a lot of laughing and swearing as we all splashed about in the marsh looking for the goose. The smaller figure, Chris, finally saw it, expertly wrung its neck, and held it aloft in triumph.

"Now we'll have goose for Sunday supper!"

It was a happy group that came in sight of our new home. To our surprise there was a police car sitting beside it.

"What are the police doing here?" said Joe sounding irritated.

"I don't know," said Connal sounding puzzled. "I think he keeps checking to make sure we're not building this grow-op everyone keeps asking about."

"If he asks about the goose, let me do the talking," warned Joe as he took the bow out of Connal's hand and gave it to Chris who was still carrying the goose.

I hoped Connal would listen to him because I realized Connal had probably shot the goose out of season and was in danger of being arrested or at least fined.

"Oh good," said Chris. "It's Arnie Stefanson and he's a decent sort."

We all gathered around the car and Connal, ever the considerate host said, "Can I help you, officer?"

"Been doing a little hunting have you?"

"We sure have," said Joe smoothly. "There's our Sunday supper and we even used traditional weapons. You can't find fault with that."

"Of course not, I just came over to check on everything."

Connal nodded his head and had a very serious look on his face.

"I appreciate that. Nu-Tec hopes to turn this into a major research facility and some of our competitors are a little too interested in what we are doing here."

Officer Stefanson took another glance at the goose, wished us 'bon appétit', and drove away. We left our wet shoes and socks at the door and trooped into the mobile home.

"I'm glad he's gone," muttered Joe. "I'm not on parole anymore but even good cops tend to make me feel uncomfortable."

"It was a fair fight," said Chris who was instantly on the defensive. "The other guy should have had more sense than deliberately picking a fight. Everyone knows how good Joe is. I guess he just wanted to find out if he was better."

"It doesn't matter," said Joe. "I'm lucky I stopped when I did. Next time I hope I walk away before things get out of hand."

"That's always the right thing to do," agreed Connal. "You must be sure to pick your own battles. When you've fought as much as I have, you'll realize how important it is to begin a fight in cold blood, not hot. Think it over for a while and you'll see I'm right."

Joe looked pleasantly surprised.

"I'll try to remember that."

Connal reached out and took the goose from Chris.

"Now let's see how good I am at turning this into dinner."

Joe and Chris phoned a friend and arranged for a tow truck to meet them on the reserve when they returned after supper. We all explained to Connal that it was illegal for anyone to shoot a bird or animal outside of designated hunting seasons. The only exception was aboriginal people, who had traditional hunting rights, and could hunt for food at any time. That's why Joe had made a point of saying they'd killed the goose.

"Thank you for protecting me. I didn't know. I am in your debt."

Both Joe and Chris told him to forget about it. I know they didn't realize Connal really meant it about the debt and would do his best to help them if he ever had the chance.

Connal did the cooking and I did all the easy jobs like setting the table. Mr. Sawirski had given us a bottle of his wine as a housewarming present. Connal used some of it to cook the goose and divided the rest into four glasses. He saved a few drops in the bottle which he sprinkled on the stove just before we started to eat. He also said a few words in his own language while the wine bubbled away into the air leaving small black spatters on the shiny stove top.

Connal explained how his people always did this to mark the first meal in a new dwelling.

"In the beginning any kind of drink was poured into the fire. If people were very poor it would only be water. However, tradition has it the stronger the drink the luckier the home will be. This is very strong wine and I hope it brings us much luck."

Joe had taken a tentative sip of the wine and started to chuckle, "This is one of Andy's wines. You should have luck coming out of your ears. You can't get much stronger than this."

"To good fortune and good friends!" said Connal.

It was a great meal and I was only a little irritated because I had to do clean-up duty all by myself while Connal drove our new friends home.

After everything was spic and span, I thought it would be nice to go out to the practice circle and work on my skills with the quarterstaff.

The practice circle was on the west side of our new home in a small space carved into the brush. Mr. Sawirski told me this was where the garden used to be when the farmyard still had buildings on it. There was only meadow land and marsh left when the property was sold.

Connal had made another replica of the Broadsword Circle and fastened it to a nearby fence post. It was nice to have a little time to practice without the distraction of helpful fairies. I composed a little chant to help me focus on the twelve different strikes. It had a nice rhythm to it. "One down, two down, three right, four left, five point, six point, seven up, eight up, nine point, ten point, eleven head, twelve head. When you do this over and over and over, it soon becomes automatic.

I had worked up a nice sweat and was considering switching to something else when two cars drove into our lane. The first car contained several unkempt teenagers and the second car held a grey-haired man and his wife. Something about the teenagers worried me. I was glad the elderly couple was there as well.

Strangest of all was the reassurance I got from holding my quarterstaff. I knew I was hardly able to do the simplest of things with it, but there was a good chance I knew a lot more than they did. If things turned bad, even a slight edge might be all the difference I needed. I also saw Churchill standing near the corner of the house staring intently at the intruders. It wasn't as if he would be of any use but at least he was there.

The teenagers swaggered over to where I was standing and formed an aggressive semi-circle in front of me.

Teenager one: "Hey, everybody the kid's green."

Answer one: "We're trying out a different kind of sunscreen"

Teenager two: "Are you building a grow-op?"

Answer two: "No, we're building a storage battery."

Teenager three: "What's with the big stick?"

Answer three: "It's my quarterstaff."

Teenager four: "What do you do with it?"

Answer four: "It's a kind of weapon."

Wrong answer! They were looking for trouble and I had just given them an opening. Now what was I going to do? At that moment the elderly lady appeared at my side carrying Churchill. She must have been a real 'cat person' because Churchill rarely lets strangers get near him let alone pick him up. I also noticed the elderly man had moved into a position directly behind my opponents.

"Oh, good," I thought. "There are four of them and four of us if we count Churchill. We're not outnumbered and we've got them surrounded. What more can I ask for?"

Connal's gallows humor must be catching for I found myself starting to laugh. I gave a shrug and shook my head.

"There's not much to see. Come on and I'll show you around."

I tried to follow Connal's example and be as charming as I could. It worked beautifully.

The eight of us wandered around the site and looked into the unfinished basement that was to house the storage battery. I say eight because Churchill allowed the lady to carry him all over. He was quite silly about it. I thought she must have catnip or something hidden in her clothes. The elderly gentleman had brought his camera and insisted in taking pictures of me, Churchill, the teenagers, the hole in the ground and anything else that took his fancy.

We looked at the practice area and the Broadsword circle and I demonstrated the twelve different moves. I was very relieved when Connal showed up at this point because I had run out of things to show them.

Mr. and Mrs. Johnson insisted on taking more pictures of me and Connal. They were fascinated with our green skin. Churchill finally decided he had enough and disappeared into the nearby brush. The teenagers however wanted to see Connal use the quarterstaff. He said it was getting late so he'd just show them how to disarm an attack. I knew what he wanted and he quickly dumped me in the sand twice when I took a swing at him.

A good time was had by all and we parted in a flurry of smiles and waves.

Connal however was worried.

"Next you will come with me. I won't leave you alone. This is such a solitary spot I didn't realize there might be visitors. This lot was friendly but the next group might be real trouble."

I wondered how friendly the teenagers might have been if I had continued to provoke them. I didn't say anything though because I didn't want to bother Connal.

CHAPTER NINE

Life On The Construction Site

Monday morning Connal and I were up just after sunrise and the rest of the day disappeared in a blur of activity. There were several work crews assigned to different jobs. Two or three groups worked at finishing the bunkhouse and control center. They built cupboards, shelves, and counters, installed the plumbing, finished the wiring, and put up the rest of the dry wall. Tomorrow the painters would arrive and the floors would be tiled. Two other groups worked on the outside. They built a large deck for the mobile home and another deck for the bunkhouse. They spread several loads of gravel on the lane that led to the access road and put up one of those portable plastic garages for Connal's pick-up truck.

Mr. Sawirski patiently drove back and forth to Selkirk to fetch all the things that had been forgotten and other items no one had realized we needed.

Connal decided he liked the idea of putting sod down to cover the bare earth created by all the construction, so we needed a load of sod. Our well would provide us with lots of water but we needed a hose to water our lawn if we wanted it to grow. It was just one thing after another. I was glad the mobile home had come completely equipped. Once it was in place all they had to do was move in the furniture. The furniture for the bunkhouse would arrive in two days.

I know all this because I became the person who kept track of everything and sent out for more supplies when needed. As soon as the portable garage was set up, I used it as a temporary office. I had a large crate for a desk, a smaller crate for a chair, a large pad of paper, several miscellaneous pens and pencils, and Connal's cell phone. My filing system consisted of several fist sized rocks set out on another large crate. I put papers under different rocks using a method created out of thin air and understood only by myself. It worked surprisingly well.

I thought it was amusing when the electricians ran a power cable to the garage and installed a plug for the truck. The only time you plug in your vehicle is during very cold weather and every day so far had been over thirty degrees Celsius. Oh well, Nu-Tec was nothing if not thorough. Did I mention the mobile home was air conditioned and the bunkhouse was ready to be hooked up as well?

I learned the workers were being paid a large bonus if everything was completed by a certain time. The only problem was, if someone wanted to cut corners so they could claim the bonus, this might lead to shoddy work and could be dangerous. Connal and the eagle-eyed Mr. Sawirski continually prowled about making sure that never happened. It was almost magical how quickly everything was coming together.

After everyone left, Connal and I worked together to prepare dinner. He kept having me do more and more food preparation and I realized, if this lasted for the summer, I would soon be a fairly competent cook. We were just about to begin eating when there was a knock at the door.

Standing outside on the new wooden deck was the very pretty woman from the restaurant. She looked so shy and nervous I found myself playing the affable host just to set her at ease.

"Hello, Ethne. It's nice to see you again. We're about to have dinner and we'd be delighted if you'd join us."

I felt Connal looming behind me and I was sure he was wearing his most radiant smile.

"Please do come in. There's plenty of meat in the pot. I can show you around after we've eaten," added Connal.

Even with his smile and all those pheromones there was a good chance she might have left. However, because I was there, she probably felt it would be safe enough to have dinner with us.

I have to admit I'm at the age when I'm starting to notice girls and Ethne was beautiful. She had a great sheaf of dark hair that in moonlight would look inky black and in sunlight would glow into a rich dark auburn. Her eyes were a soft yellow color that reminded me of Churchill the cat, who promptly arrived on the scene and began to rub against her ankles.

Ethne leaned down and picked him up and carried him with her as she came into the kitchen. She seemed to be using him as a shield to hide her nervousness at being alone with two almost strangers. It probably didn't help that we were still a rather vivid lime green.

I used to spend a lot of time with my brother Gordon and his friends who were all ten years older than me, so I've had a lot of experience with courting rituals. For the introductory stage it was useful to have me around. The girls felt more in control when there was a third person there and they seemed to be impressed that the boys would willingly cart a child around with them. The trick is you are expected to disappear when things begin to get interesting. I spent our very pleasant meal thinking up a good excuse to make myself scarce when the moment was right.

Tonight I had lots of help with the dishes. Ethne kept putting me between her and Connal. She seemed quite determined not to get too near him. In my opinion she was more afraid of herself than she was of Connal.

Finally, we all went outside to look at the unfinished hole and the bunkhouse. I spotted a trouble light someone had left on the deck and it gave me an idea. I picked it up and said, "I'm going to work in the garage for a while. There's some paper work I've got to do."

An excuse that was actually true. Just before quitting time a special delivery had arrived for me. It was a laptop computer accompanied by a note addressed to the site manager requesting a written report on our progress. Mr. Sawirski gave a slight twitch of a smile when he told me I was the site manager and to get busy writing.

So the garage's electrical outlet came in handy the first day it was installed. I plugged in the trouble light and hung it over my 'desk'. There were lots of assorted insects that came to fly around the light but none of them bothered me. This seemed to be one of the beneficial effects of my green skin. When I looked up from my keyboard toward the bunkhouse, Connal had his arm around Ethne and they were walking back toward the house. I watched them disappear inside before I turned my attention back to the report. I had a very clear idea of what they were going to do.

The report took longer than I expected because I wasn't sure what they wanted. I decided to have three categories in point form; work completed, work in progress, and things that needed to be done or purchased. I didn't think much of my effort, so I was surprised to learn later that my report was being held up as a model of efficiency and clarity. Head office obviously didn't realize the site manager was a twelve year old who didn't like writing long reports.

When I came out of the garage, Connal and Ethne were sitting side by side on the deck. Ethne was nestled in the curve of his arm with her head on his shoulder. As I approached, they both stood up and Connal kissed her gently on the forehead.

"Good-night, James," said Ethne and gave me a pat on the shoulder as she walked over to her car. I was surprised she was leaving.

"She could have stayed over," I offered. "It wouldn't bother me and you know I'd never tell."

"Your friends know you're the soul of discretion, James. However, it's a lot more complicated than that."

"Didn't she want to stay?"

"Yes, she did, and I would have been delighted to share my bed with her. Instead, I made her leave. I had to warn her how dangerous it is to be near me and give a chance to make up her own mind. We'll see what tomorrow brings."

"Do you think she'll be back?"

"I have fond hopes, James, fond hopes."

Then Connal walked into the house singing softly under his breath. The song was in his own language and I had the feeling the words were very naughty. The more I got to know him, the more he reminded me of my brother Gordon.

The next morning new work crews arrived and everyone was kept busy. This was just as well because Connal was getting jumpy. Ethne had not returned but that was only part of it. A lot of the supplies Connal had ordered still hadn't shown up and it was time for him to start building the battery. We had received word another fairy had fallen ill. Time was running out.

I breathed a lot easier when, shortly after lunch, Ethne arrived bringing a large suitcase and a small overnight bag. I learned she had volunteered to help out and was now our cook. Connal's fond hopes had come true.

Just before we quit for the day, Connal's supplies appeared and he was as excited as a child at Christmas. He couldn't wait to check everything out so Ethne and I were left to prepare the supper.

That's when I got a surprise. Ethne didn't know how to cook. One of the reasons she hadn't come earlier was she'd driven into Selkirk to buy a cookbook. Now she was in a dither because she really wanted to impress Connal.

"What will I do," she moaned. "I can't even think where to start."

She looked as if she were going to cry.

I rolled my eyes toward the ceiling and declared, "What must I do to be saved? Have you ever heard of the KISS principle?"

"No. What's that?"

"Keep it simple stupid. Just start at the beginning and see what we've got on hand."

Mr. Sawirski had gone shopping for basic supplies for our kitchen and I noticed we did have zucchini, tomatoes, onions, cheese, and breadcrumbs. That gave me an idea.

"I'll show you how to make a zucchini casserole. Connal seemed to like the one Mr. Sawirski fed us the other night. We can have ice cream and fresh fruit for dessert."

With two of us working together it took very little time until the casserole was bubbling away happily in the oven and a nice selection of strawberries and fresh peaches were waiting in a bowl in the refrigerator. We even had wine with the meal because Ethne had picked up a bottle in Selkirk to celebrate what she called 'the beginning of our relationship'.

All I could do was pat her a little awkwardly on the back and wish her much happiness. I knew in my heart it wasn't going to be easy but they were good people and deserved a little joy.

When Connal arrived the table was set, the meal was ready, and there was even a little nosegay of green leaves and small flowers on the table. Ethne had an eye for those small touches that add grace to any occasion.

The meal was quite festive. We finished every bit of the casserole and drank all the wine. The Ethne shooed us outdoors while she cleaned up after the meal. She also told Connal that I was the one who had organized the meal and she was not good at cooking anything. She was painfully honest when it came to admitting her faults.

"That's all right. I'm sure you'll learn," responded Connal airily.

He and I tumbled around in the practice circle for a short time then went on an equally short run. I knew Connal had other things on his mind. I stayed outside for a while longer than he did because it was such a fine evening and when I came in they were both behind the closed bedroom door.

It had been a long day so I went to bed early myself. Churchill often slept with me but I hadn't seen him for a while. I wondered about that briefly before I drifted down into sleep.

The next morning we discovered he'd fallen asleep in the back of Mr. Sawirski's truck and had spent the night at his place. Andy said it almost seemed as if he wanted to stay there, but he didn't object to being brought back either.

The feverish pace of the construction was beginning to subside. Now, Connal could start on the things only he knew how to do. The remaining workers spent most of their time installing the lightning rods. There were two on the house, three on the bunkhouse, and four forty foot contraptions, each one placed a yard or so from the corners of our hole in the ground. These would carry an electrical charge from a lightning strike safely to ground and would also deflect some of the power to the storage battery. There was even a lightning rod on the plastic garage. To me that was just overkill.

Later Connal told me Guy had an idea about using these rods in conjunction with the geo-thermal power system he'd already installed.

There was also a specially designed sheet of super tough plastic with elasticized edges that would fit snugly over the top of the battery hole to keep out the rain. Eventually, a permanent building would be placed over the battery but this would have to do until then.

Mr. Sawirski took one look at it and promptly dubbed it the 'shower cap'.

Once Ethne had recovered from last night's panic attack, she proved to be clever, efficient, and good natured. She said she would cook for us and cook she did. How much she relied on the cookbook and how much on her own instincts I don't know, but no one had cause to complain about the food when she was on the job. It made me think better of Connal's choice of a girlfriend.

Just before bedtime the three of us went outside and sat on the deck for a while watching the water sprinkler's gentle arc go back and forth over the new sod. Ethne and Connal were curled up on the patio swing while I dangled my bare feet over the edge of the deck where a few tiny drops of water could reach them as the spray went back and forward. The wind had dropped and the air was soft and sweet. The slanting rays of the sun made opalescent patterns on the few fluffy clouds. It was one of those absolutely perfect moments.

I heard a soft rumbly noise behind me. I turned around to see Ethne massaging Connal's neck and shoulders.

"Connal are you purring?"

"I do believe I am," agreed Connal.

"He does that a lot when he's very, very happy," said Ethne with a mischievous smile.

Yes, right! I could just imagine what other things might make Connal very, very happy.

"It seems to be a side effect from bonding with the cat," continued Connal. He seemed rather pleased with his new ability.

I just shook my head. Just when things began to feel more normal, something new and strange happened.

A short while before sunrise a thunderstorm roared though. July is the thunder moon but there had been no rain since we came here even though several storms had passed close by. We could see the huge anvil shaped clouds in the distance and see the lightning flashes but no raindrops fell to soothe the parched earth.

Tonight was different. We were right in the middle of the storm path. Connal and I ran out and quickly put the 'shower cap' over the hole that was soon to become the storage battery and the reason for all our efforts. It was a fairly heavy storm with a considerable amount of rain and we quickly realized the water was collecting in the middle, the plastic was sagging into the hole, and the elastic sides were moving up. If we didn't do something, all the water would be in the hole anyway.

We each grabbed a discarded plastic container and Ethne came out to help. She sat on the edge and pushed down on the plastic sheet with a spare two by four. This made a depression near the edge which collected the water. Connal and I would lean over and bail. It was sloppy but effective. The shower cap stayed in place.

"Why don't we wedge a pole under the plastic sheet so it's higher in the middle the next time it starts to rain?" I suggested.

"That's a good idea," said Connal. "We'll try it the next time it rains. It just might work."

It might, but I made a mental note to phone Evan in the morning and see if he could come up with something better.

We were drenched to the skin and laughing like idiots and like idiots didn't know when to stop. I tripped and fell into a puddle, Connal leaned down to help me, and Ethne pushed him from behind. Connal has great reflexes and managed to shift his weight so Ethne ended up in the puddle with me while he stood laughing at us. We both scrambled to our feet with mud in our hands which we promptly threw at Connal then ran madly for the house.

Before we reached the door Connal bellowed, "Stop!"

We both froze. I wondered how he could do that.

"There's no need to take all this mud into the house. Take off all your clothes and leave them on the deck. We can clean them up after breakfast."

I could tell Ethne didn't like this even though it was a very sensible idea. Associating with Connal made me a lot more relaxed about wandering about in the buff so I said, "Turn your back Ethne and I'll go first."

I left the two of them giggling out on the deck.

The morning dawned bright and sunny but it was still too wet to do much. Connal came out to the garage and helped me move my things into the real office space in the bunkhouse. It seemed to be a good time to ask him a question that had been bothering me.

"When elves have sex is it something like what humans do?"

"I wouldn't say 'something like', it's 'exactly like'. The differences between elves and other humans are essentially trivial. Do you know a lot about sex, James?"

"I believe I do," I replied. I was prepared to defend my answer but Connal surprised me by taking me at my word.

"You realize, James, that Sean, Max and I have given our oaths to the Core in return for sanctuary. This means we have proved to the Core's satisfaction that we believe in the same things they do. One of these beliefs is that humankind is all of one blood and every human on Earth is pretty much the same. In the eyes of the Core my being an elf is of no particular importance. It's like being French, or Turkish, or Bantu. These kind of cultural categories mean little to them and so does being an elf. They believe, and so do I, that I'm human first and the elf part is just window dressing."

"How do you become a member of the Core?"

"Well, since you already know about them that makes you eligible. Whether you ever join the Core is really up to you. You see, you are the one who has to create your own small group or 'core', and this requires friendship and loyalty. Leave it at that for now."

Connal had certainly given me a lot to think about.

I worked the rest of the morning putting entries in a ledger book. Yes, I do know how to do simple double entry bookkeeping. Remember, I'm good at math and my father and grandfather are both accountants. They showed me how it works when I was in primary school. I could have used the computer but my Grandpa Duncan always says, "Leave a paper trail."

My stomach was beginning to tell me it was time to eat when two familiar figures walked into the office.

Clifford walked over and punched me in the arm.

"Get out of that chair, James. It's time for lunch."

"Who's the pretty lady in the mobile home?" asked Kelsey from the doorway.

"She's Connal's new girlfriend, Ethne. She's working as the camp cook. How long are you two here for?"

"We're here for the rest of the summer," crowed Clifford with a big smile.

I wasn't surprised Clifford wanted to be near Connal. I knew what a bond was like. It also made sense Kelsey would come along. He wouldn't be far from his brother if he could help it. I wondered how he would manage when September came and Clifford was off to university.

Lunch was on the table when we came inside. Today it was plates of cold cuts, sliced tomatoes, cheese, and lettuce. There were also several kinds of relish and a large basket of fresh buns, so we could make our own bunwiches.

When we were all seated at the table, Connal turned to me and said, "We've got some new neighbors. All of the fairies are now living in Mr. Sawirski's basement. Michael decided it was too dangerous to leave them in Winnipeg and Bissett."

"Andy's a very brave man," added Evan. "I know he'll be well paid, but it's starting to look dangerous for anyone to get near our small friends. They've started to gain weight."

"You mean they might explode!" I exclaimed.

"Not for another month or two. The gain is very tiny as yet. It was only noticed because the people in Bissett kept careful track of their weight. They think that might explain why some are falling ill.

Andy knows what's happening but we haven't told the fairies yet. They have enough troubles. Andy says he plans to keep them busy learning English so they won't have time to realize what is happening."

"I hadn't expected to lose Andy's help," said Connal with a worried frown. "Now what are we going to do?"

"That's one of the reasons I brought Clifford and Kelsey with me. They're both very reliable workers. I also thought you and I could take a trip up to Sandycreek and talk to an elder I know. I'm sure she can arrange for a few young men to come here to work."

"I suppose that will have to do. Some of the fairies would know how to build the battery but their size makes it impossible. As long as these men are willing to do exactly what I tell them, they should be able to handle it. I knew I would have to teach the whole procedure to anyone you hired. The first part is going to be pretty nasty work. I hope you're going to pay them well."

"It's one hundred dollars a day and I wonder if that's enough," sighed Evan. "Max has sent word he wants everyone working on the battery to take the sunscreen potion. That means they'll all have to consent to turning green."

"Kelsey and Clifford, too?" I laughed

"Especially, Kelsey and Clifford. Connal's to give them their first dose tonight. We can use them to set an example for the others. More important than that, I can be sure they'll be safe."

"What's so dangerous about building the battery?" I asked.

"It would be extremely safe if we weren't trying to do it so fast and without the proper equipment," replied Evan. "We're using the same procedure to make the battery walls that you've seen in Andy's basement. Andy's dad and I installed the white coating in a week with nary a scratch or a blister. I must admit we needed only three coats and it was minus 40 at the time, so we could keep the basement windows open. We'd have finished in two days except we also did the ceiling and that's very tricky.

To keep on schedule here, we need six coats in three days, and it's going to be very hot. Unfortunately, no one in Nu-Tec's engineering department could come up with a practical way of keeping things cool. They looked at fans, refrigerating units, everything.

The problem is there are two different substances that combine to make each coat and when they combine it produces intense heat. The reason for taking the sunscreen lotion is because it helps the body to protect itself from both ultra-violet and infra-red light."

"Will I need to take more of the sunscreen?"

"No. You and Connal will be just fine. It's the others Max was worried about."

I'd been glad the green had almost faded and Connal and I were now a warm golden tan. I quite liked the way I looked in the mirror. The only startling thing was, while the green faded from our skin, our eyes changed color, too. We now had greenish eyes instead of blue. Connal said it was a little like mixing yellow and blue and getting green. He also said that people with brown eyes usually found their eyes a lighter color, sometimes golden and occasionally violet.

After lunch Kelsey, Clifford and I wandered down to the lake. We waded in the water but didn't go for a swim. I think they liked being near the water even if the little sand beach couldn't compare with the ones near their home. It had its own cozy charm. I noticed with some surprise that someone had graveled the path to the beach. It looked neat and tidy but I missed its former unspoiled look.

I showed them the practice circle, the fire pit, the outdoor showers and Connal's tiny garden. I'm not sure when he found the time to make it.

When I asked him about it he said, "James, my boy, both Max and I are wizards and making gardens is something wizards always do."

It was only later I realized he was talking about ingredients for potions not vegetables. I thought it was quite funny Connal had made a kind of grow-op and didn't know it.

Late in the afternoon Connal and Evan drove up in the truck and Evan promptly left. He had promised Mr. Sawirski he would have supper with him. The rest of us trailed into the house. We found Ethne on her hands and knees muttering curses.

"I can't believe it. What can have possessed that blasted cat?"

"What's the matter, Ethne?"

"Your grey alter-ego has been chewing into quite a number of the little paper packages you keep in the bedroom closet. I tried to bring the opened packages in here to put them in plastic bags and now I've dropped two of them."

"How did he get in there? I kept the closet door closed."

"So did I," fumed Ethne.

"Churchill can open doors," I volunteered. "If you want to keep him out of somewhere, you need to tie the door shut."

"Here, let me see what he got into. I don't think he took anything fatal but he might be very sick and it would serve him right."

Churchill was nowhere to be found. Kelsey joked that he was lying low to avoid Connal's wrath.

I didn't think so. I'd lived with that cat for a long time and I was quite sure he didn't care whether you approved of his behavior or not. Like Kipling's cat he would wave his wild tail and walk his wild lone according to what seemed right to him.

It had been decided Clifford and Kelsey would share the big bedroom and I would continue to stay in the smaller one. Connal announced that he had made arrangements to board with the cook. This produced raised eyebrows and grins from

Kelsey and Clifford. Both he and Ethne were probably glad of the chance for a little more privacy.

They were walking toward the door when the phone rang.

It was Mr. Sawirski. One of the fairies had been out patrolling the area around the house and had found Churchill asleep under a clump of snowberry. They couldn't wake him and Andy had carried him into the house. Cormac was of the opinion he'd come over in Evan's truck.

Ethne stayed behind while the four of us drove over to Mr. Sawirski's to retrieve the cat. Connal was muttering under his breath about unpredictable felines when he suddenly sat up straight.

"No, he couldn't have," he said softly. "That would be just too strange, strange enough to chill my spine."

I prodded his arm.

"What are you talking about?"

"I've been going over in my mind which herbs and other ingredients Churchill ate and I'm not sure, but we may have a much bigger problem on our hands than a cat with an upset stomach. We may end up with a very large cat."

"How large?" asked Clifford.

"Well, if it doesn't kill him, he might become larger than a bobcat but hopefully smaller than a mountain lion. The mixture he ate causes things to grow abnormally large. That wouldn't be so bad if it didn't produce some very weird side effects. Let's hope he doesn't grow an extra head or tail."

"Why would he eat that stuff, anyway?" continued Clifford.

"I feel I may be responsible. Churchill, like most pets, had a small but useful store of words he understood, like his name or the word 'no'. More intelligent animals have quite considerable vocabularies. I suspect one of the effects of our bond is he now understands most of what he hears.

A few nights ago I foolishly left James alone and I remember talking to Churchill and telling him I wished he was bigger so he could help me protect James. Today he probably heard me telling Evan I was worried about the fairies because I was needed here and they also needed my protection there.

What I find alarming is that he appears to have acquired my knowledge of herbs and potions. Oh well, I now know the secret of how to purr."

"You know how to 'what'!" exclaimed Kelsey.

"How to purr. It's actually a rather useful skill. For example, it relieves pain and speeds healing among other things. I've been too busy to check out all the possibilities. For example, Ethne seems to find it very appealing.

If Churchill lives, he'll probably stay at Andy's and help protect my people. I know it sounds impossible, but I believe it's true."

Cormac was sitting on the gatepost waiting for us.

"The cat's started to wake up. I think he'll be up and around very soon. Your friend Andy's a good man, Connal. He's got all fifty-odd fairies properly intimidated," he announced with an appreciative chuckle.

"Several fairies started to fuss and complain the moment they arrived. Andy just tilted his head to one side, gave them his icy stare and said, 'You realize I'm going to get paid for taking care of you whether you survive or not?' Then Ansel, who is not noted for his quick wit or charm, said, "We will do as we like. Why should we listen to you?" Andy never blinked an eye. "Because I'm bigger than you and this is my house." There wasn't another word out of anyone. That man has a truly evil grin."

"You think this arrangement will work," asked Connal.

"It's quite amazing. Everyone is on his best behavior. It's, 'yes, Mr. Sawirski this' and 'no, Mr. Sawirski that'. Andy's got everyone organized and assigned various duties. I found Churchill while on patrol duty which is now part of our regular daily routine. English classes will begin first thing in the morning. Andy wants to get everyone's personal time switched over to sleeping at night. I think that white basement of his helps. It makes all of us feel more at home."

"Who are we talking to?" hissed Clifford. "I hear a voice but I can't see anything."

"I think it's Cormac," whispered Kelsey.

I was surprised to learn that while Kelsey shared my ability to see and hear fairies. Clifford could only hear them, at least in low light conditions.

I could tell Mr. Sawirski didn't like the idea of keeping Churchill around while he recovered, especially since there was a good possibility he was soon to become much, much larger.

Connal picked up the cat and was gently stroking his fur. Churchill looked dyspeptic but otherwise normal. They moved nearer to Mr. Sawirski and Connal appeared thoughtful.

"Consider this Andy; you've got everything nicely under control inside your house, why not let Churchill help you with maintaining control on the outside?"

Mr. Sawirski thought for a moment then he nodded.

"Let's see how that works."

Before we left, I sat with Churchill for a while and rubbed his back the way he always liked. I had a feeling he would be just fine even if he became a super-sized cat.

Clifford and Kelsey each got a dose of the sunscreen and we all went to bed. I drifted off to sleep that night hoping tomorrow would bring fewer distractions. We really needed to get working on the battery.

CHAPTER TEN
New Arrivals

Connal's worries about security must have filtered up to Michael Flynn. A very green colored Kelsey and Clifford were watching me to see if I knew how to cook their eggs when there was a knock on the door. Four men in very official looking uniforms were standing on the deck.

"Is Mr. Ferryman here?"

"Not at the moment, "said Clifford. "He should be along any minute now. May I help you?"

"That's all right; we'll wait till he comes. Pardon me for asking, but why are you green?"

"It's a new kind of sunscreen," said Clifford and quickly closed the door.

I was already hitting the speed dial button on the cell phone. Connal answered on the second ring.

"I'll be right there. Don't open the door again."

The three of us didn't feel particularly worried so we rescued the eggs and ate our breakfast.

The new arrivals were here to provide security for the next stage of the project. They found it hard to believe such important research was taking place in the middle of nowhere without any precautions for the safety of the personnel or the protection of the site.

They started to give Connal orders, but ran into his impenetrable charm. All of their ranting and raving only splashed harmlessly against his iron-clad resolve to do everything his way.

"Gentlemen, gentlemen," he said sweetly, "I know you will do your jobs to the best of your ability and so will I. However, I am the only one who knows how to build this battery and if I walk away there's no project at all. Everything you do has to meet with my approval and nothing I do is under your control. You are welcome to phone the head office for confirmation."

Actually, things weren't nearly as lax as they appeared. We had our own early warning system. The fairies were able to make quite amazing leaps with very little effort. This made it easy for them to travel over surprisingly long distances when compared to their tiny size.

Connal had approved of Andy's decision to have regular patrols of his farm, so he arranged for some of the fairies to make regular patrols here as well. With fifty-odd fairies to choose from there was plenty of help available. Mr. Sawirski seemed to like the idea of keeping everyone as busy as possible.

The security people finally agreed to begin in a very small way. Two of them went back to watch the gate, one of them stayed around the site, and the other was sent to watch the lake. They wanted to set up cameras everywhere but Connal wouldn't allow it. I think he was worried the fairies might show up on film.

Connal took Kelsey and Clifford out to show them what we had been doing and I went inside to clear everything away. I wasn't quite finished when I heard a lot of shouting out by the gate. Two vehicles were stopped nearby. Our helpers from Sandycreek had arrived.

"You can't come in here," shouted one of the men. "Your names are not on my list."

"What list?" demanded Connal. He arrived so quickly the guards must have felt he popped out of the ground.

"Nu-Tec gave us a list of authorized personnel. No one is supposed to be here if their name isn't on the list."

"I'm sure the list is a good idea," agreed Connal. "However, this is how I want you to use the list. Everyone is to be allowed into the site. People on the list may come in immediately, those who are not on the list will be allowed in but they must have someone who works at the site accompany them at all times.

I will only say this once. This project must appear as ordinary as possible. If you try to make it a secret, it only makes others more curious. However, the one thing I want you to insist on is absolutely no cameras."

"Can we at least install a gate and a guard post?" pleaded the shortest of the men.

"Yes, that does seem to be a good idea. I'm quite willing to accept your help and advice. Just make sure you clear everything with me first."

We had expected four men but we got five men and one woman. Connal was annoyed.

"It would have helped if they could count," he grumbled to me. "Perhaps, it's best though, because from the looks of them, I wonder how many of them have the stomach for a lot of really difficult work. Oh well, they did arrive on time."

Then he turned to the group and said, "Everyone follow me into the bunkhouse. We have a lot to talk about."

I could see what Connal was worried about. Except for one very big fellow, the men all looked grubby, unkempt, and very queasy. They sported a fine assortment of cuts, bruises, and one black eye. The woman kept her head down and scowled at the floor.

I was pleased to see both Chris and his Uncle Joe in the group. It was their bedraggled appearance that puzzled me. They hadn't looked like that on Sunday.

"I take it most of you are hung over. I believe that's the correct term. It must have been quite a party," said Connal.

"It wasn't exactly a party," said the big fellow, "and, from what I saw, no one had more than one glass of punch. I was just lucky because I didn't have any. I try to stay away from sweet things whenever I can.

Yesterday evening we were all called over to the band office and Laura George told us what you wanted. Everyone was excited about the chance to work here for the summer. Joe and Chris said you were good people."

There was a long pause and it was Joe who finally continued the story.

"We were standing outside Chris's house when several people we know came over with a big cooler of what they said was punch. We all decided to drink a toast to our good fortune. That's when the trouble started. Paul over there threw up immediately. Then everyone joined in. We knew it had to be the punch but nobody would admit to it. The people who brought it over were just as sick as we were."

"Then there was a fight about who spiked the punch," added Chris.

No one seemed ready to say anything more. I believed they were telling the truth even though their story didn't add up. It smacked of outside interference and I wondered who would do something like that? There were a lot of possibilities.

Connal just shook his head.

"James, put the kettle on. I'm going to make us all some tea. It's an old family recipe and is good for most kinds of poisonings."

I wondered what the effects of the tea might be. If Connal had the kind of ingredients that could accidentally produce a two headed cat, this could be very interesting.

Both Clifford and Kelsey accepted a cup and I didn't want to be a chicken so I took one as well.

"Just sip it slowly and you'll start to feel better in a few minutes," advised Connal.

The effect began almost immediately. It was very pleasant. First you began to feel peaceful and calm, then you became awake and alert, ready to move mountains if there were any handy.

Chris suddenly became aware of his surroundings. He blinked when he realized both Clifford and Kelsey were bright green. Then he nudged me and said, "Those two people are green."

"It's the new kind of sunscreen," I wearily replied.

"That's weird," said Joe. "Are you sure you aren't all aliens?"

While the tea was working its magic, Connal began pacing up and down the room.

"What we are doing here is very important to me. If we succeed it will save the lives of a good number of my friends. Except during the first three days, you are free to leave at anytime if you become ill or the work is too difficult for you. The next three days are going to be like something out of your worst nightmare. After that the work will be less challenging. On the bright side, there is a possibility of long term employment.

You will live here, eat here, and sleep here. You will be paid one hundred dollars a day for every day you are on the site whether you work or not, though I'm sure there'll always be something that needs doing. My word is law. Don't ever forget that.

Oh yes, you will be required to take a substance that will turn you green. This is to protect you from the worst effects of the next three days. James and I took it a little over a week ago and Clifford and Kelsey took some last night. As you can see the green color does fade with time."

I'm sure they had many questions but Connal just walked toward the door and beckoned for them to follow him.

I started to follow him but he turned and said, "James you stay here and phone Andy. Ask him what we might use to make a gate and a guardhouse.

Mr. Sawirski said he'd phone over to the building materials store and see what kind of portable building and gate they could deliver by lunch time. We were becoming such good customers he was sure they would oblige.

He was right. Everything was out at the gate by eleven thirty.

I went out to tell the security guards and they were rather impressed. Later, they were even more impressed when the guardhouse was finished and the gate installed before quitting time.

They told me what their names were; Mr. Anderson, Mr. Bychan, Mr. Chan, and Mr. Duchin. They were quite nice when you got to know them. Chris was the one who first called them Misters ABCD 'the alphabet guys' and the name stuck. There were also four other men who took the night shift but we never did get to know them very well.

After lunch Joe, Clifford, Paul, and Alfred, the big fellow who didn't like sweet things, were told to put up the garden-shed-guardhouse and build the gate. I asked Clifford if he thought they'd be all right. He grinned at me and said, "I think everyone here knows which end of a hammer to use."

Kelsey, Chris, the fifth man John, and myself were delegated to help Connal. So far, I hadn't heard John say anything. I wondered if he could talk.

I asked Connal if he knew why the woman, whose name was Gracie, had come along with the others.

He just shrugged his shoulders.

"I don't think it would be polite to send her back. I'm sure Ethne can use the extra help."

I wasn't so sure about that. Kelsey and I had been in the kitchen when she first came and what we saw was more of a fight than the beginning of a friendship. However, later in the afternoon I heard peals of laughter from the bunkhouse. I wondered if they were drinking extra cups of Connal's tea.

I asked him about that.

"Connal, is your tea a kind of drug? You know, is it addictive."

"There are a lot of different kinds of tea. Some of them might be addictive, but the tea I made today is not. It makes you feel better because you really are better. It's a remedy that helps your body get rid of various kinds of poisons and balances the body's own chemistry. The expression, 'it's good for what ails you', comes to mind. You feel happy and alert because your body tells you that all is well."

When I thought about it, that was exactly what it was like.

After I'd talked to Evan, he'd arranged for the manufacture of a series of very light weight rigid panels to cover the battery opening when it rained. These arrived after lunch and we set them in place to see if they fit properly. We could leave them to the side when we were working. That made the 'shower cap' unnecessary.

In the spirit of 'waste not, want not' Connal decided to punch a lot of small holes in it and hang it between the four huge lightning rods. He had paid attention to the alphabet guy's warnings about aerial photographs taken from planes and satellites. The shower cap would offer some protection from both cameras and the sun while allowing a free flow of air over the hole. They had suggested putting barriers on the open three sides, but Connal was adamant about not doing anything that would increase the heat risk.

"Barriers will also increase people's curiosity and we're quite conspicuous as it is. The 'shower cap" will look like a forty foot high orange umbrella."

After the umbrella was in place, our group of four went down into the hole and helped Connal install four heavy iron bars, one in each corner. We painted these with something sticky. Then Connal asked everyone to climb out because he said he wanted to offer a blessing.

"We'll see if all those years of learning to be a wizard really helped," he said grinning mischievously.

"Are you wizard?" asked Paul.

"At home they call me the Warrior Wizard, but you can call me just plain Wiz. I hope you peasants will be suitable impressed."

Everyone crowded around the hole to watch.

It actually wasn't that impressive, and we all began to wonder if Connal was serious or joking. It was hard to tell.

The better I got to know Connal the more I realized, while he was very good about telling you whatever you needed to know, he didn't always tell you everything. If you really wanted understand what was going on, you had to fill in a lot of the gaps on your own.

All he did was stand in front of each of the iron rods and utter a brief chant. Then he threw a sparkly powder at the rod. This stuck to the surface and caused the rod to glow briefly. Then he grinned up at everyone and said, "We're finished for the moment, so let's wash up for supper."

As soon as supper was over, we gathered in the common room of the bunkhouse and Connal gave us what he called his "Beware of Stupidity" lecture.

"It's been a good day. We've accomplished everything I wanted to do and I've learned you are all willing workers. Laura George made good choices when she sent you here.

Now it's you who have to make the choice. I want you to be aware that some very ruthless people are interested in this project. It is quite possible your lives will be threatened. Steps have been taken to keep us secure but there are no guarantees. If you choose to leave tonight, no one would blame you. If you stay and danger threatens, save yourself, 'Better a live coward than a dead hero'.

You also must make a choice regarding the first three days on this job. Once you begin the work tomorrow morning, I will expect you to finish all three days. Those who wish to leave after that may do so. I have friends whose lives depend on this project being finished very soon. With the weather being so hot, conditions down in the hole will be quite dreadful. The only good thing is your lives will be quite safe even though you might not believe it at the time."

There was a long silence.

"If you choose to leave, go now. Otherwise, come over to the counter and I give each of you a dose of the sunscreen."

Everyone took the sunscreen including Ethne and Gracie.

The five young men found comfortable seats in the common room and turned on the television. The rest of us went back to the mobile home. We had to get the sleeping arrangements sorted out again. Kelsey and I were to share the large bedroom, Clifford moved his things to the bunkhouse, Gracie would have the small bedroom, and Connal would continue to board with the cook. That way there would be one spare bunk if one of Michael's people wanted to stay over.

I thought Guy would probably want to do so. He had been very upset when he was told he would spend most of his time working in Winnipeg. Evidently, he was wonderful with anything abstract but practical and mechanical details often escaped him. Leaving him near machinery could be dangerous.

As Michael had ruefully remarked, "Guy, just doesn't think outside the box, he lives outside the box."

It was still early in the evening so Connal, Kelsey, and I went for a short run, and then returned to the practice circle. Clifford came out of the bunkhouse and joined us and Chris tagged along. Ethne and Gracie were already outside sitting on a blanket and enjoying the evening air.

Connal was a very organized teacher. He began with unarmed combat, the same way he had started with me. We practiced defensive moves and falls. Then he paired me with Kelsey and Clifford with Chris. Clifford was only a little taller than Chris so they made good partners. I was quite a bit smaller and lighter than Kelsey. However, I'd had a couple of weeks start on him and that evened things out a little. Especially, when I discovered myself using Connal's tactic of watching to see when Kelsey was a little distracted before making an aggressive move.

Thanks to Connal, protecting myself at all times had become second nature whenever I stepped into the practice circle.

My whole attitude toward life was changing. What I'd learned inside the circle was both challenging and fun. I was gaining confidence in myself. Even protecting myself outside the circle was much easier because my new mind set began to warn me of life's unwelcome surprises. There were bound to plenty of them and you could side-step most of them if you paid attention.

Clifford and Chris really enjoyed the unarmed combat lesson. On their way back to the bunkhouse I heard them laughing and joking together.

"When we get good at this, we should form our own warrior's society. We could call ourselves the Red Warriors or something," laughed Chris.

"By tomorrow we'll both be green," corrected Clifford.

"That's right," continued Chris. "Let's make it the Red-Green Warriors. We can save the world with duct tape."

They both dissolved in laughter at this apt reference to a popular television show. Clifford must have told the others what Chris had said because soon we all began to refer to our group as the Red-Green Warriors which was soon shortened to the Argees.

In the morning, when we walked out of our climate controlled luxury inside the buildings, we were met by a wall of warm air. It was going to be a scorcher. I began to understand what Connal was worried about.

Working on the walls of the battery was simple enough as Connal demonstrated on a four by four foot sheet of plywood.

"First you apply the clear coating. Be sure to use a lot because you don't want to leave any gaps that might weaken the surface. Next you apply the grey coating before the first coat has time to dry. That is why you must work on areas no larger than this board. Then you have about ten seconds to move to the center of the battery and wait there until the area cools down."

Here Connal paused and counted softly to ten.

There was a flash of light and the whole section began to glow. You could feel the intense heat against your skin. We watched in surprise as Connal reached out and picked up the board. He handed it to me and I took it before I thought. The board still gave off a steady heat but was much cooler than you would think. I passed it around so the rest could touch it.

"You have been divided into four pairs, one for each wall. One man will do the clear coat and the second man will do the grey coat. Under no circumstances will you change jobs. I don't want anyone putting his brush in the wrong coating. That would cause a very violent reaction, an explosion."

We all nodded wisely and clambered down into the battery. We were a strange looking crew. Nu-Tec had provided a selection of coveralls some white, some orange and some dark green. They had decided to see which kind worked best. I never did notice any difference. They were all uncomfortable. We also wore welder's helmets. The fact that everyone but me was green made it even more bizarre.

As we stood at the on the floor of the battery, Chris took one long look at the lot of us and mournfully remarked, "I've heard of being green on the job, but this is ridiculous."

We had a good laugh and settled in to work.

Once we began the process didn't seem difficult or dangerous. Everyone worked on his small 'patch' then stood in a circle Connal had painted on the floor and waited for the flash. The trick was to time doing your 'patch' so all eight of us were in the circle at the same time. After the first few tries we developed a good working rhythm.

The problem was the heat, both the heat from the flash and the steady warmth radiating from the walls. Connal told us his people called the process making liquid fire. It was something like the way plaster of Paris becomes warm when it sets, but much more intense. You couldn't stay down for too long. Everyone felt sick and dizzy at one time or another. When that happened, they would call out, "Everyone out!" and we would climb up the ladders to cool off.

If you wonder how we could cool off with the outdoor temperature in the high thirty degree range, it was because of our two outdoor showers. There was one for the people doing the grey coating and another one for those doing the clear. While we were working, we tried to keep the two groups as separate as possible. We stood in different parts of the circle, kept the containers of clear and grey liquid as far apart as possible, and even slung our coveralls over different clothes lines when we showered.

Connal told us we could fall into a vat of either material and come to no harm. The danger came when the two combined.

At one point Mr. Sawirski watched us staggering out of the now glowing interior of the battery and said, "Lo, the escapees from the white hole of Libau."

"What's he talking about?" muttered Clifford.

Chris picked up the reference and laughed. "I think he's comparing us to the people who survived the heat in the 'Black Hole of Calcutta'. I read about it somewhere. It's a good comparison."

When we finished for the morning, we were each given a blanket and told to rest in the shade. Everyone fell asleep almost immediately.

We ate a hearty lunch and everyone seemed to be in good spirits. We knew we had survived something physically difficult and potentially dangerous. The Argees had passed the first test.

Putting on the second coat of liquid fire was even more difficult than the first because the heat was worse. It took every ounce of your will power to keep going. After it was over, all I wanted to do was grab my blanket and sleep forever or at least until suppertime.

It would have been better if I could have slept in my nice soft bed, but Connal seemed to think going back into the air conditioned buildings would be too sharp a change after the heat.

That evening we found out why he'd built the fire pit. All the coveralls were thrown into the fire.

"Our enemies might be able to discover a lot of things I don't want them to know if they got their hands on this clothing," he explained.

It was very pleasant and peaceful sitting out under a velvet sky watching the flames dancing in the dark. We had used poplar wood to build the fire and Connal admired the purple shade this gave to the blaze. This fire was even more special because of the bursts of sparkles produced by the residue on the coveralls. Gradually one or two of the others drifted down and we all enjoyed the light show.

The next two days were much like the first, intense periods of absolute misery punctuated by sleep and food. In the evening everyone started coming down a little early to help Connal set up the fire pit. The coveralls weren't the only things we burned. Those few things the fire refused were neatly packaged and sent off to a high grade incinerator at the bunker near Bissett.

While the fire was being started, Kelsey and I were detailed to make a patrol around the site. Ostensibly, to check for intruders, but in reality we went out to get reports from the fairies. Since we could both see and hear them, we sometimes went together and sometimes separately. Connal told us to vary our routine.

There was only one report of an intruder. He had retreated swiftly after becoming ill. The fairies used some kind of poisoned missiles launched with throwing sticks. It may have been primitive but it was highly effective.

The fairies weren't completely satisfied with this success. They were already working on something even more deadly. I always felt, even though they were small, they knew how to look after themselves. Both Kelsey and I began to develop a healthy respect for these tiny warriors.

The morning of the fourth day Connal assembled everyone around the battery. The sides now glowed white in the early morning sun but the floor was still ordinary concrete.

"Now, comes the fun part," laughed Connal. "I left it until it there was enough natural light so we shouldn't disturb the neighbors too much."

He started to descend the ladder, and then he stopped and came up again.

"I think I wore this shirt and my shoes last night when we were cleaning out containers. It shouldn't be a problem, but I'll leave them up here to be safe."

This was the first time the others had seen him without his shirt. The network of scars on his back was clearly visible against his glowing golden skin.

Joe whistled. "What happened to you?"

"I was touched by evil a long time ago and I'd rather not talk about it," replied Connal with a grim smile. Then he straightened his shoulders and went back down the ladder.

Once inside the battery he rolled up his jeans and began to pour out all of the clear liquid that was left. He walked around in it barefoot for a few minutes making sure every part of the floor was covered. Then he threw the empty containers out of the battery and came up and ladder whistling.

"All right everyone! Take one of the grey containers and when I give the word, throw the contents into the battery. Try to get as much as you can on the floor rather than on the wall. Then you should have about two minutes to find a nice piece of ground to lie on and cover your eyes."

We each picked up a container and Connal placed us at regular intervals around the battery. Ethne, Gracie, Guy, who was on one of his regular visits, and even the on-site alphabet guy joined in.

"Are you ready? Now!"

We all dumped the grey liquid over the edge of the battery and watched as it flowed smoothly over the clear liquid. Then we ran quickly for a spot to lie down.

It didn't really make a bang sound. It was more of a very loud whoosh. I felt a slight tremor in the earth and I was aware of the flash of light even though my eyes were closed. However, when I looked toward the battery, everything was back to normal except for the persistent glow that lasted for about half an hour.

Connal was delighted with everything.

"I've heard of my people doing this occasionally and I've always wanted to try it. The chemical reaction is quite spectacular and it makes an instant floor. You can't do it on the walls, of course. I've always loved fireworks."

Connal may be two hundred years old but sometimes he's just like a big kid.

We were just standing there feeling pleased with ourselves when three carloads of people drove up filled with friends and relatives from Sandycreek.

The second day on the job Chris got a message from his mom. She and some other friends wanted to drive out to the site to see where he was working. They'd learned the whole group was green and she particularly wanted to take pictures. Connal and the alphabet guys declared they'd have to wait until Thursday and the walls were finished. He had to promise her that everyone would still be green by then before she would agree to wait.

We spent a good hour or so giving a tour of the site. Everyone admired the softly glowing floor, the air conditioned bunkhouse, and took lots of pictures of the green men and women. Ethne and Gracie finally corralled our visitors, fed them tea and cookies, and sent them happily on their way. This was the first of many, many tours.

We all became very good tour guides. We learned to talk glibly about anything and everything except what we were really doing. I was amazed at how careful everyone was about not giving anything away. Connal never asked them to keep anything a secret but they did it anyway because they knew how important it was to him.

The one question we got tired of was, "Is this the grow-op?" It didn't help that Joe made a sign on a spare piece of cardboard that said, "Welcome to the Grow-Op" and nailed on a post near the gate. The alphabet guys wanted him to take it down, but Connal thought it was funny and told them to leave it where it was. I was often tempted to make another small sign that simply said, "Grow-op", and stick it beside Connal's herb garden. I didn't though because it was a little too close to the truth.

It seemed local gossip had decided that, if this wasn't an illegal grow-op, then it must a government sponsored grow-op like the one up in a mine at Flin Flon where they grow marijuana for medical purposes. They seemed to think the battery was being built to make sure there was enough electricity.

I was glad when the walls and floor were finished. Working in extreme heat had required every bit of strength I had. I no longer hoped for a relaxing vacation. All I wanted to do was to survive until the end of the summer.

Everyone felt elated with our success, but we wondered what the next part would be like. The work was supposed to last for at least another month and I don't think anyone wanted to keep working at something as hard as finishing the battery walls.

CHAPTER ELEVEN

Friends Forever

When the visitors left, we began with a class in braiding. That's right braiding. Connal explained how the technology involved in making this battery included a special electrolyte and cell cores designed to increase electro-magnetic resonance. Actually, what he said was something like this...

"I have asked James to demonstrate a very simple fuel cell for us."

Feeling more than a little embarrassed, I stood up with a lemon, a strip of copper and a strip of zinc. I shoved the copper strip into one end of the lemon and the zinc strip into the other and demonstrated how copper wires attached to each could complete a circuit that would light up a small electric bulb. Mr. Sawirski had provided me with all the materials. Since he once taught school and he knew about these things.

Connal continued, "The metal strips are the positive and negative poles of the fuel cell and the acidic juice inside the lemon is the electrolyte that allows the electricity to flow between them. There are a lot of substances you can use for the electrolyte. Over two thousand years ago people living near Babylon made a fuel cell of sorts using grape juice. It is known as the Bagdad battery.

A single fuel cell isn't very powerful so we and others began joining them together. That is how you make a battery. My people use batteries about one quarter the size of the one we will build to power our underground strongholds.

About fifteen centuries ago certain wizards started to experiment with different kinds of batteries and over time created many interesting improvements.

The special electrolyte for our fuel cells I will make myself using an old family recipe. It's not difficult to do. The complicated part is the special core each fuel cell contains. This is the part you will do by hand.

My people have always been interested in all kinds of vibrations, light, heat, sound. We were particularly interested in creating resonances. It's like singing a high note and breaking a wine glass if you have the right frequency. You can get a lot more power if everything resonates properly.

Think of these braids as a kind of resonating electrical cable that will be placed in the center of each fuel cell."

We spent the rest of the morning practicing the very complicated braid with short pieces of the materials we would require. We used linen strips, copper wire, zinc wire, and lots and lots of fine silver wire. Our first attempts were only eighteen inches long. Then we learned to make a braid with strips about fifteen feet long. The long pieces required two people to handle them, one at each end. This produced ten feet of finished braid.

John, who hardly ever said anything, proved to be surprisingly adept. Connal was quick to take advantage of this and used him to sort out mistakes when any of us made errors in the sequence.

Paul told us about John. When Laura George had chosen Paul for the job, he'd asked if he could bring John with him. John was 'different' and sometimes people picked on him. Paul always considered himself his protector. Laura George told him to take John along and ask us if it was all right. That's why five men had arrived instead of four. She'd included Gracie because there was trouble at Gracie's home and Mrs. George thought it best if she were away from Sandycreek for a while.

In the afternoon, we moved outdoors and worked on long trestle tables set up on the rigid covering of the battery. It was still very hot but after the last three days we hardly noticed.

We would braid for an hour or so, take a break, then return to braiding. Sometimes two people would be sent to do other work or take someone on a tour and then return to braiding. This became the pattern for the rest of the summer. I wondered if keeping us in pairs was a safety precaution, but I never did ask Connal about it.

At Connal's insistence everyone began doing a little jogging on our breaks. We would jog up to the gate and back, or down to the lake and back, or both if there was time. Connal was convinced that, if we'd spent a couple of hours doing somewhat sedentary work, only an idiot would want to take a break by sitting down and drinking tea or coffee. A break should consist of doing something different.

This was really no hardship because we certainly didn't lack for companionship or conversation while we were braiding. All the time we worked we talked and laughed and drank lots of water because of the heat, or tea when we needed a lift.

The young men loved to make jokes and teasing was something of an art form. They also liked to gossip about their friends and family. They found out Clifford and Kelsey's family was related to Alfred's family. This made Connal something of a distant cousin which amused them to no end. They took to calling him cousin Connal when he wasn't there and occasionally when he was. Connal didn't seem to mind as long as they remembered who was in charge.

They asked Clifford how Connal got the scars on his back and Clifford more or less related the story we had heard from

Max. The difference was they got an updated version, in which Connal's father was some psychotic rich guy who murdered his wife but the cops couldn't prove anything. Then Child and Family Services became involved and returned Connal to his father. This was a mistake because his father tried to kill him, so Max's family took him to live with them. The whole group was properly sympathetic. I never realized Clifford could bend the truth so convincingly. Perhaps, it wasn't so much bending the truth as translating Connal's history into something easier to understand.

They wondered if working for Connal was really as dangerous as he'd said it was. They agreed it probably was. Listening to them I realized no one showed even the faintest signs of wanting to leave. The Argees seemed quite fearless.

They talked a lot about girls and sex. These conversations sounded so similar to those of my older brother and his friends that I found them oddly comforting. It was like suddenly feeling at home in strange city.

At one point I caught Paul looking at me with a knowing smile on his face.

"You're not shocked by any of this are you?"

"I've heard it all before," I replied.

They'd seen the scars on my lower legs because the heat made it more comfortable to wear shorts, so I told them about my accident and then about being looked after by my brother and his teenage friends who had good research skills, access to the internet, and over-active hormones. I related how I would sit quietly in a corner playing with a toy or pretending to read a book while I soaked up information that I never repeated to anyone because I'd promised my brother I'd never tell.

They immediately gave me a quick pop quiz to see if I had my facts straight. I easily answered all their questions which they found rather amusing, especially when I tried to explain that my knowledge was still theoretical rather than practical.

"Give it time, kid. Just give it time," advised Joe with a tolerant smile.

Another time when we were braiding with most of the group, Joe started teasing Alfred about girls in general. It seems he didn't have a steady girlfriend and Joe wanted to know what he wanted.

"Well I'm a very big man and I feel nervous around small women. I think I'd like someone closer to my size," he said thoughtfully.

"What about Gracie," suggested Chris? "She's certainly big enough."

"She's damaged goods," snorted Joe. "He wouldn't want her."

"That's not fair," retorted Alfred. "You know what happened wasn't her fault. I've always thought she's a very nice person."

Everyone fell silent. Alfred was a very big man and, even though he had the demeanor of a gentle giant, you didn't want to provoke him.

I was seated looking toward the door and I saw something the others didn't Gracie was standing outside and had heard everything. I noticed she didn't seem angry, just thoughtful.

Quite often, when I was paired with Kelsey, we would help Ethne and Gracie with such things as laundry and meal preparations. We soon learned a lot about both of them. They came from very different backgrounds but shared many areas of common ground.

They discovered that neither of them knew how to cook. This became a bond rather than a barrier because they sensibly realized their best chance of success lay in helping each other. They were both bright and resourceful and the results were remarkably good and tasty. Together they decided, since we were working so hard, our food should help promote good health and they became very fussy about what we ate.

Joe and Chris teased them about being 'the food police' or 'health food junkies' but no one really complained because what they did prepare was really quite delicious.

They both loved books, any kind of books. The printed word was their way of escaping from the aches and pains of reality. For example, over the few short weeks of the summer they managed to acquire a formidable array of cookbooks, historical novels, and romances.

One morning, Ethne brought in a paperback romance she had just finished and handed it to Gracie.

Gracie looked sadly at the cover and said, "I used to dream of being a princess when I was little. That's before life kicked me in the teeth."

"My dad always called me his fairy princess," mused Ethne. "That's why I've always been fascinated by stories of long ago with lots of kings and queens and castles in them. Life kicked me in the teeth, too."

"It's wrong. I can accept reality, but our dreams shouldn't die just because they can't come true."

They were silent for a long while, and then Ethne sat up and declared, "Let's not let a little thing like reality defeat us. Did you ever pretend when you were little?"

"Yes," replied a wary Gracie.

"Then, let's pretend we're princesses. What's to stop us?"

"That's easy for you to say. You're so beautiful you look like a princess already. I'm big, and fat, and ugly."

"That's just not true. You are tall, but usually the royal family comes from a line of warriors and, if you pretend to be a princess, you should look at your height as a symbol of your lineage. Besides, all the top models are tall. You were a little pudgy when you came here, but we've both been running and exercising and eating properly and you've slimmed down a lot. Those sloppy T-shirts you keep wearing are hiding the kind of body any woman would envy."

"Maybe, but I'm not pretty. You can't change that."

"Oh, but I can! You've got everything you need; wonderful hair, beautiful eyes, a lovely oval face, and one of the most elegant profiles I've ever seen. Let me show you what to do with yourself."

Ethne was as good as her word. She had a real talent for what she called 'gilding the lily.' Over the next few weeks the transformation was amazing. It helped that they were able to fit personal shopping expeditions into their regular trips to Selkirk for other supplies.

What I noticed most was the way we followed them with our eyes whenever they walked by. We were all discrete, mind you, because Ethne was spoken for and no one wanted to offend Gracie because of her awesome temper. I often wondered about female pheromones.

One other thing they had in common was that both of them had been badly mistreated by men, Gracie by her stepfather and Ethne by her husband.

One afternoon Kelsey, Ethne, Gracie, and I were working in the kitchen when the two women began to exchange confidences. I don't know if they'd forgotten we were there or if they didn't care. We just kept quiet and learned a lot of interesting facts about both of them.

It was like watching the afternoon soaps on TV. Kelsey and I sat quietly and pretended we weren't listening. We did exchange a lot of significant glances though.

Ethne was very angry about something.

"My soon-to-be ex-husband is making more demands. It would be lovely if this whole divorce was finished, but he keeps asking for things that don't belong to him."

She shook her head and her mass of dark auburn hair swirled around her shoulders like an angry storm cloud.

"Why is he doing that? I thought those kind of issues were settled," said Gracie.

"I'm sure it's the girlfriend's doing. I always thought she was out for everything she could get and, since she's already carrying his child, she's pushing him to get as much as he can so she can have it all.

I wouldn't mind giving up more just to get it over, but it galls me she's the one who will end up with everything."

"If you're sure you don't mind losing something more to reach a settlement, why don't you have your lawyers draw up papers that will place all the extra stuff in trust for the baby? It's the only innocent in the whole affair. If you want to create a little trouble of your own, you could insist on a paternity test so you are sure the baby is really his," said Gracie displaying a Machiavellian streak I'd never noticed before.

"Oh, Gracie, that's such a wicked idea," laughed Ethne. "I wonder if it would work. I'll have to ask my lawyer. I don't know if Connal and I would ever marry but it would be wonderful if I were free."

"Don't you want to marry him? Most women would, he's gorgeous."

"It's not that simple. Connal seems very pleased I can't have children and that worries me. What does it say about him as a person?"

She wasn't asking me so I kept quiet. However, I thought it showed good sense. He'd already lost at least one child because of who he was. Having more children would be very risky.

Gracie thought about that for a moment then shook her head.

"I think he likes children. He's been so good with those who have been out here to see the battery. It's probably something else. Why don't you ask him?"

"For the same reason you avoid talking to Alfred. We're both scared of what the answers might be."

"I'm not afraid of what Alfred's answer might be. I'm sure he likes me. It's his family that scares me. They are very religious and everyone knows what my stepfather did to me while I was growing up."

"I think you should try. If his family really are practicing Christians, they should be able to forgive you for something that wasn't your fault. Look how I forgave you for being so nasty the day you arrived."

"Forgive? You just kept giving me cups of Connal's tea until I couldn't see straight. It helped though. When I arrived, I hated the whole world and everything in it. Laura George is a smart woman. She said I needed to get away from my family before I did something I'd regret. She was right. Since I've been here, I feel as if I'm finally getting some control over my life, thanks to you and Connal's tea."

"Perhaps you should make some tea for Alfred's family?"

"Soup might be better. Remember what happened the first day I was here. That soup would definitely put an end to the problem."

They both broke into peals of laughter. This was too much for Kelsey.

"What did you do?" he asked.

"We nearly poisoned the whole camp," said Ethne.

"Luckily, Connal popped in for a minute and saw what we were putting in the soup. The recipe suggested using herbs to improve the flavor and we decided to try some of the ones Connal had in small bags in the cupboard. We had that problem with Churchill, but he thought keeping things up in the cupboard would be safe. Now he keeps everything dangerous under lock and key."

"He was rather startled," chuckled Gracie. "I can still see him peering over your shoulder. Then he gave that wicked smile of his and said, 'Ethne, dear heart, if you no longer wish to share your bed with me, all you have to do is say so. There's no need to commit mass homicide.'"

When they left, Kelsey turned to me and said, "I see what you meant about sitting quietly in a corner and learning far more than anyone thought you were."

"Are you going to tell anyone what you heard?"

Kelsey thought for a moment.

"No. It might cause trouble and I think we should protect their privacy, even if they didn't."

"Good man," I said feeling relieved. It was as if Kelsey had passed some important test in our friendship. I wanted to be his friend but my computer program told me it would be dangerous to become close friends with anyone who couldn't keep secrets.

As soon as they discovered Connal was holding classes in unarmed combat everyone wanted to learn, even Ethne and Gracie. We had to enlarge the training circle so there was enough room. I think they all realized this was a good way to protect themselves when trouble did come knocking.

One of the alphabet guys, Mr. Duchin, knew a lot about unarmed combat and he often stayed after his shift to practice with Connal. This really pleased Connal because now he had someone who knew how to fight and this made their bouts really interesting. Back in Winnipeg he was always dragging Max out to the practice circle so he could stay sharp. From what I saw Max was very good and seemed to like it. However, he was always preoccupied with other matters and unarmed combat skills were not his first priority.

I still spent a little time each day using the broadsword circle. Sometimes I used my quarterstaff and sometimes just a short stick. I usually did this on my own because the attention of the others was focused on unarmed combat.

One evening Mr. Duchin walked over and watched me for a while.

"Is this anything like kendo?"

"I think so. You should ask Connal. He's a real expert with the quarterstaff."

He immediately walked over to Connal and asked whether it would be possible for him to bring his bo (that's the name of the big stick they use in kendo ... the small one is the do) and try it out against the quarterstaff.

"I've heard about kendo," replied Connal. "It would be fun to try, but without practice armor it would be too dangerous. I assume you are very skilled in its use."

"I like to think so," said Mr. Duchin.

The next day he bought two suits of kendo practice armor out to the site and they had their first contest. I noticed Connal wasn't using his special staff; just the one we'd made out of a branch of carrigana from our backyard. When he saw me looking at it, he smiled and said, "My wizard's staff I usually save for mortal combat. This fight is for fun. I have no intention of harming our alphabet guy."

I could tell right away Peter, that's Mr. Duchin's first name, was very good. Connal's eyes glittered and he had that slightly manic smile he gets when he's being pushed to exert himself. He relished the fact their styles were different because he was always eager to learn something new. Also, there was a possibility Peter might get through his guard and give him a good whack. He had to be on his toes every minute and he found the challenge invigorating.

Peter must have known immediately he was out-classed but he never backed down. He kept trying to break through Connal's seemingly effortless defense. After three or four minutes, Connal neatly dumped him on the ground and stopped with the end of his quarterstaff hovering just above Peter's throat.

They went at it twice more with pretty much the same results. When Connal offered his hand to help Peter up after the last fall, Peter just shook his head.

"You're amazing! Would you be willing to teach me some of those moves?"

"Willingly! It will be wonderful to have a skilled partner to practice with. Take my hand on it."

Everyone was in a good mood when we gathered around the fire pit as it grew dark. I wanted to tell Connal that Kelsey and I had seen Churchill while on our evening patrol. He had started to grow and was now over a foot high at the shoulder. He looked very well otherwise and the fairies said they were glad of his company. There were foxes in the area and Churchill was large enough to keep them at a distance. We had to wait till later in the evening to make our report because both Clifford and Connal had disappeared.

We didn't think anymore about it because Chris's mom had brought him his guitar and we all enjoyed singing together as the night grew darker.

The first chance he had, Kelsey asked Clifford where he'd gone and Clifford showed him the quarterstaff he and Connal had selected. Now that Connal had discovered where he could obtain suitable practice armor he wanted to start training Clifford.

Clifford was very enthusiastic. He said he was going to see if Chris would be willing to practice with him. I noticed Kelsey felt left out so I said, "Come on Kels. Let's go out and cut a quarterstaff for you. We can practice together. It works best if you're close to the same size."

Once our routine was established life began to seem quite ordinary. Everyone gradually became a nice golden color, we produced endless amounts of braid, we took friends and strangers on tours, and our unarmed combat sessions were beginning to produce results. We were all relaxed, trim, and glowing with good health.

The hot weather lasted for another week and a half before another big thunderstorm came along. The cover on the battery worked just fine but the whole area was soaked so Connal declared a paid holiday. There was a wedding at Sandycreek on Saturday and our friends wanted to go. The timing couldn't have been better because Michael, Guy and some others were coming up for a visit and this small break meant we wouldn't get in each other's way.

Before they left Joe asked Connal if he was willing to train some of the others in how to use the quarterstaff.

"Using the quarterstaff requires a lot of work and dedication. If you are prepared to put in the time and effort, I'll be happy to teach you. First of all you must find your own piece of wood and prepare it for use. Remember, it should be a hand span taller than you are. If you bring it back with you, then I'll know you're serious."

CHAPTER TWELVE
The Salt Oath

That evening Cormac and Kelda paid us a visit. They had been on patrol that afternoon and made an interesting discovery.

Kelda leaped gracefully to the table top in front of Connal where she could look him in the eye.

"Why didn't you tell me Gracie can both see and hear fairies?"

"I wasn't aware of that. Is it important?"

"Yes, it is. There are many things she and Ethne should know for their own safety and comfort. I am responsible for all the females involved in this quest. I wish I'd known of this ability earlier."

Back in Fairyland Kelda was a very important and powerful person whose vast experience allowed her to function as a sort of living encyclopedia of general knowledge. She was also an expert healer and a strange combination of judge and police officer; responsible for seeing everyone obeyed the rules.

"You've entered into a serious relationship with this young woman, Connal, and it's time she had some idea of is expected of her." The small figure with its halo of flaming red hair radiated authority.

"She's right," said Cormac. "You can't argue with our very own 'fairy godmother'." He was teasing but the reference has slightly sinister overtones to it, rather like the term 'godfather' when talking about a crime lord.

I could see Connal looked uneasy and was about to say something when he thought better of it and just nodded his head.

"Come, Gracie, Ethne. We have a lot to discuss."

Kelda was very tiny but you felt she was in total command and seemed to sweep the two women before her into the large bedroom.

"Gaia, help us all," said Connal. "That woman just can't leave well enough alone, can she?"

"I think she's right," retorted Cormac. "It certainly won't hurt your love life and it's essential Ethne is accepted into the women's circle. She's going to need all the help and support she can get.

Kelda's been fretting because she couldn't talk to Ethne before this. Discovering Gracie is like gold and diamonds to her. I was very surprised, myself, when we discovered Gracie could see and hear fairies. It's not unexpected that Kelsey has the ability because of his grandfather, Evan, but Clifford can only hear us."

Connal shrugged.

"I talked to Evan about it the other day. He thinks it may have something to do with Ojibway blood. Some of the elders he knows have similar special abilities.

I wonder if we should find out if any of the young men working with me have the same talent. It wouldn't surprise me that there were others."

Cormac nodded his head. "We'll definitely be more careful from now on.

There something else I have to tell you that may upset you."

"What's that?"

"Evan doesn't want there to be any secrets between you and him and he's feeling slightly guilty about a request he made."

"And what request was that?" Connal did not sound pleased.

"He hoped you would help Clifford develop some male lifelong friends, rather like the hunting packs of a free clan. He's had lots of casual friends, particularly girlfriends, but only Kelsey is very close to him.

Evan's a member of the Core and you know how essential friendship is for them. He felt Clifford won't reach his true potential if he can't form lasting friendships. I told him not to worry, you knew what you were doing, but he still wasn't satisfied. Finally, I said I'd get things started and Cian said he'd help me."

"Oh and how did you do that?" Connal's tone was sweet but very dangerous.

"Do you remember how sick and miserable everyone was when they arrived that first morning?"

"Go on..."

"Well Cian and I were in the truck with you and Evan on your first trip to Sandycreek. We knew you were hiring some young men from the reserve. So we stayed behind to see what we could cook up.

When the group started to drink the punch, it was too good an opportunity to miss. We had a full complement of toxic darts and between us we managed to hit all of them on an area of exposed flesh. The darts were very tiny and with all the mosquitoes they are exposed to I doubt any of them felt a thing. We did notice the big fellow didn't take a drink so we deliberately left him out. If everything was blamed on the punch, then you weren't likely to look further.

This way you only got men who were determined to come here because no one but the very strong willed would ever make it out of bed the next morning. Also, they were feeling so miserable they willingly went along with whatever you asked of them and Alfred simply followed their lead.

You were a captain in the army when you were young and you know what is done with men from the free clans when then offer their swords. They would kill you if there was any hint of a fairy bond, but you do put them through a kind of initiation. They expect it and consent to it. First, you get them drunk enough to be very sick, then you give them a cup of your special tea, and then you assign them a series of tasks that are usually hard, dirty and dangerous, tasks where they have to rely completely on each other. And there you have it, a hunting pack or an army unit, closer than brothers.

You, of course, recognized an opportunity when you saw it and felt no particular obligation to explain what you were doing."

"I don't appreciate you and Cian putting us all in such danger," said Connal stiffly.

"Oh, you weren't in danger because we cleared everything with both Evan and Michael before we went ahead. Michael is very interested in the results. In many ways it's more like the old way the Core used to bond before they had an absolute ban."

"In that case, I'm glad I didn't know," said Connal. "In any event, Evan has his wish. Clifford is now a part of a group of eight who will be lifelong friends."

'I'm part of the group of eight,' I thought with surprise. What Cormac said was true. I knew these young men would be my friends for the rest of my life. When I thought about it, I was surprised at how well I knew each of them in such a short time.

I felt it was natural to know a lot about Clifford and Kelsey. I had known them the longest and their lives were completely entangled with my own. Now there were five other people whose lives had been joined to mine.

Chris was the brightest and best of all of us. In the fall he would be going to university on a full scholarship. He wasn't just bright. It went far beyond that. His mental gifts would have turned a Druid wild with jealousy. Often, someone like

Chris ends up being envied and disliked by his peers but this didn't happen. He was blessed with a delightful sense of humor. His quick wit caused him to move through life buoyed up on a wave of laughter. He could turn his hand to anything. This past year he had taught himself to play the guitar. He was handsome, physically strong and graceful. When you met him, you knew he was destined to do great things.

Joe was the youngest brother of Chris's mom. She had taken him to live with her family after their parents died. Both she and Joe were exceptionally strong willed individuals, but, though they often clashed, there was nothing they would not do for each other. Early on they recognized how special Chris was and were united in protecting him from any kind of unfair treatment.

Joe, like Chris, was also handsome, strong and well coordinated. The difference was he knew it and used it to his advantage. Women found him very attractive. He never backed down from a fight and had a local reputation for stubbornness.

While he was in prison, he had been approached by various gang members. He refused to join at that time because he'd promised his sister he wouldn't be pressured into anything he didn't want to do. When we first met him by the lake, he was trying to decide what he would do with his life if he didn't move to Winnipeg and join a street gang. There weren't a lot of options.

Alfred was the largest and strongest of the group. He was interested in Gracie before he came to work and even more after Ethne began to 'gild the lily'. He had been raised in a very strict but loving household. He knew they wouldn't consider her to be good enough for their son. However, if he did decide he truly wanted her, I don't think anything would stop him.

In many ways he was very gentle and this created the illusion he was a little slow in mind and body. This was just not so. He had lightning fast reflexes and a mind like a steel trap. I had a feeling he deliberately hid these talents so anyone who foolishly crossed him would be in for more trouble than they ever dreamed possible. I'd watched him doing unarmed combat and he had a real killer instinct. Any fight with Alfred would be brutal and brief.

My first impression of Paul was of someone so average he was almost invisible. Then, bit by bit, I came to realize Paul lived most of his life inside his head where it didn't show until you hit the right buttons. One of these buttons was his sense of fair play. He was the social conscience of the group. Chris called him the 'white knight'. He claimed nothing for himself but was absolutely fearless in the defense of others. This could be dangerous.

A few nights ago, everyone had driven over to Selkirk. There were five of us in Connal's truck and Guy took the others in his large van. Gracie and Ethne were on a shopping expedition for food and other supplies and the rest of us felt like getting away from the battery for a while.

Most of us trooped over to the local fast food franchise for a big juicy burger with everything on it and lots of greasy fries. Chris said it was our gesture of defiance toward the 'food police'. It made everyone feel just a little bit wicked to eat something that would annoy our very health conscious cooks, so we were in a particularly good mood as we stood around waiting for the two of them to reappear with their purchases.

Not everyone was enjoying a friendly gathering in the warm evening air. Only a few feet away from our group several people began yelling at each other and someone was screaming. It was hard to tell what was going on and we all stopped to watch. It looked like some kind of domestic dispute and getting involved in something like that can be dangerous. Everyone, but Paul, just stood there and waited for something to happen.

Paul walked up to the angry strangers and said earnestly, "You shouldn't do this. It isn't right."

As you might expect, one of the angry men hit Paul and knocked him down. The man was very angry and the first blow might have been overlooked, but he also kicked Paul when he was down and it looked like the others might join in. Joe immediately started forward.

He was stopped by an iron grip on his shoulder and familiar voice.

"No, Joe. Stay here and watch my back. I need the exercise."

Connal stepped into the middle of the hostile group and announced, "You shouldn't have kicked him."

It was just like one of the martial arts sequences in an action movie. Connal always told us he was very fast and could handle anything he could see coming. The real danger was a sneak attack from behind. We had learned to pay close attention to everything he said, so we immediately fanned out into a circle around the strangers. That way someone was always in position to protect his back. Then we more or less sat back and enjoyed the show.

I remembered the night we rescued Clifford when Connal had said speed could save you when nothing else would. He now demonstrated how true this was. Every movement was swift and sure and every blow so rapid he appeared to spend most of his time standing still. They came at him singly, or in twos and threes, several pulled out knives. The result was always the same. Connal was left standing calmly in the center of the circle with at least one assailant groaning on the ground. It was over very quickly.

John was the only one who didn't stay for the whole show. He followed Connal into the hostile group and calmly helped Paul to his feet and then escorted him over to sit in Connal's truck. It struck me he was the bravest one of all. He placed himself in danger with almost no chance to defend himself. Getting his friend to safety was all that mattered to him.

John was very different. In an e-mail I sent to my dad, I told him about the young man who was so silent. He understood everything that was said and he did not have any obvious speech impediments because his rare utterances were clear and concise.

My father suggested it was probably an auditory processing problem.

Sometimes a person's mind works differently than the rest of us, in John's case it was likely something to do with expressive language. His hearing was normal and the message arrived just fine. It was sending messages out that was difficult. As a child he was probably a late talker.

Don't get the wrong idea. Being a late talker has little to do with intelligence. Someone told me Thomas Edison didn't talk much until he was almost four years old. I often wondered what I would do if I were locked inside my own head. John seemed to have developed other skills to compensate for this. Once in a while, he displayed an extraordinary understanding of very complex situations.

One afternoon, John, Joe, Kelsey, and I were coming back from a run down to the lake. For some reason we were all very quiet, so Connal and Ethne didn't hear us coming. We stepped around the corner of the bunkhouse and there they were. They had obviously been kissing and Connal was running the tip of his tongue gently along the side of Ethne's slender golden neck.

Joe, Kelsey, and I were quite amused at catching them together because they were usually quite formal during working hours. We would have smiled, averted our eyes, and strolled nonchalantly into the bunkhouse, but not John. He stopped and stared intently at them. Then he spoke.

"Does she taste good?"

"Yes, she does," laughed Connal. "It's the salt."

There was a long pause while John continued to stare at them. Connal shrugged his shoulders and went on to explain the custom.

"A long time ago, salt was highly prized. In some places it was used in place of money. The Celts called it white gold and the Romans paid their troops with it. In fact, this payment in salt is where the word 'salary' comes from. Animals sometimes need a salt supplement to remain healthy. Hunters know about 'salt licks' and will stake out a likely location so the animals come to then. Salt also improves the flavor of your food. It was also used to preserve meat. Salt had real value and importance.

Centuries ago, among my people, there was a salt blessing given by a family member to honor a departing guest. Translated it went something like ... "You've shared our salted meat, you've shared our hearth and home, now you're a part of our blood and bone."

There was also a more intimate variation of this blessing that lovers use when their relationship deepens into lasting love. It probably arose from someone enjoying the salty taste of a lover's body.

"I've shared your salt, I've shared your bed, now you're a part of my blood and bone."

That version is very poetic in my own language but not in English.

Licking salt is never something that is done lightly. It is something like the ritual for becoming blood brothers. We have a similar blood ritual and use it and the licking of salt almost interchangeably. It acknowledges that someone is your kindred spirit forever, in this world and beyond."

It was an interesting, if somewhat long explanation, and Joe, Kelsey, and I turned to go when John spoke up.

"May I taste you?"

We quickly turned back.

"What?" exclaimed a startled Connal. "Do you have any idea what is involved?"

"Yes," said John.

Connal stood for a long while looking deeply into John's eyes. Finally, he shook his head wonderingly and murmured, "I believe you do."

He put his hands on John's shoulders and pulled him close enough to run his tongue along John's neck and John did the same. Then he stepped back and they clasped hands.

"Blood and bone," intoned Connal solemnly.

"Blood and bone," replied John.

We all knew something important had happened even if we weren't sure what. John looked wonderfully happy and Connal seemed surprised and oddly pleased. I believe Joe, Kelsey and I all realized John had picked up on some implied message we had missed.

From that time on, John seemed much happier and more confident. I think he finally felt he was a real part of our group. He also spoke more and every so often would teach us a little ASL, that's American Sign Language. He had learned it in school because it took a while before anyone realized he could talk. We began to discover what an interesting person he really was.

Our visitors arrived early Saturday morning with a truckload of metal hexagons that were to form the cell grid for the battery. It took most of the day to put everything in place so Kelsey and Clifford decided to walk over to visit the fairies, Churchill, and Mr. Sawirski. I said I had to stay behind because I had some paper work to do. That was true, but what I really wanted was to have a private talk with Michael.

It was mid-afternoon before I had my chance. He actually came into the office to see how I was doing. I asked him to sit down and offered him a cup of tea.

"Michael, I told you about the new ability I developed after bonding with Max."

"Yes," he said, suddenly all attention.

"I've been using it to think about what happened. Why it isn't what anyone expected."

"This sounds very interesting."

"It's like this. When we were all in the tent and I knew we were in real danger, I was the one protecting Max and Connal. Remember I'd been told to look after them and at that moment I was much bigger and stronger than either of them so I felt responsible for their safety.

I remember Max said something about bonding as equals and he seemed surprised this had happened because I was only a child. Elves don't bond with children. It's not considered proper because the child is so vulnerable. However, I didn't feel the least bit vulnerable then and I don't feel vulnerable now. I even wonder if I might be the dominant personality in the bond, perhaps not now, but when I'm grown.

I really like Max and I'd like someone to warn him. It may be me who has to free him and not the other way around."

Michael looked startled. Then he shook his head and gave a rueful laugh.

"I'd say your idea is definitely possible. I'll talk it over with Sean and we'll both talk to Max. The world gets stranger every day."

CHAPTER THIRTEEN

A Fight For Survival

On Sunday we settled back into our normal routine. Our friends returned from the wedding a little weary but in good spirits. Everyone brought his handmade quarterstaff and John and Chris even brought shorter fighting sticks as well. The world was unfolding as it should.

We still had a lot of braiding to do, but Connal was now ready to start assembling the battery and set up the control booth in the bunkhouse. A crew of workmen came and began to put up the wooden framework for the outside walls of the battery. It would give us better protection but I missed the open spaces. The rest of the braiding would now be done in the common room in the bunkhouse.

Connal divided us into three groups; one group to help with the connections inside the battery and the control room, another to work on brewing the electrolyte, and the rest to continue braiding.

My parents kept in close touch with me during the summer. I called home frequently and Dad often checked on our progress and advised me how to keep track of our expenses. After the computer arrived we sent frequent e-mails.

It wasn't as easy for Kelsey and Clifford's grandmother and grandfather to keep in touch, but my mother made a point of phoning out to Newago to talk to them. Evidently my mother and their grandmother were both feeling lonely with all their chicks away from home.

When Mrs. Williams had to come to Winnipeg for a medical check-up, my mother invited her to stay at our house. That's when they both decided to hold a surprise birthday party for Clifford. He would turn eighteen on August 18th.

It was a nice treat for everyone when Mom and Mrs. Williams arrived with two big red velvet cakes. A moment or two after they arrived, Chris's mom drove in carrying something wrapped in aluminum foil and tied with a bright red bow. She walked up to Clifford and gave him a big kiss and thrust the shiny silver package into his hands.

"I made a dream catcher for you to protect you from bad dreams. Now only the really, really good dreams should get through," and she gave him a roguish wink.

My mom had brought some ice cream and a couple of bottles of her home made wine. The three mothers and the two young women immediately set about laying out the food while the rest of us piled more brush on the bonfire. It leapt up merrily challenging the fiery red and gold of the setting sun.

An eighteenth birthday is rather special in Manitoba because you are considered to be an adult. You can vote, join the army and drink alcohol. Often your friends take you out to a bar.

The older guys were too busy to do this but we still had fun. Most of the group never tasted red velvet cake and it proved to be a big hit. Even Albert, who always tried to avoid sugar, had a small piece. Connal brewed a special tea. We all sang songs and told silly stories. Our group displayed a real talent for turning any gathering into a really good party.

Guy was at the site on one of his periodic trips to check on our progress with the battery. He decided to stay late and join us for the birthday party. It was the first time I'd ever had a chance to talk to him. He was very friendly and easy going. For some reason he reminded me of a tall, gangly, very young, Abe Lincoln.

He was wildly happy about working on this project and spoke warmly about working for Michael's company. Michael, he declared, was a truly wonderful person. His enthusiasm was so overwhelming it gave me an idea.

"Are you bonded to Michael?" I asked.

He paused for a moment, and then he smiled and said, "I belong to a Core group and, while we prize loyalty and friendship, we don't bond in the same manner as yourself and Max. It is absolutely forbidden. That doesn't mean the ties within a selected group aren't strong. We believe our freely given loyalty is even more complete than an elfish bond. And, yes, Michael has my absolute loyalty."

There was a pause before Guy continued.

"He has your loyalty, too, hasn't he?"

"Yes, he does and I've been wondering why."

"Were you aware that Max, Connal, Sean Kerry, your grandfather, and yourself were close to being killed when you were in Bissett?"

"My Grandpa Duncan said as much but I never knew why we were spared."

"You were spared because the knowledge Max, Connal, and Sean could give us was too valuable to be refused. However, in order to protect ourselves we had to sacrifice Michael."

"You had to what?"

"Michael was our brightest, best, most trustworthy member. He never let power corrupt him and he never wavered from his belief in the prime importance of individual freedom and social responsibility. He was the one person we knew would remain loyal to our group even when he acquired the bonds of who knew how many elves of the White Court.

It wasn't hard for Sean and Max to give Michael their bond because what Michael believed in was what they had been seeking for years. However, Michael had to become part of what he most hated so our group could make use of their knowledge. It was fortunate for all of you that we were so desperate to find a way to counteract this new kind of bonding.

It was a hard choice for him to make. It went against everything he had worked toward all his life. Perhaps, he just couldn't see you all killed when there was a chance he could save both you and our own people."

"I thought Grandpa Duncan and I were spared because Evan asked for our lives."

"That helped, but we never could have trusted any of you without Michael's sacrifice.

Don't think too badly of us. It's just that we would never have survived this long if we weren't quite ruthless in protecting ourselves. Evan said he would silence you himself if he ever thought you would betray us."

"Have Max and Connal been able to help you?"

"Absolutely! It will be a long and difficult struggle, but we now have a good chance of winning. You have no idea what a great weight has been lifted from my heart."

"Do you think Connal's battery will be able to save his friends?"

"If there was more time, I would definitely say 'yes'. The elves understand different forms of resonance far better than we do. It's how they were able to travel to Fairyland in the first place. Unfortunately, they used it in very limited ways and never bothered to do any rigorous scientific studies. There are lots of gaps in their knowledge and that could cause real problems."

"Problems, like coming to Manitoba instead of Ireland?"

"Exactly! Still, it's always better push ahead, concentrate on all the successful steps we've taken, and journey in hope."

Rather than being downhearted, Guy glowed with enthusiasm. It was obvious he liked challenges and I found his optimism encouraging. I believed, even if we there were still many problems, we were going to make it. I had a strong feeling luck was with us.

Guy brought a small hand drum down to the fire and proceeded to teach everyone what he called a 'family chant' for us to sing around the fire. He also showed us a few dance steps that were traditions of the Core. They were very easy and soon the fire was surrounded by stamping chanting figures. The long forgotten past sprang to life around the leaping flames.

I was feeling thirsty and wanted water not wine so I wandered back through the narrow path to the well. The cool sweet air caressed my face and stirred my soul. As I started back I caught a glimpse of three familiar shapes outlined by shimmering moonlight; my mother, Connal and Ethne. They were so beautiful you could believe they were mysterious beings from an alien world.

The powdery dust of the path stole the sound from my footfalls. I moved as silently as a wraith through the silver sheen of this moonlit world and drifted close enough to hear their voices.

Connal turned to face Ethne and I heard him say, "I'd like you to meet Mary. She's the beautiful woman who often walks in my dreams." The two women nodded and smiled. Then Connal took my mother in his arms and kissed her.

I don't know what I might have done or said, but suddenly I was aware of Kelda sitting on my shoulder and whispering softly in my ear. "Don't worry, my child. Certain things are different in Fairyland and all three of them know the rules. Your father also understands."

My father might understand but I didn't. Watching your mother in the arms of a powerful elf lord is a shock. I'm quite sure Kelda would have explained everything if I asked her. Did I really want to know? I just stood there and watched as Connal put an arm around each of them and they walked together back to the bonfire.

I found it strange I wasn't more troubled. I still liked Connal and loved my mother. Perhaps this was because Kelda said it was all right and fairies don't lie. Explanations could wait for another time.

My Jewish friend, Marty, says eighteen is a lucky number. Perhaps, Connal should have run the first battery test on August eighteenth. He ran it on the nineteenth and the results were a little strange.

Albert, Connal, and I were in the control room when he began to test the battery. Connal decided he would teach Albert how to control the power flow from the battery. Joe also wanted to learn the procedure but the control booth was rather small so he was standing in the doorway.

The controls allowed you to access as many fuel cells as you needed. He planned to test each individual fuel cell to make sure they were all working properly. Unfortunately, Guy tried to be helpful and had already connected three or four cells in series. Bad idea! Or perhaps, good idea??

The large silver oval that was supposed to contain the portal was leaning against the south wall opposite the control room. Its bottom edge was in contact with one of the fuel cells. There was a small poof of light and two tiny figures tumbled out onto the floor.

"Gaia help us!" exclaimed Connal.

"Look at those blurry lights going up the wire," said Albert.

I was speechless as I watched two fairies shinny up a loose piece of electrical wire to the top of the wooden wall and disappear over the side.

"James, get out there and find them. If you can't get them, alert the patrols. Bring them back here as soon as you can."

I ran outside and around the battery walls. I tried to think where I would run to if I were looking for shelter. There was a lot of brush on the far side of the battery so I headed for there. When I reached the edge of the clearing, I discovered John was there first. I could hear him talking as I ran up.

"Are you the friends Connal is trying to save?"

"Yes, we are," said a small voice.

"If you would like, I can take you to him."

"Can he be trusted?" said a second small voice.

"I believe so," replied the first voice. "If he tries anything, we can always kill him."

"I hope you won't. Connal wouldn't like that," I interjected.

"Oh James, there you are," said the second voice.

"How do you know my name?"

"It's all in the reports. Now that I look more closely, this bigger one must be John. Come along both of you we have to see Connal right away."

John and I each carried a fairy back to the battery while the tallest of our new arrivals explained how the fairies here had sent continuous reports back to Fairyland. They were even able to make hand drawn pictures of everyone who worked at the construction site. It is true, elves really do keep written records of everything. These two fairies seemed to think we were a couple of dolts not to have figured this out on our own.

Somehow the fairies had calculated the approximate location in Fairyland where the portal would be opened relative to the battery near Libau. They narrowed it down to a certain stronghold on the border of territory that belonged to the Misbegotten. They had been busy fortifying it and bringing all those who wanted to return to Earth close enough so they could leave as soon as the portal opened.

Our two new arrivals were walking through a corridor in the stronghold when this tiny portal opened. They immediately created two fairies and sent them through to find out what had happened.

Connal was both startled and surprised.

"Eddi, Murdo! Is it really you? If you two are involved, things must be really dangerous."

The taller one, Eddi, gave a contemptuous snort.

"You would have to build this blasted battery in a spot that is practically on one of the Misbegotten's trade routes. Next time you might put it on the side of a volcano. It would be a lot safer."

"Do you have any idea how much longer it will take? Remember each day on Earth is equal to two or three days in Fairyland. Some of your friends might not last much longer," added Murdo the smaller more delicate looking fairy.

Connal smiled.

"If all goes well, it should take about five Earth days. You should be able to hold out, Gaia willing.

Now get back to the battery and go through what's left of the small portal before it closes. You need to have all your attention concentrated in Fairyland for the next few weeks."

Alfred, John, Joe, Connal and I crowded into the control room and watched as the two tiny figures ducked down and pushed through the portal.

Connal sighed and said, "There go two of the most dangerous elves in Fairyland. I feel much better about our chances now they are there to protect my friends."

John surprised me by asking a question.

"Are all your friends small?"

"No, John," said Connal. "Most of them are my size. What you saw was like a picture of the person who lives on the other side of the door we hope to open with the battery."

"Can I go through the door sometime?"

"I don't know if you would ever want to. Fairyland is very beautiful but very dangerous. Also, your friends and family are here and you might not be able to come home again."

Connal's estimate of the time it would take to finish the battery was accurate. In four days the battery was tested and hooked up to the geo-thermal power sources. Guy hoped this extra power source would provide back-up power and boost the strength of the battery even further. The battery seemed to be working properly.

The permanent roof over the battery had not been built as yet. This was because there was no way of knowing exactly where the portal would appear. When it did, the silver oval would be hoisted into place by a crane. The oval would stabilize the location of the portal.

That evening we ran into trouble. Joe said it was Nanabosho, the trickster, playing games with our plans. We were so close to being finished when it started to rain. It was another tremendous thunderstorm. I began to wonder where our nice normal weather had gone. So far this summer we had searing heat punctuated by violent storms with nothing else in between. I suppose I should have been thankful there were no tornados.

The only bright spot that evening was the arrival of the training armor Peter had ordered for Connal. Everyone was excited because now training could begin in earnest. We were all in the bunkhouse trying on various pieces of equipment when our enemies arrived at the gate in two black vans. It is likely they were using the storm as a cover.

The first thing they did was take out the man at the gate. Luckily, there were several fairies watching or the guard would have died. One of the fairies at the gate was a particularly skilled healer. Under his guidance this small group managed to keep him alive until other help arrived.

All of the intruders weren't so lucky. One of the fairies, I think it was Cian, scored a direct hit with a tiny poisoned dart to the eye of one fellow. He died on the spot but the rest got through.

The fairies also managed to keep the guard near the water safe. They created some mysterious lights just off the trail to the beach. When he went to investigate, they hit him with another dart. This dart put him instantly to sleep but was otherwise quite harmless. When the attackers came to look for him, he was sleeping behind a screen of cattails. The fairies then made short work of this enemy patrol as they stumbled about in the marsh trying to find the guard.

The raiders were very professional. They left several of their group outside the bunkhouse to patrol the area. The fairies down by the lake made quick work of them as well. These men may have been trained assassins and the fairies very small, but the fairies had centuries more experience in warfare. In a few moments the outside of the battery site was cleared of intruders.

Peter was with us in the bunkhouse demonstrating how to wear some of the armor. Everyone was in the common room except Alfred and Gracie who were in the control room. She said she wanted to see how the controls worked, but I think she wanted to get Alfred alone for a few minutes.

When the attack started, there were twelve full-sized people plus three or four fairies in the bunkhouse. The attacking force had over twenty assailants if you counted the ten or so who arrived later in a huge military helicopter. The common room was certainly crowded when our enemy came crashing through the door.

I should have been scared but it all happened so fast I wasn't. No one else seemed very worried either. Everyone now knew there were fairies patrolling the bushes and realized that even though they were tiny they were quite prepared to defend themselves.

After Eddi and Murdo returned to Fairyland, the fairies no longer tried to hide and even if most people couldn't see them unaided, they believed in them and knew they were dangerous. John, who could see and hear them, spent quite a lot of time talking to them. Most of those who couldn't see them well had taken to wearing blue tinted sun glasses.

Everything outside the bunkhouse was now returned to our control. Inside the bunkhouse was another matter. The fairies in the bunkhouse disappeared even before the door burst open. Not because they were afraid. It's just that it's much easier to defeat an enemy if they don't know you exist. I saw Cormac dart around the edge of the door to the control room and thought to myself, "I'll bet he's up to something."

The common room was now very crowded. The invaders took up defensive positions and trained their assault rifles in our direction. The person who seemed to be the leader looked contemptuously at our strangely attired group. Most of us were wearing bits and pieces of padded armor and blue tinted sun glasses.

"Which one of you is Connal Ferryman?" he demanded.

"I am," came back as a chorus. Every male in our group had responded together. Confusion to our enemies!

"Well, I'm sure you're not," said our interrogator and calmly shot John in the stomach.

John never made a sound. He just crumpled to the ground and lay there with tears streaming down his cheeks. The pain must have been dreadful.

Suddenly, I was way beyond fear or anger. I was ice cold. Nothing would stop me from selling my life as dearly as I could if only I could destroy the person who hurt John. I was only waiting for Connal to pick the right moment.

"Everyone, except Connal, down on the floor. Now!"

Connal eyes glittered and he nodded. He seemed to be enjoying some kind of private joke.

We obediently lay down on the floor. It reminded me a little of nap time when I was in day care.

"I hope you realize you've made me very angry," he said slowly and with great deliberation.

At that moment Churchill walked into the room. He was well over twenty inches high at the shoulder and definitely attracted attention.

"MEOW," said Churchill.

"Gaia!" shouted Connal as he dived for the floor.

Before he even landed, Churchill was back through the door and the control room wall blew out.

Anyone standing was peppered with flying debris. The padded armor helped to protect Connal and the rest of us. The fairies popped out of their hiding places and made short work of our disoriented foes.

It wasn't time to start cheering though because we could hear a helicopter landing out in the yard.

Connal shrugged philosophically and murmured, "They know I'm a wizard and they really aren't taking any chances, are they."

We all straggled over into the space that was once the control room. Ethne and Clifford helped Alfred and Gracie to stand. Alfred was wearing both padded jackets which had provided some protection even though they had been torn to shreds by the blast and I could see the blood oozing through. Gracie had an assortment of scrapes and nicks and Cormac was unscathed.

Since Gracie could also see and hear the fairies, Cormac was able to tell her what he wanted them to do. At his urging she made Alfred turn all the controls to high and protect his back and head as best he could with the padded armor. He used his body to shield both Gracie and Cormac and stood with his back to the small window and control panel. When everything was in place, they waited till they heard Connal call, "Gaia!" Then Alfred had reached around behind his back and flipped the switch. The end result was spectacular.

The giant electrical surge blew out not only the control room wall but the other three walls as well. The battery itself appeared to be quite untouched. The old orange shower cap was just a few plastic remnants fluttering in the wind. Most remarkable of all was the enormous glowing oval that floated peacefully about three feet above what was left of the rigid battery cover.

We could see the helicopter had landed and another group of armed men were starting to emerge.

"Move all the intact floor panels under the portal," shouted Connal.

This was the first order he'd given any of us and we scrambled to get it done even though we didn't understand it. We were very used to moving the panels around and it was only a second or two before they were in place.

I wondered why the men from the helicopter weren't firing at us. I suspected they had orders to take Connal alive and still weren't sure which of us was the elusive Mr. Ferryman.

That few seconds saved us because the minute the panels were in place a horde of elves came pouring out of the portal.

Connal yelled, "Everybody down!" and we flattened ourselves against the damp sweet smelling earth.

The elves streamed out of the portal shrieking and screaming with swords and other assorted weapons at the ready. They were wearing some kind of bulky mid-calf robes and chunky cloth covered helmets. The robes and helmets had brightly painted words and pictures in various eye-catching locations. They certainly looked as if they were not of this Earth.

The men from the helicopter continued to run toward us and now they began to fire their assault rifles. I saw several of the elves knocked off their feet, but to my amazement they got right up again and continued to charge.

It was all over in a minute.

We were just starting to catch our breaths when Mr. Sawirski drove into the yard with those fairies who had remained at his house. They started driving over even before the portal was opened. The elf Cormac in Fairyland was the one who made the decision to open the portal and the link between the fairies and their true selves was rather like being in two places at once. It was a little confusing but it worked.

It was strange watching the tiny fairies becoming part of the elves. An elf would hold out his hand and his fairy would jump into it. It must have been pleasant to rejoin because they both would smile and the fairy would fade into the hand. I was told later losing your fairy could be quite painful.

The first order of business was tending to the wounded. I went over to one of the elves who had been hit by a bullet. He seemed to be complaining about a cracked rib. One of the others came over took off his shirt and bound his chest tightly then gave him a drink from a small green bottle on his belt.

"How did you do that?" I asked.

I hoped he might be one of the elves who knew English. He did.

"Break a rib?" He looked puzzled.

"No. How did you get hit by a bullet and live?"

"Kevlar," he replied with a smile.

"What?" I didn't think I'd heard him correctly.

"Kevlar and glue and Velcro."

All the television and endless questions had produced some strange results. Mr. Sawirski realized it was more effective to teach his students English if they talked about things they were really interested in. They watched the war news, police and crime shows and learned about modern body armor. They asked Mr. Sawirski to let them see some and he'd obliged.

Back in Fairyland there were now several workshops turning out a product similar to Kevlar. Light body armor is a wonderful protection for a people continually at war. The problem was they hadn't worked out the bugs in tailoring it into form fitting clothing. They were making long narrow blankets of the stuff and fastening it together with their own glues and a modified sort of Velcro. No wonder their clothing looked so strange. My computer program wondered briefly about patent infringement.

The other thing that was startling was the designs painted on the armor. The elves had time on their hands while waiting for Connal to open the portal and to amuse themselves they painted all sorts of slogans on everything. They got this idea from all the t-shirts their avatars saw on TV. Most of the slogans were in their own language but a few were in English. The one I remember was painted on both Eddi and Murdo. I think it originally came from Texas. It said, "Come and get it", and there was an artistically rendered knife dripping blood beneath the words.

Poor Alfred was rather embarrassed when two tall young women insisted he remove his clothing so they could cover his many bruises and cuts with some kind of ointment. They also treated Gracie's cuts at the same time and told her to take him somewhere where he could sleep on his stomach for the night. He'd be fine in the morning.

I walked back into the bunkhouse because I wanted to find out how John was doing. There was a fair sized group gathered around him. Connal was kneeling beside him and he looked very grave.

"Don't you dare touch him," said Cormac sternly. "You're in enough trouble with the Core over Clifford. This one you'll have to let go."

"I agree," said a richly musical baritone. "But, who's going to stop me it I choose to step in?"

I turned around and felt an instant shock run through me. There was Connal the way he was before taking the sunscreen. The brilliant blue eyes, flawless ivory skin, and honey gold curls were all there. The difference was this was someone who had never tried to hide his beauty with ragged peasant clothing and the grime of hard labor. Here was someone who had spent his life developing a polished easy charm that overcame every obstacle. I had a vision this must have been what Connal's father was like before madness destroyed him. No wonder his people adored him.

Connal stood up and clasped hands with the newcomer. He looked surprised and very, very happy.

"Edan, my brother, it's so good to see you. You didn't have to come. It's a great risk."

Edan's answering smile lit up the room.

He made a slight movement and I had the fleeting impression he was going to kneel before Connal. However, Connal's eyes flashed a warning and there was an imperceptible shake of his head.

Cormac was standing behind me and whispered in my ear.

"You saw that didn't you James. It's good you can keep secrets. That one could cost Connal his life. Get Max to explain."

Out loud he said, "John's yours for the taking if you want him Edan. He won't live if he doesn't get proper care and soon."

Edan just smiled.

"Your hatred of bonding is well known Cormac, but sometimes there is no other way."

"Not so," snapped Cormac. "There's always death," and he stomped away.

"If you'd like my brother, I'll try your trick of bonding him to a search for freedom and hope it works," Edan offered.

Connal just nodded and Edan took John's hand. Like my bond with Max, this one happened in a heartbeat. Then he lifted John in his arms and carried him through the portal.

A goodly number of our rescuers returned to Fairyland. For them it remained home and well worth saving if that could be possible. Before they left a very dark looking wizard shrouded in a black cloak used some of the 'liquid fire' ingredients to turn the helicopter and the dead bodies into a heap of molten metal and ash.

While he was driving over with the fairies, Mr. Sawirski had phoned Paul's uncle on the reservation and talked him into bringing one of the school buses down to drive a group of stranded tourists a.k.a. the elves into Winnipeg. Michael and Max would have to take responsibility for the lot of them when they arrived.

Mr. Sawirski, Cormac, and Garridan broke open two hay bales and spread them around on the truck bed. Then they wrapped the two injured guards in blankets and drove them in to the hospital in Selkirk.

The storm had caused a huge power failure over the area and Cormac gave the admitting clerk some story about our two alphabet guys being too near a lightning strike. They had valid Manitoba Medical cards so there was no problem getting them admitted to the hospital. It was just another small incident in a very eventful night.

It took a bit of shuffling but everyone found somewhere to sleep. Peter, the security guard, slept in the bunkhouse with the rest of us. We closed the door to the common room and turned up the electric heat. We should have felt triumphant but we didn't. I think we all missed John.

CHAPTER FOURTEEN
A New Beginning

The garden where I found Connal was a kind of threshold to a very different world. Did it lead to the new Eden or did it harbor the seeds of Armageddon? I've decided I don't want to know. Let the future take care of itself, the present is all I'm going to have.

We spent the next five days picking up the pieces and making repairs.

Our training in unarmed combat continued because everyone realized we had a lot to learn. It was fortunate the elves were able to help us during the attack because I don't know how we would have managed without them.

Connal finally relented and allowed cameras and motion sensors to be placed in strategic locations and the Argees now handled the regular patrols of the battery site. Once a proper fence is constructed these patrols could be discontinued. I wrote my final status report just before Grandpa Duncan came to take me back to Winnipeg to start school.

Chris and Clifford went off to the University of Winnipeg together. Michael Flynn managed to arrange for them to take many of the same classes. He also purchased the six small apartment blocks at the end of my street. The people who lived there had been offered a bonus if they would move to other quarters all expenses paid. Most had accepted the offer. This freed up enough space to accommodate all the recent arrivals.

There was enough space for Chris and Clifford to room together in one of these blocks. The bus service made it very convenient for them to travel from there to the university. Chris's mom liked the arrangement because it was so close to my house. She's already enlisted my mother to keep an eye on her son.

The block nearest the park has a very nice three bedroom apartment attached to the rear. It was built for the original owner of the property and even had its own pretty little yard with a white picket fence. Max had already moved there.

None of the four problems Connal outlined in Bissett just two months ago were solved but we'd made a lot of progress.

Still undaunted, Connal, Max and their friends picked themselves up, dusted themselves off ... and they lived happily ever after.

Well, almost.